MEET ME IN THE DARK

BAD HEROES
BOOK 3

JO BRENNER

HIGH RISE PUBLISHING

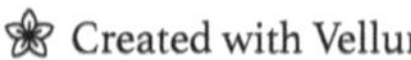 Created with Vellum

AUTHOR'S NOTE

At Yom Kippur services this year, one of my rabbis gave a speech on joy. He said that (and I'm not quoting verbatim here, sorry): "Joy isn't the absence of suffering, and joy isn't happiness. Joy is full commitment, full participation, in the present moment."

It's something I've thought about a lot over the past few months, as I wrote the ending to Kara, Conor, Luke, and Micah's story. There's a lot of pain in this one—there's *been* a lot of pain in the series—and it made me question myself at times: If my purpose, as an author, is to entertain and hopefully help create joy, then how can I write so much about suffering?

And then I realized: It's about fully immersing yourself in the story. Committing, participating, letting yourself feel the good and the bad. And trusting that whatever darkness there is, will lead you back to the light.

This story contains a lot of darkness. **This one, I think, is darker than the other two, and therefore potentially more triggering. Please, please visit my website, www dot**

jobrenner dot com, for content notes and warnings before proceeding.

But I also think it contains a lot of light. Kara's been through a lot of shit—and is about to go through more—on her way to finding joy. And along the way she'll realize this: That joy, for her at least (for *me*, at least), is fully participating in your own happiness, despite the darkness surrounding you.

For those of you sticking around, I hope you enjoy this one. This story and these characters have lived with me fir so long, and giving them their HEA was bittersweet: sweet, because after everything they've been through, they deserve their happiness together, and bitter because it's hard to say goodbye. But Kara, Conor, Luke, and Micah have lived through a lot of darkness. It's time for them to find their joy.

Thank you for saying goodbye to them with me.

Yours,

Jo

1

———

Where was she?

Why did everything hurt?

Why was she so cold?

And why were her feet wet?

Kara forced her eyes open. Her head felt like it was being cut open by a chainsaw.

Her eyesight blurred, then focused.

She was still in the car. They all were.

And they were beginning to sink below the surface of the Pacific Ocean. Water was pouring in through the open windows and the sides of the car, pooling on the floor and drenching her feet. It started slowly, then began to pick up in velocity, and as water rushed into the car, everything came rushing back to her.

The bombing at *Vixen*. The drive down the coastline. They'd never even reached Catalina. Sucking Micah off while Conor fingered her; fucking Luke in the backseat. Luke's declaration that she had power over them, when she'd always been sure it was the other way around. Telling them what it would take to make her stay. Luke saying,

"Sweetheart," before they were rammed into from behind. Her men shooting at the car behind them, the people in the car behind them shooting back. Getting hit again. Their car swerving off the road. Being airborne.

Luke saying, "I love you."

And then:

Nothing.

She'd seen videos about cars crashing in bodies of water. There was a window of thirty seconds to two minutes to get out of the car before the weight of the water caused the car to flip over, nose first, completely submerging the vehicle and its passengers underwater and making it impossible to open a door or window and swim to the surface.

Kara had no idea how much time had passed since they'd hit the water, but she knew this: they didn't have long before they were goners.

The sun was setting. It would be dark soon.

"We need to get out of the car," she groaned.

No one answered her.

No.

One.

Answered.

Her.

She twisted her neck—which hurt like hell—to look at her men. They were all knocked out—Micah's head on the steering wheel, a bloody gash on the back of his head. Luke's head back against the car seat; Conor's sagging against his partly opened window, water spilling in on top of it. None of them moved.

"Micah?" she leaned forward to shake him, gently at first, then more urgently.

"Micah."

Nothing.

"Luke. Conor." Her voice cracked as she looked at the men on either side of her. "Please."

No answer.

More water poured in.

"Damn it!"

She could barely hear herself over the rushing water, which was now up to her knees. They didn't have long. Soon they would flip, wouldn't be able to breathe or escape. Kara had an easy way out—she wasn't wearing a seatbelt, after all, and the window was open. All she had to do was swim out the window and to shore.

She didn't even consider that option. She wasn't leaving them behind. She couldn't leave them there, trapped in the car.

She refused to lose them.

Not now.

Not like this.

Not ever.

The water level rose to her stomach, making her sundress cling to her skin, tight and claustrophobic. Panic tried to take her in a chokehold but she fought it down. The normal breathing tricks weren't going to work when she was drowning and she didn't have time, anyway. She could have a breakdown once they were all safe. She only had to figure out how to get them out of the car.

Think, Kara.

In the videos she'd watched, they'd said to open the windows immediately—already open, thank god—and then swim out of the windows before the car flipped.

The only problem with that was that her men were unconscious.

No matter. She wasn't leaving them.

She reached for Micah's seatbelt, her hands fumbling with the release.

With a groan, he sat up.

"Oh, thank god."

He was awake. *Alive.*

He looked at her through the rearview mirror, his eyes telling a story she didn't want to read.

"No," she said.

"Baby," he said, as blood dripped down his forehead. "Have you seen these shoulders? There's no way I'm fitting through. None of us are."

"No!"

"Kara," Conor said startling her. He was conscious, thank fucking god, but the look in his eyes when he turned to look at her, brushing the water off his face, made her want to scream.

"Is Luke..." she trailed off.

Conor moved his hand to Luke's throat, checking his pulse.

"Breathing," he said shortly. "But the only one of us who will fit through these windows is you."

The water was up to her chest by now. She shivered from the cold, the wet, the fear. They didn't have much time left.

"I'm not leaving you." Her throat stung with tears. "I only survive if you all do. So I suggest you help me get us the fuck out of this car."

Neither Conor nor Micah responded.

"Help me get us the fuck out of this car!" She shrieked the words so hard this time, she was surprised the sound didn't break a window on its own.

Finally, Conor nodded, pressing the button to roll down the windows further.

"Boss, what the hell are you doing?" Micah asked.

"Saving us all."

After a pause, Micah held out his hand to Kara.

"Gun," he said. She handed it to him. The water was almost up to her shoulders now, and Luke still wasn't moving.

"Baby girl, if this doesn't work..." Micah warned.

"It's going to work," she said.

It had to.

Micah shot the gun at the windshield, once, twice, three times. With a crack and crash, the windshield gave, shattering into pieces. Kara pulled her soaked dress over her head and handed it silently to Micah, who used it to clear out the glass.

Oh god, they were going to make it.

Except Conor was gritting his teeth as he tried to undo Luke's seatbelt.

"Stuck," he said. "And he won't wake up."

Her brain screamed a denial, but Micah and Conor were having some silent conversation and then Conor was lifting her out of the water and pushing her through the left rear window. The front of the car was bobbing in the waves.

"Swim to shore!" Micah yelled at her.

She ignored him. He could go to hell—but only if he took her with him.

Taking a deep breath, she swam around to the passenger-side, pulling on Luke's door.

Conor glared at her from the other side of the backseat. She ignored him. He must have said something to Micah, who shook his head. And then Conor was ripping at Luke's seatbelt with his teeth and hands, and then finally, *finally*, Luke was free.

The next moments were a dreamlike haze; Micah and Conor dragging Luke through the broken windshield, the car flipping moments after and sinking down, down, down, and that could have been them, *that could have been them*, but there was no time for that, no time to think about that, only to swim, swim, swim until her body wanted to give out. As they swam, her arms and legs slicing through the water, it was like the water resisted, the ocean fighting to keep them and swallow them whole like it had their rental car.

Finally, she spotted land ahead of them: a tiny sliver of beach broken up by large rocks jutting out of the sand and water. Waves crashed onto the rocks, spraying them with white mist.

"There," she tried to say, swallowing a mouthful of cold saltwater in the process and gagging.

There was an arm around her waist—Micah's—and then he was pulling her along to shore, Conor swimming next to him dragging Luke along. When they reached the strip of beach, Micah released Kara, and all three carefully pulled Luke toward the shallows and laid him out on a flat rock, before collapsing beside him.

Unable to help herself, she crawled over Conor to check Luke's pulse.

Steady.

Strong.

Alive.

And then he was conscious and coughing.

Thank god.

She helped roll him to his side.

"Kara, sweetheart, why are you crying?" Luke coughed.

"You almost died," she explained, she thought matter-of-factly, but it came out as a sob.

Conor was helping him sit up. "We don't have time for this," he said. "They must be watching. They'll be down here at any moment to finish off the job. We're sitting ducks right now."

Luke scanned the area, quickly figuring out the situation.

"Micah, take her and run. We'll distract them," he said, coughing up more water.

"You fucking idiot," Kara cried. "We are not leaving you. We won't let you die here. You don't get to play the martyr. You don't get to die. You're not my hero. You never have been. Don't start acting all gallant and sacrificial now."

In what seemed like minutes but was probably only a few seconds, the three soaked, shivering men stared at each other, some silent conversation passing between them.

"You sure?" Micah said to Luke.

"You're not the only one who's good at planning," Luke said. "I'll figure it out. You take her."

"Time for you to be the boss," Conor said, and the sad smile on his face terrified her.

Micah shut his eyes.

Darkness grew around them, but the sun was putting up a good fight as it sank, resisting the night.

"What's going on?" Kara asked, trying to stave off the panic. "Tell me."

Conor cupped her cheek. "I need you to listen closely to me. In a moment, you're going to follow Micah. Go wherever he takes you, do whatever he tells you to do."

"And what about you two?"

On her other side, Luke stroked her hair. "We love you, sweetheart. Please believe us. We're only men, and often bad ones, but we're yours, and we love you."

"Luke?" her voice sounded frantic. "Conor?"

Conor buried his face in her neck. Luke hugged her waist, kissing her above her ear.

Then they straightened, pulling away at the same time. "Go."

"But—"

Conor's voice was so rough, it hurt her ears. "There's no time for this. Kara, we meant it when we said without you, there's no living for us. We know we've taken so much from you, but give us this one, final thing—go."

And then she was being carried back down the beach and into the water.

"No," she yelled at Micah, trying to fight him as he began to swim, dragging her with him. "I won't leave them."

"Kara." His voice was harsh. "We stay, we all get taken. This is our only shot. And theirs."

At that moment, she heard propellers chopping through air. Lifting her head, she watched as a helicopter descended on the beach.

"Is that…"

"Not anything good."

"Oh god, oh god, oh god." She couldn't stave off the panic anymore.

Micah pulled her hair, hard, the sting snapping her out of her spiral.

"None of that. You need to be strong now, baby."

She watched as Conor stood, his hands raised. He was shouting something but she couldn't hear him. The helicopter landed, and two men dressed in all black hopped out. One took off toward Micah and Kara, but Conor grabbed him and swung. They grappled on the rock, but even though Conor had the opportunity to smash the man's head against the rocks, he didn't.

"What's Conor doing? Why isn't he—"

"He's not going to kill him because he's acting as a distraction," Micah said roughly. "He's saving us."

The orange sun gave up its fight, sinking below the water, and as it disappeared, darkness fell over them, casting the beach and rocks in shadow and hiding them from whoever else might be searching for them. And making it harder for her to see what was happening to Conor and Luke.

"Micah…"

"No." His voice was unbending.

She started to argue again but stopped herself. If this was their only shot—theirs and Luke's and Conor's—she'd do what Micah needed her to do. They were a team, and she was a part of it, and that meant listening to the new boss.

"What do we do now?" she asked instead.

"We take a deep breath."

Kara inhaled and exhaled, picturing the four of them together, back at the cabin, happy and whole.

She'd make it happen, or she'd die trying.

"Now," Micah whispered.

And they ducked their heads below the surface.

2

———

Then

Micah didn't understand how that fucking woman had dug so deep into Conor's head.

Micah had watched as Conor hit on the curvy redhead—just like his friend, boss, and sometimes lover had done hundreds of times with hundreds of women. Except that night, something was different. As he'd watched Conor flirt with her, it was like electricity leapt between them. There was a twinge in Micah's gut, and the sense that if he wasn't careful, the foundation he'd worked to build between Conor, Luke, and himself would crack.

Micah shouldn't have ignored the feeling; he always trusted his own gut. His sixth sense about things had saved his team's lives more than once.

But Conor was determined, and so was the girl, and at the time Micah tried to convince himself that it was just business as usual and there was no reason to cockblock even though everything inside him had screamed otherwise.

But something had changed. The man that left the bar

with a stranger two nights ago was not the man who showed up at Micah and Luke's apartment that morning, dark shadows under his desperation-filled ees.

"I don't know, man," Conor said when they pressed him about it. "She just... I...we..." Micah's friend, Micah's always calm, always centered, always focused friend, pinched the bridge of his nose and shook his head like he was trying to dislodge water.

Like Conor was drowning.

As he watched Conor, that gut sense that everything was going to change came back in full force.

"She, you... what? What, Conor?" Micah had asked, keeping his tone even.

Conor's eyes flashed in warning before his shoulders and head slumped. "It was different. *She* was different. I don't know."

"Pussy that tight, huh? Maybe I should give it a try," Luke joked lightly, trying to dispel Conor's mood and bring them back to familiar ground.

Conor had Luke up out of his chair and shoved against the fridge, hand around his lover's throat, before Micah could stop him.

"What the fuck, man?" Luke choked out.

"Conor," Micah warned, maintaining that even tone.

Conor ignored him.

Micah tried again, appealing to his lover's deepest fear. "Conor, take a breath, okay? Look at what you're doing. You're out of control."

That did it. Conor released Luke, both men breathing heavily, staring at each other.

"Okay," Luke finally said, capitulating for once. "You're obviously into her; take her out to dinner, wine and dine her, see where it goes."

Conor groaned. "I tried. She wasn't interested. And she left town already."

She was gone. Micah waited for the relief to sweep in, but instead there was just...loss. And Micah, who always understood his emotions, couldn't figure out where that came from. He didn't even know the woman. He should be happy she'd left.

"It's more than that," Conor added. "It felt like... she felt like... I'm worried about her. Taking a stranger back to your hotel room is a reckless move, and the things she said, it's like she doesn't care what happens to her."

Micah glanced over at Luke. Luke's jaw was tight; unsurprising, based on the way Micah's teammate had lost his mom.

Conor saw it, too. "Not like that. Just not willing to be safe. Or smart. And a woman like her..."

A woman as beautiful as her, he meant. A woman as alluring as her. Micah hadn't talked to her at all, but he'd seen that much.

"She could get hurt easily," Micah surmised.

He'd never really worried about what would happen to their triad if, or rather when, one of them met someone else. Even though Conor and Luke never admitted to their feelings for each other or for him, they'd die for each other. Period, end of. No one could ever break up what they had together.

But based on Conor's reaction, this one was different. This one was a game changer. This one could take Conor away from them.

Unacceptable.

Conor began talking again. "I'd go after her, but I promised Mom I'd come home for a week. Maribelle just had her baby, and they won't forgive me if I blow them off to chase a woman who doesn't even want me. And after that, I'm off on that mission with Team Four. It's going to fuck with my head, knowing she's driving alone in that car to who the fuck knows where. The next guy she picks up in a bar," Conor swallowed, "well he might be a scarier asshole than me."

Luke cracked a smile. "Not possible."

"We'll keep an eye on her," Micah offered. The words seemed counterintuitive, but they came from his gut. He wasn't sure where he was going with this, yet—he had no plan—but he wasn't about to risk Conor's head not being in the game. Besides, Micah could spin this in a way that suited all of them. He knew himself, knew what he was capable of.

"We'll do what now?" Luke asked, not following Micah's mind's trajectory. Luke was smart, but his infallible honesty made it hard for him to see manipulation and maneuvering for what it was. He was too straightforward; his imagination didn't allow for the twists and turns that Micah took to get what he wanted and they needed.

"From a distance," Micah added, mind whirling. "Watch her, make sure nothing bad happens to her. Only interact if it's absolutely necessary."

"And you'll keep your hands off her," Conor said.

"That goes without saying," Micah said.

It wouldn't be an issue. No woman—no person—could get under his skin enough to fuck up what he had with Conor and Luke.

Conor relaxed, looking less troubled than he had when he first showed up. "Thanks, bro. I honestly don't know what I'd do without either of you."

"Good thing you'll never have to know," Micah said, careful to make sure it didn't sound like the threat it was.

And thus began "Operation Kryptonite Pussy"—so dubbed by Luke, behind Conor's back, of course.

Micah followed Kara for a few weeks—she'd bounced from Santa Fe to Albuquerque to Austin, without any seeming destination in mind. Micah had sat at the back of bars or pulled over at rest stops, shaking his head every time she chatted up or was chatted up by a bartender or fellow patron.

"Just passing through," she'd tell each fucking guy, and each one so obviously wanted to get in her pants, they might as well have waved their dicks in her face. "Yes, I'm traveling by myself. I like it—no one to fight with over the music selection."

The first few times, he'd considered maybe she just liked sex with strangers, that this was her M.O. It would be easier if it were—he could tell Conor this when he got back and maybe the evidence that Conor was just one dick in a line of dicks would knock the sense back into his friend. But she never followed through with any of the dudes she talked to; she refused all of them. She never took a single jackass back to her motel room or followed him home or got it on in the alley behind a bar.

His second thought was that she was naive or stupid, but between stalking her online and listening in on her conversations, it was obvious she was neither. She knew how the world worked. She knew that people did horrible things, especially men, and especially to vulnerable women. He'd seen her watch out for drunk women at bars, watched her tell two younger girls to "always keep an eye on your drink and don't touch it if you take your eyes off it for even a second."

No, it was like—there was this gleam in her eyes, like she was purposefully goading disaster. Like she knew that any of these fuckers could've followed her out to her car, that any number of awful things could happen to her, but didn't care.

Why?

The question haunted him. It kept him company when he showered in hotel and motel bathrooms, when he tailed her on long stretches of highway, when he went for a run in the morning. It kept his ass up late into the night, and Micah never had issues sleeping.

That fucking question, *why*, was how Micah found himself sitting at a table near the back of a swanky New Orleans restaurant about four months later—on Christmas Eve, no less—pretending to ignore the redhead in the killer black dress sitting at the bar and flirting with the bartender. Micah wanted to punch the poor bartender in the face, and he didn't know why.

Well, that was bullshit. He knew why. Just didn't want to admit it to himself.

Seemed like he and Conor had the same kryptonite.

He should call it. The mission was heading in a direction he couldn't foresee and therefore couldn't control. Better to wash his hands of the whole thing, come up with some excuse for why he couldn't keep watching her, and let Luke take over. Luke wouldn't be able to walk two steps without tripping and falling into Kara's unintentional trap, but fine, let him. Conor could marry her, for all Micah fucking cared. Conor and Luke could kick each other's asses over the woman, for all Micah gave a shit at this point.

Liar, his brain sang. Micah lifted his glass to suck down his bourbon and hopefully drown out the taunting voice, only to realize his glass was empty. He raised his head, searching for the waitress, but as luck would have it, the waitress was on the way over to him—and she was already carrying another glass of bourbon.

"This is great place," Micah remarked when she reached him. "I was thinking I needed another drink and here you are, three steps ahead of me." He didn't mention that he hated when people were a few steps ahead of him—any steps ahead of him was a cause for alarm.

"Oh!" She grinned at him. "I'm not that good of a waitress; this is from the redhead at the bar."

Micah's stomach dropped to his feet, his vision blurring, a warning roaring in his brain and drowning out whatever else she was saying. He'd been tailing Kara for months, and this was unprecedented. She flirted all the time, but she never made the first move—especially not such an obvious one. Had he been made? What was he going to do if she knew he'd been tailing her?

"—read it so I can let her know if it's a yes or a no," the waitress was saying.

"Sorry, read what?"

As Micah's vision cleared, he noticed that the waitress was holding out a paper napkin, folded into fourths like origami. Morbid curiosity moved him to take the napkin from her and smooth it flat.

The handwriting was full of loops and uncertainty. Something had been written and then crossed out, repeatedly—Micah couldn't make out what it said, so he focused on what she'd replaced it with.

For the Tzedakkah you did earlier. Can I join you?

Micah swallowed, hand going to the Magen David hidden below his shirt. How had she seen it? Furthermore, how had she seen him, period? The night before, he'd left her safely ensconced in her sublet in the Marigny, asleep and alone. He'd made his way back to his hotel downtown, his thoughts churning with how hard it was becoming to walk away and how useless the whole mission had become, when he'd come across a homeless veteran and his dog on Delphine. The guy was clearly broken, had basically given up—just sitting on the street, head in his dirt-encrusted hands, not even bothering to ask passersby for money. His sign *Homeless Vet, Need Money to Feed Me and My Dog* had fallen over, and the tragic wastefulness of the whole situation made Micah stop in his tracks. Reaching into his wallet, Micah pulled out a wad of fifties, probably a thousand dollars' worth, tapped the guy on his shoulder and handed it over, along with the number for a national organization Luke liked that helped veterans get back on their feet, no questions, no judgment, no fine print. The guy had cried, he'd been so thankful, life coming back into those dead eyes, and Micah had mumbled a "don't mention it" and gotten the hell out of there.

It was completely unplanned—Micah only carried that kind of cash because he hated the security nightmare of credit card accounts—a moment of vulnerability. It was okay, because he was the only one who was supposed to have known about it.

Was that what Kara was talking about? How had he missed her?

"...Sir? Should I tell her you're not interested?" The waitress prompted. Micah ignored her, his gaze going straight to Kara, who watched him from the bar, her head tilted in question.

Watching him. *She* was watching *him*. Like she could see into him. Micah's chest—and groin—heated and tightened.

He nodded at Kara, then jerked his head to the seat across from him. She swallowed, biting her lip, before hopping off her bar stool and murmuring something to the now-disappointed bartender. Micah was almost amused at the sense of jealous satisfaction he got from knowing Kara had chosen him over the other man.

Because that was the thing, wasn't it? This time, she hadn't waited for someone else to make a move. She'd picked him out of all the fuckers at this restaurant and moved first. She'd chosen him. He didn't know *why,* but he was going to find out.

"I'm hoping this seat isn't taken, or this is about to get really awkward," Kara commented beside him, her soft, throaty voice smoothing over him like the rough side of velvet. It felt so good hearing her address *him* for once, it practically hurt.

"I could say, 'taken by you,' but that would be cheesy," Micah said, relieved that she couldn't hear his heart pounding in his throat.

"We can't have that." Kara slid into the seat across from him and ran a hand over the back of her neck. Micah wasn't sure if it was a nervous gesture or a come on; he'd seen her do a lot of things, but he'd never seen her do that before. He liked that he wasn't sure, which was a real mindfuck for a guy who usually hated mysteries.

"I'm Micah."

"Kara."

There was a moment while they digested that information; or pretended to, on his side.

"So how'd you know I was Jewish?"

Kara sighed. "Right. I'm sorry, that was a real creepy stalker move, wasn't it."

Micah laughed. She had had no fucking idea.

"Stalking can be sexy, depending on the circumstances," he said.

"Uh, as relieved as I am to hear that you aren't going to

file a restraining order against me—you aren't, right?—I'm going to have to disagree and say there's literally nothing sexy about stalking."

She delivered this with a straight face, and Micah would have believed her—except that he'd been hacking into her computer searches over the past few months, even the ones sent to her privacy filter, and he knew what kind of smut she liked to read. *Stalker, kidnapping, nonconsensual* had all made appearances at various times. Micah wasn't a dick or an idiot; he knew that just because a woman fantasized about dangerous meetings with men didn't mean she actually wanted to have one. But even knowing it was a fantasy of hers...it brought up interesting fantasies for him, too, ones that made his cock thicken under the table.

He hid his thoughts from her, making sure to lower his voice for the next part.

"No? Someone behind you in the dark, cataloguing your every move, his breath on your neck, putting all that time and energy and focus into knowing where you go, what you eat, how you sleep, someone who knows what you like and how you like it, someone who's made it his mission to give it to you that way? Nothing sexy about that, not at all?"

Silence. Had he gone too far?

"Man, you're good at that," she finally commented, seeming torn in two. "Just a little smooth talking and here I am ready to flip all my beliefs upside down. The military should hire you to handle its PR."

Micah didn't respond. Did she know? Did she know who he was, what he did? Was this some game she was playing? What was her angle?

"Oof, tough crowd," said Kara. "Not a fan of Uncle Sam, noted, won't joke about it again."

That hit too close to home, and it seemed clear she was

just guessing, so Micah redirected the conversation towards safer territory.

Well, safe-ish. Micah wasn't going to lie to himself—the second she'd sent over the drink and note, he should've cut his losses and run. Staying was dangerous, in a way that even his riskiest SEAL mission hadn't been. Not physically. Worse: emotionally.

But something wouldn't let him leave. He needed to see this through.

"How'd you know I was Jewish? And what's this charitable action you assume I did?"

She sighed. "I woke up in the middle of the night and couldn't fall back asleep, so I did a—remarkably stupid thing, quite honestly—and went for a walk around the Quarter."

"By yourself?" His voice was sharp with reprimand, and he hastened to soften it. She wasn't his, and his protectiveness wouldn't be easily accepted by her. "What I mean is, this isn't a great spot to walk around at night by yourself."

He was usually smoother than this. What was this woman doing to him?

She waved him off. "Like I said, remarkably stupid. Anyway, I decided to go over to King PoBoys and get myself some fried oysters smothered in bread when I saw you giving that unhoused man an incredibly generous amount of money." She looked at Micah from under her lashes, not flirtatious, not accusatory, just...seeing him, clearly.

She continued. "I was impressed. Shocked, and a little concerned that someone I'm kind of doubting is a drug dealer carries that much money on their person in the first place, but still, impressed. The Magen David necklace slipped out from under the shirt you were wearing, so I nicknamed you the Good and Sexy Jewish Samaritan in my head and figured I'd never see you again. But New Orleans loves to prove how small it is. And then here you were tonight, nursing a bourbon and looking like you wanted to murder someone."

She glanced down at her hands, as if her nails were fascinating. Sighing, she glanced back up at him, holding his gaze. "It's not my style to send a guy a drink. It's not my usual move. I don't really have moves at all, per se, but I don't know... it's Christmas, there was another Jew alone at my favorite restaurant, and my curiosity sometimes gets the better of me, and I figured, well... what did I have to lose?"

Everything. She had everything to lose. So did he, apparently.

Micah had never in his adult life considered committing long-term to a woman, much less keeping one, but dear god, *this* woman needed a keeper.

Kara wasn't done. "For someone to give that much money to a homeless veteran—even if you're obscenely wealthy—you had to have a deeper reason. There was meaning behind the action, I could see it. And I just..."

She shrugged.

"I can't stop thinking about it. I needed to know why."

No one ever saw Micah that deeply. No one. That hot, tight feeling intensified, and Micah didn't know if he should just get up and leave her at the table alone and get the hell out of New Orleans, or Louisiana, or maybe the whole of North America... or pick her up, throw her over his shoulder, and take her to his hotel room so he could get so deep inside her neither of them would feel anything but each other for a while.

He settled for a third option.

"I've got a soft spot for veterans," he told her. "Something about them making a huge sacrifice for our country, only to be basically shoved out of the airplane without a parachute, pisses me the fuck off. That guy should've been smooth sailing for the rest of his life. He shouldn't be, he shouldn't..." Micah swallowed, choking on the words, an unfamiliar burning in his eyes.

Kara watched him carefully. "...shouldn't be on a street corner, forced to beg to feed himself and his dog, no matter if he's an addict or not. They deserve better. We owe them better." She finished for him, like she was in his goddamned head.

Micah nodded once. She turned her head away and shut her eyes, but not before he saw her eyes were wet and glassy.

"Are you crying?" He asked.

"Are you?" She countered, still looking away from him like she couldn't bear to let him see her so vulnerable.

"Well," he laughed. "Fuck. I guess I am."

She whipped her head back around, and then laughed too.

"Guess we're a pair."

"Guess we are."

They sat in silence for a moment, Micah sipping his bourbon, Kara a glass of red wine—Malbec, he knew. She was a one-wine-woman. Micah had begun believing that Kara might also be a one-man woman, and that Conor was that man, except here she was, sitting with him instead.

"Why the note? Why not come straight over here?" he asked, curious.

"You're lucky you got the note you did. I was going to write *do you find me attractive* and make you circle yes, no, or maybe, but that felt too middle school, even for me," Kara said, and although she attempted to sound casual, it was obvious she felt anything but.

Micah felt the corners of his mouth lift. "What do you think I would've circled?"

Kara grinned. "'Maybe.' You're tricky like that."

The laughter rolled out of him. "Tricky?"

She shrugged again, but this time there was no uncertainty in her voice. "Most people are easy to read. Their mannerisms, their eyes, the tone of their voice. You aren't. Not exactly poker faced, but like there's a whole iceberg beneath what you say and how you listen. I like that, I think, even if I don't think I can trust you."

Micah's whole body tensed back up. For her to just put that out there—no insinuations, no beating around the bush—was brave as hell, but also a little terrifying. He could placate her, of course, make her think she could trust him, but he preferred the honesty between them. How often could he be honest, even if it was only one layer of honesty covering a core of deceit?

"Good," he finally said. "You shouldn't trust me."

Kara nodded. "Okay. Let's order. I'm starving."

As she turned to the menu, he found himself saying, "I bet I can guess what your favorite flower is..."

The walk back to her rental was tense and silent, fraught with sexual tension and, if he were honest, a little fear. They hadn't directly discussed the fact that they were about to fuck—the look in Kara's eyes had been clear enough.

She'd suggested they go back to his hotel room, but Micah had quickly countered that he'd been wanting to see the Marigny. Although Micah was meticulous about keeping any telling information locked and hidden away, he couldn't risk that Kara would surprise him again. If she realized he was stalking her, she'd no longer be torn on whether it was sexy; she'd go straight to the police. Micah would be fine, of course, but it would create a mess he didn't need, especially when Conor found out he'd done the opposite of what he'd promised.

She'd relented easily, but she hadn't said a word to him in the last twenty minutes. Since it was Christmas Eve, Frenchmen Street was also silent—all the jazz and funk musicians home with their families for the night, or booked up at private parties. Without the music and crowds, the neighborhood felt ghostly and a little magical. Micah glanced at Kara a few times to see if she noticed the weirdness, but her shoulders were stiff and she seemed lost in her own head.

Was this what she'd been like with Conor that night when they'd made the much shorter walk from the bar to her hotel on Coronado? Distant? Preoccupied? Ambivalent?

Fucking Conor. Micah didn't want to think about him at all. Micah doubled his pace, closing the distance between them and placed a hand on her back. She startled.

"Kara…"

"I swear to god, if the next words out of your mouth are 'you don't have to do this,' I'll fucking stab you," she told him, whipping around to face him.

Micah chuckled, relieved to at least get a rise out of her, to have her present with him.

"I wasn't going to say that. You're a grown woman; you make your own choices. I just want to be one of them."

She stepped away from him and into the glow of the streetlamp. It bathed her in gold, almost like a fantasy. His throat burned. He hadn't meant to tell her something so revealing.

But then she said, "I haven't always been proud of my choices. I've done a lot I regret, and then a lot to punish myself for those regrets, and then I turn around and regret those, too." She shook her head at herself. "I never say shit like this out loud, I don't know why I'm telling you, but I just... you should know, Micah—regardless of what happens after this, sending you that drink tonight will end up in the *things Kara Blum did right* category." She shared a small, tremulous smile with him, lit by the streetlamp behind her.

Kara reached out her hand to him. When he took it, wrapping her small, soft hand in his, something settled in his chest. Like she was making a promise and he was accepting it.

"Just don't regret choosing me, okay?" she asked, and the vulnerability in it made him hate himself. A better man would tell her the truth. A better man wouldn't take advantage.

She needed a better man.

She needed a keeper.

He wasn't a better man, but he still wanted to be the one to keep her.

It wasn't because she was reckless and lost. Micah didn't have a savior boner for lost women. It was the addictive mix of confidence and vulnerability that made him feel like the latter was something precious he had to protect. And, mostly, it was the way she'd seen through him—seen *him*—and liked what she'd seen. No wonder Conor felt this way about her.

"No one could regret you, Kara," he told her. It sounded like he was making a promise back, and he hated himself for it. None of this fit his plan, and for once he didn't care. He'd figure out a way to deal with the wreckage later.

They walked holding hands, the silence no longer tense

with distrust, but fraught with anticipation. They hadn't discussed their jobs or their backgrounds; it was like there was this unspoken agreement to leave all backstory and subsequent potential bullshit out of this. And yet they'd connected on a level Micah didn't think was possible unless you were putting your life in someone else's hands. When he'd first met Conor and Luke, it was like their puzzle pieces had snapped into place. He'd never felt that before, never expected to feel it again, and yet here it was: the puzzle piece he hadn't realized was missing. He felt that snap like a tangible thing.

He buried the thought, and the guilt that came with it, as they reached the front door. She released his hand to let them into the little shotgun house and he followed her in.

"Well," she said, trying to dispel the sex in the air with humor, "I guess—"

Micah never gave her a chance to finish the sentence. He pulled her to him by her hand, wrapped one arm around her waist to keep her anchored against him, and wrapped a hand around her jaw so he could guide her moving mouth under his. She gave him a small gasp of surprise in response, and he used it kiss her, open-mouthed and insistent. He was almost shocked by how turned on he already was. Kara gave as good as she got, switching between letting him take and taking herself, so their kiss kept alternating between war and armistice.

At one point, she pulled away, gasping.

"Give me a second."

"No." Micah went after her mouth again, unwilling to take a break from the taste and heat of her. In retaliation, he shoved his hands under her ass and lifted her up.

"Wrap your legs around me," he ordered, not even bothering with seduction. What was the point? He knew what she liked.

She hesitated for one second, then complied—like he'd known she would. Triumph warmed him, or maybe it was the caress of her fingers over his shirt. He wanted to feel them on his skin. He wanted nothing between them.

He started walking while kissing her—not the best choice. Micah was good but he wasn't a superhero with double vision, so he bumped into a few pieces of furniture before Kara pulled away from his mouth again to direct him to the bedroom. They banged into the wall once or twice, but Micah couldn't bring himself to give a shit; his hands were too busy squeezing her delectable ass, listening to her gasp as he discovered the terrain of her mouth with his tongue. He was going to map the rest of her body with his tongue, too.

Kara melted against him, surrendering herself fully, bravely. Softness and strength in one messy, brilliant, beautiful package. No wonder Conor had lost his mind when she'd left. Micah would lose his, too, if he weren't careful.

Operation Kryptonite Pussy, indeed, he thought grimly.

"Fuck!" Kara cried, and Micah realized he'd squeezed harder than he'd meant to.

"You like it when I'm rough with you baby, don't you?" Micah spoke against her mouth as he spotted and walked them into the bedroom, flipping on the light. He wanted to see this. "You like when I get so worked up, I grip your ass too tight," he continued.

She panted against him, and in retaliation for making him feel so goddamned much that he forgot his mission, his lovers, himself, he tossed her on the bed. She bounced once, and he watched with satisfaction and not a little bit of anger, his hands going to the buttons on his shirt. He left them there—the promise of getting naked he wouldn't deliver on.

Yet.

"Your ass feeling a little lonely, huh, baby? Want my hands back on you? Well, you're going to have to get naked before I touch you again."

Fire flashed in her eyes.

"Who's going to make me?" she taunted.

She wanted to play that way, huh? Micah, who was already halfway-to-hard, felt his cock go rock solid at the husky words.

"You want me to make you? Will me ripping that dress and those tights off that needy body make your little cunt that much wetter?"

She growled at him, and he laughed, which only made her growl more.

"I don't know how you can be so cute when you're seconds away from getting your ass spanked, but then you've been surprising me all night, haven't you, baby?"

Her eyes darkened. "What did you just say to me?"

He could be getting himself into hot water. He wasn't sure how far he could go with knowing her turn-ons before she figured out it wasn't organic. But he couldn't seem to get himself to dial it back—the words just poured out.

"You heard me. Clothes off, Kara. Or you don't get to come at all tonight."

That did it. Her pupils dilated, a flush spread across her body, her nipples beaded, and her hips jerked. She looked turned on and terrified, and god save him, he wanted her that way.

Eyes on his unmoving hands, she squirmed out of her black dress.

"Tights," he said, voice like gravel and not caring.

"You, too."

"Who's calling the shots here, gorgeous?" But to reward her, he started unbuttoning his shirt. This sped her up, and she wriggled her tights down her body. He paused in unbuttoning to help her slide the tights off her feet until she was naked except for a pair of silky black boy shorts and a see-through black lace bra. He'd known her tits were big, but he wasn't prepared for the way they filled the cups, the way her berry pink nipples strained against the fabric. It had been one thing to see her, clothes on, flirting with Conor and other men. A whole other to see her almost bared, *to him.*

Just for him.

Only for him.

He finished unbuttoning his shirt, pulling it off and following it with his undershirt, tossing them on the ground. Who cared if they got wrinkled? He had more important things to worry about.

Like the wet spot between Kara's legs.

"Bra and underwear off. Now," he barked. Micah didn't give orders—he topped from the bottom, he made other people think they were calling the shots he was making, and he liked it this way. But something about this woman had peeled back his layers until he was just another bossy asshole telling her what to do. And yeah, she liked it—he only had to look at the red splotches across her body to know she liked it—but this wasn't his way.

What was she doing to him?

As if she could feel his hesitation, she stood there, head tilted and watching him.

She didn't need to be bossed, she needed to be led.

"You want to take everything off, don't you, baby? Your poor nipples are hurting, your cunt is throbbing, it's so needy. But you're not going to get what you need until you do what I want you to do. And you want to do what I want, don't you, baby? You want to please me."

Breaths speeding up, Kara worked off her bra. Micah, trying not to get caught up in his triumph, dropped to his knees and pulled her underwear off her body, slowly, letting the fabric pool at her knees, and made sure he stroked her legs as he freed them and let the panties drop to the floor, forgotten.

And then he descended on her cunt—and into madness.

That's what it felt like, as he kissed her inner thighs and nibbled on her labia and licked and sucked and feasted—he didn't feel like a man, he felt like an animal, like a bull who had been taunted one too many times with a red flag. She writhed underneath him, and he gripped her hips, aware on some level he was going to leave bruises and not caring. Kara shrieked and pleaded and mumbled nonsense as he ate her, her hands alternating between beating his shoulders and stroking his hair, pushing him away and holding him to her, and her gibberish only stoked the fire inside him higher. When he felt her tightening beneath him, about to go over, he searched for some semblance of control and forced himself to gentle his ministrations.

"Don't you dare come," he breathed against her perfect pussy, looking up at her finally and catching the look in her eyes. If she'd been turned on and terrified before, he didn't know how to categorize what she was now.

He liked it, though.

"Micah, please..."

"You chose this, baby," he murmured, placing a kiss against her trembling thigh. "Are you regretting it now? If you are, I'll stop. I'll leave and you'll never see me again."

"I don't like ultimatums," Kara responded shakily, and for that, he bit her where he'd just kissed her.

"Damn it, Micah!"

"Ask nicely."

She growled again—god, it was a cute sound—but she said, "please, pretty please, Mr. Bossman, let me come."

She couldn't know, of course, how Mr. Bossman would set him off.

"I may not be *the boss*, but I have no problem being your boss," he told her, before diving back in and edging her again, once, twice, three times, in retaliation. He was so hard he thought he might just come from the taste of her, from her writhing, trembling, helpless, needy body, her soaked and greedy cunt, and he resisted when she dragged at his head.

"Micah, Micah, please. Why are you so angry? What did I do?" she sobbed.

Fucking hell, how did she see through him that easily?

No one, no one had ever...

If he weren't careful, she would destroy him. Micah would've left her, right then and there, if he could have. If she hadn't already dug her pretty little her claws into him. If he wasn't already obsessed.

"The only one who is angry is your poor little teased and ravaged pussy," he growled, and *his* growl was not cute. "She's so red and so wet. She hurts so bad, doesn't she? She needs to come. Poor pussy," he crooned directly to Kara's cunt. "If only Kara would get with the program, maybe you'd get some relief."

For that, he got actual claws: her nails in his neck. He grinned, feeling savage and brutal.

"What's the, the—" she could barely get the words out as he licked her.

"The program? Easy. Say, 'Micah, you're the only man I want,' and you can come."

She gasped, but she didn't say the words. Rage tore through him. Micah didn't *get* jealous; he fucked two dudes who fucked him and each other and also fucked other people, and he was fine with it, for fuck's sake. And yet suddenly this redhead came along with danger in her eyes and he wanted to piss circles around her, make her wear a collar that said his name on it, give her a ring so all the other fuckers including Conor knew to stay away—

God.

God.

He pulled back, staring at her. What was wrong with him?

And why couldn't she say the words? Was she still holding onto Conor, after all these months? And if she was, why did she leave San Diego in the first place? He'd been tailing Kara for months, had hacked every single account she had, and he still didn't know enough.

He wanted to know everything.

Kara reached down and cradled his cheek in her hand, and Micah leaned into it like a cat, absorbing the warmth, the tenderness. "Micah, I can't say you're the only man I want, but I can say that I've never wanted anyone the way I want you."

Fuck it. Good enough.

"That's right, baby," he said. "You were honest, and this pussy gets rewarded for it." Diving back into her pussy, he sucked her swollen clit into his mouth, and then bit.

She came hard, her screams sweet, her taste sweeter. He drank her down, feeling a thousand feet tall. All that she'd said, all that she'd given him, all she'd surrendered, helped him feel like himself again. It hadn't been easy, but he had gotten her here.

She needs you, his gut told him. *You, not Conor. Conor doesn't know how to handle a woman like her.*

Except when he'd given her the opportunity to swear off all other men—and he'd been pretty damn persuasive—she'd refused and instead opted for something else.

She couldn't say he was the only man she wanted, because he wasn't.

Fuck this.

Orgasm denial had shown up on her private search history, but so had *forced orgasm*. She wanted to come again, and she was going to come again. He swiped his tongue down her wet pussy, chasing any remaining juices.

"Micah," she gasped, "enough, please."

"No," he said stubbornly. "Not enough. You'll come for me again, and then I'm coming in you."

With that, he clamped onto her clit with his lips and worried it with his tongue, sending her screaming into another orgasm, the "yes, oh god, yes," that came from her sending satisfaction clawing at his balls. Releasing her, he climbed his way up her body and unzipped his fly, pulling himself out, barely remembering to grab a condom.

"Fuck," he groaned, tearing the package open and putting it on in record time, before grabbing her wrists in one hand, and guiding himself inside her with his other, catching her gaze with his.

"Mine," he growled.

"Yours," she sobbed.

He thrust home.

Holy. Fucking. Shit.

Tight, heavenly, out of this world wet heat clasped around his cock. Kara cried out, coming for a third time, milking him for all he was worth. He got off two, maybe three thrusts before he came harder than he ever had in his entire existence.

Micah caught himself on his elbows before collapsing on top of Kara, rolling off to the side and bringing her with him. Sweat plastered their bodies together.

She started laughing, wheezing, really, and without knowing why, he joined her.

"Holy shit," Kara breathed, before laughing again.

"Holy shit," he agreed.

"Merry Christmas, I guess," she said.

He moved sweat-dampened hair off her forehead and lifted his head to plant a gentle kiss there.

"I always thought Christmas was stupid. Guess I've been doing it wrong," she mused.

"Yeah?" The words, *well we can do Christmas this way together forever* were on the tip of his tongue, but he caught them just in time. He couldn't promise her that.

Not when he'd already gone back on a promise to his best friend.

He wasn't supposed to be here.

He should never have touched her.

But fuck it, he had, and here they were, and he wasn't about to walk away from her. Not even for his relationship with Conor and Luke. What did he have with them, anyway? No one was willing to admit to anything real. He thought he was okay with that, but was he? Didn't he deserve better?

On top of him, Kara stiffened, almost as if she could sense his inner turmoil.

She moved as if to slide off him.

Micah gripped her tighter.

"Going somewhere?" he asked casually.

"Figured you might want some space."

"You figured wrong."

"Well, maybe I want some space. That was… intense."

"It was," he agreed amiably, although he felt anything but.

"Look," the words burst forth from her. "Usually, I'm the one to clear out or make it clear that nothing can come from this, and maybe I'd wait until the next morning to do that, but for some reason I don't want to say any of that *at all*, and it's scaring the absolute shit out of me, and you're already a scary enough dude. So if you want to leave, I'm giving you the space to do so. No hard feelings. But if you're going to go —" her voice broke a little here, making Micah feel like even more of a shit than he already did, "—you need to go now. Anything else would be drastically unfair and unforgivable."

Micah opened his mouth and shut it. She groaned.

"Damn it, now I sound vulnerable and pathetic," she muttered against his chest. "What the fuck have you done to me? You do need to leave."

He rubbed his hand over her back soothingly. "I like this vulnerable side of you. And I'm not going anywhere. We'll fuck again and then sleep and then in the morning find out if Cafe Du Monde is open on Christmas or if we need to go to Popeye's for food."

She lifted her head. "Are you asking me to have breakfast with you?"

Micah stroked further down her back, until his hand landed on her ass again. He smacked it lightly.

"Not asking. Telling. You just gave me the best orgasm I've ever had in my entire life, and I also don't entirely know which way is up, but I know this—we'll be together in the morning, we'll eat, and then we'll figure it out."

She lifted his head, gifting him with another smile. Like

the smile she'd given him earlier when they were outside, it both solidified his decision and threatened to upend everything.

He kissed that smile, telling himself he'd worry about whatever threatened them later.

Later came too quickly.

It came with the vibration of his phone.

Micah opened his eyes to the dark room. At first, all he could see was the pile of curly red hair in front of him. He'd fallen asleep spooning Kara. Micah was rarely the big spoon, and it felt nice, to hold her against him that way.

His phone vibrated again. He twisted away from her and reached to the ground, searching around in the dark for his pants before pulling the phone free.

Luke: **I always forget, am I allowed to say Merry Christmas to you?**

Micah laughed, responding.

Micah: **Merry Christmas, asshole. Sorry I'm not there with you. Hope you aren't masturbating and crying about how lonely you are without us.**

Luke: **Don't worry about it, I'm saving it all up for you when you get back. Hope you're ready for my whip.**

Even though Micah had come three times in the past as many hours, he felt his guts tighten at the image.

Luke: **How goes Operation Kryptonite Pussy? Got enough evidence of her fucking other dudes to turn Conor off her forever? I'm still not sure that'll work—he seemed pretty gone over her.**

Fuck. Micah pinched his nose between his fingers, before

freezing, remembering Conor doing the same thing some months back.

What could he say? Luke couldn't—and wouldn't—lie unless his and his teammates' lives were on the line. But that was to enemy actors, never to each other. Could Micah convince Luke to keep his mouth shut? Could he lie to Luke? What the fuck was he going to do?

Luke: **Man, you're freaking me out a little.**

Micah responded.

Micah: **I'm handling it.**

His phone started ringing. He contemplated refusing the call, but that would only spur Luke on, and he wasn't sure how he could keep Kara from getting suspicious if he was getting called relentlessly on Christmas Day from a contact saved as Sexy Sadist with a Huge Cock (Luke's doing).

He rolled out of bed, careful not to disturb the sleeping woman beside him. Kara curled deeper into the pillow, and he smiled, but there was no humor behind it.

Nabbing the phone, he went into the hallway and shut the door quietly behind him.

"I'm handling it."

"Where are you?"

"New Orleans."

"Where in New Orleans?"

"My hotel."

"Really? Because I'm looking at the GPS on your phone, and it looks like you're in the Marigny. I thought the Monteleone was in the Quarter."

"You hacked my phone's location?"

He could practically hear Luke shrugging on the phone. "I was worried something had happened to you. Turns out I was right."

"I don't know what the hell you're talking about."

"You fucked her, didn't you?"

Micah's stomach dropped. Was this when he lied? What would happen to his relationship with Luke when he lied?

He heard Luke inhale sharply. "Damn it, Micah! You were supposed to keep your hands off her. It was your idea, remember?"

"I know. Fuck. I know," Micah concluded. "There's something about her, man…"

Luke laughed, incredulous. "You sound just like Conor. I guess I was right, her pussy is kryptonite."

"Bro, you have no fucking idea."

"Maybe I should take a turn," Luke joked.

Micah growled. "Don't even think about it."

"Fuck. Micah. You can't be serious about this girl. She's Conor's."

"She isn't Conor's. She isn't mine either. She's no one's."

Not even her own. She was too lost for that, and Micah wanted to help her find herself—on her way to him.

If she hadn't already.

There was silence on the other side of the phone.

Then Luke said, "Come home. Clear out now, get in the car, or I don't care, leave the car there and get on a plane and come home, we'll get it shipped. Just come home. Clear your head, get away from her before you do something you can't take back. Conor and I are your family, man."

"I can't leave her," Micah argued, part relieved by the option Luke had offered, part horrified by the idea of not having her in his arms, her taste in his mouth, after this. "Not after tonight. Besides, I promised I'd watch her."

Luke snorted. "A little late for that argument. Whatever. I'll take over." Before Micah could say anything or growl again, Luke hurried to say, "I won't touch her. Won't get near her. I've learned y'all's lesson, man." Luke's southern Texas only came out when he was stressed. "I don't need kryptonite pussy in my life, got enough problems, right?"

Micah laughed tersely. "Right."

"See you soon." Luke hesitated on the phone, started to say, "I—"

Micah froze. Was Luke finally going to admit his feelings? "You what?"

"I'm excited to see you, that's all. I've missed your conniving ass."

Of course. Luke was always able to cut through Micah's bullshit but refused to address his own.

They hung up. Micah opened the door back to the bedroom. Kara was still asleep, curled on the bed, auburn hair almost black in the dark. Even though a voice in his head screamed at him to get back in bed, wake her up, fuck his way back into her body and then tell her everything, he ignored the voice. Forget what it would do to his relationship with Conor for a second; Micah couldn't stay with Kara for his own sake.

He'd been right when he'd first seen her all those months ago in the bar. She was dangerous. But not for the reasons he thought. Not because she threatened to take Conor away from him, but because she threatened to shake the foundation of his entire existence. She'd dug her way into Conor's head; she'd dig her way into Micah's heart.

Better to leave now. It hurt, a little, after having promised her breakfast, to ditch her in the middle of the night, knowing she'd think he was just another asshole. He considered leaving her a note, apologizing, but to what purpose? Better for them to end this game now, for her to hate him, than for things to go sour later.

Micah pulled on his clothes and shoes, watching her breathe, committing the image to his memory. He leaned over and kissed her gently on the back of her neck. She murmured something in her sleep.

Then forced himself to turn away from her and walked out the door and out of her life.

For now.

3

____

Now

Micah couldn't sleep. He'd been lying in bed for hours, watching the time tick away on his phone as shadows moved across the ceiling of the seaside motel.

After Conor and Luke had been tied up, knocked out, and dragged onto the helicopter, which took off not long after, Micah and Kara had swum back to shore and started the long, grueling hike up the beach back to the highway. Waterlogged and terrified, Kara had followed him silently. They'd flagged down an SUV driving past: two young surfers. Micah hadn't worried about their safety; he was the scariest thing on the road.

The surfers had dropped them off at the motel, and Micah had gone inside to use the phone—and grab them a room. A short conversation with Marcus later, and a room was procured from the suspicious older woman who ran the motel. She clearly didn't trust Micah, but Marcus's money had a way of making the wariest people shut their eyes and pretend they didn't know something was wrong.

Micah and Kara had checked into the room and he'd gotten her into the shower, briefly leaving her to go find food, hair dye, and to clean and dry their only clothes. When he'd come back, Kara had been prostate on the floor, gasping for air.

"We have to find them," she cried. "We have to—"

Micah didn't bother to tell her he was doing everything he could, or that Marcus was sending Billy and a car. He didn't tell her that he already had a lead, but that she wasn't coming with him. She could barely breathe, and the only thing that mattered right then was helping her.

That was only the first panic attack she'd had that night. Usually, Micah could help break her out of them with Luke's guidance, but she was spiraling, and all he could do was hold her and remind her *breathe, Kara, just breathe with me.* She'd clung to him tightly, like she'd needed the reminder that he was still there.

Finally, exhausted from the ordeal, she'd stood quietly while he dyed her hair purple, and then let him lead her to the bed, where she'd passed out. Now, Micah lay there, holding her, finding comfort in the feel of her in his arms. He'd shut his eyes at first, hoping to get some much-needed sleep to fuel him for what came next, but sleep wouldn't come.

Micah was familiar with functioning without sleep—it had been both a part of his time as a SEAL, as well as when he lived on the streets and sleeping meant leaving yourself vulnerable to other predators. But he'd gotten used to sleeping, especially with Kara wrapped in his arms, asleep on his chest, Luke and Conor framing them on both sides. Sleep was reserved for being with his family, knowing they were safe. And they weren't now. Not him, although he didn't care about that. Not Kara, who was the real target of Chris Johnathan's wrath. And not the two men he loved, who were god knows where, surviving god knew what.

God, he hoped they were surviving. They had to be alive. The maniacal professor was too vindictive to kill them quickly. And they'd been trained for torture. All they needed to do was live through it.

But he wasn't sure how much time he had left, which was why he needed to leave, now. Leave *her.*

As if she'd heard him, the woman in his arms, warm and soft and oh-so-vulnerable, cried out in her sleep.

"Micah? Luke! Conor!"

He didn't know what she was dreaming, but her obvious pain ripped his heart out. Just like he was about to rip out hers.

He'd been here before, long ago, holding her for a few moments in her sleep before sneaking out the door. He'd never planned on leaving her again. In fact, he'd promised himself he never would. But then, god laughed whenever a man made the mistake of making plans. Even at Micah, who was a planner down to his core.

He didn't have much of a plan, now, but he would do anything to protect his family, to rescue the men they had lost. And that meant forcing his ass out of bed so he could leave Kara in Billy's safekeeping and start the long, lonely journey into the dark to reunite them.

There was a part of him that wasn't sure leaving her was the right choice, especially with the state she was in. But the only thing that would stop the panic attacks, that would help her, would be to bring Luke and Conor home. She'd be safe; Billy was going to take her to Marcus's compound and watch over her there, indefinitely.

But even that rationale couldn't stop him from feeling like he was betraying her, all over again.

He kissed the back of her neck, light as a butterfly's wings. He'd done this before—that Christmas Eve when he'd first felt this unbreakable connection to her, and then left. *Fuck.* Still, no matter how much his body yearned to stay and pull her tighter into his arms, he had a job to do.

Slipping quietly from the old, musty bedsheets, he rose off the bed and dressed, while wracking his mind for a way to soften the blow. To make it clear he wasn't leaving her, that he would come back—or at least try to.

Finding a half-dead pen in the desk, he scribbled a note:

Baby, I'm sorry, but I need to go rescue them, and I can't risk your safety in the process.

Do what Billy tells you to do.

I love you. More than is measurable.

M

There, that would have to do. Last time, he hadn't left a note.

He took one last look at her, memorizing the way her hair fell across her face as she curled into a ball and reached out a hand, seeking him out even in sleep. They'd come so far in their relationship, and even though he accepted he might never see her again—might not make it back alive— he was glad for every second he'd had with her.

He hadn't told her he'd loved her enough times. She'd never said it to him. But he knew.

Time to go.

Closing the door behind him, he turned toward the bald man who stood outside the door, facing the railing, smoking a cigarette, eyes on the desolate parking lot, empty save for two cars. Billy's car, and Micah's temporary getaway.

Holy hell. He shivered, not because of the cold, just

remembering the freezing water they'd been submerged in as their rental car sank into the ocean. Kara had gotten them out, had saved them. She could've left them there to die. Probably should've. But she was strong, and she had a big heart, and she cared deeply about them.

Although she was going to kill him for leaving her.

That made him smile.

"You sure about this?" Billy asked.

No, he wasn't. But what choice did he have? He couldn't bring her with him, and trust that she'd be safe while he did what he needed to do. She'd be fine with Billy. He'd take her to Marcus's compound. She'd hate it, but she'd be safe. If she wasn't, Micah would destroy Marcus, Billy, and the Doctor—blood ties to Marcus be damned.

"Keep her safe. Give her whatever she wants. And if we —I–don't make it..." he swallowed. Breathed. Accepted the possibility of that reality. "...then make sure she has a good life."

Billy tapped him on the back—his version of a promise —and with one last look back at the door, Micah headed down the stairs with peeling paint and out to the car waiting for him. Thank fuck Marcus was willing to help. For a favor, of course. Blood ties only went so far with his half-brother... you always paid a price for his help.

And Micah would pay any price.

4

———

When she woke, the bed was empty. Someone had dressed her while she'd slept—leggings and an actual bra with underwire and everything, underwear and a sweater and socks. The bra hurt, unfamiliar, the underwear tight and alien. When was the last time she wore socks? But then it was fall in Idaho, and socks were a necessity now.

There was a hoodie folded on the bed. She zipped it on, feeling claustrophobic, trapped. Strange that it was clothes that made her feel trapped now, when before it was being naked in front of her men.

Where were they?

A warning sounded in her head, discordant, like a broken chord on a guitar. Something was different.

Something was wrong.

"Micah?"

Silence.

"Luke," she called out sharply. "Conor."

More silence.

Reluctantly, she went downstairs. The house was just

waking, the early dawn light filtering over the trees out the window. The tops of the Tetons were white from snow and orange from the rising sun. Maybe they'd go for a hike later.

But the men weren't in the kitchen, the office, the workout room. Finally, she found them, in the vestibule by the front door. Micah held a backpack, Luke, sneakers. Luke saw her and glanced away. Were those tears in his eyes? Conor stood in the center, hands clenched, eyes wild.

"Are we going somewhere?" she asked.

Conor started toward her, only for the other two to drag him back, arms around his waist, his chest, holding him tight.

"We aren't going anywhere, baby," Micah said. "But you are."

Her throat felt tight. It was hard to swallow.

"What do you mean?"

Conor spoke through clenched teeth. "A gilded cage is still a cage, right? Love without freedom is just possession. You wanted your freedom more than you wanted us, so now you have it."

He jerked his head. Kara followed his gaze. She wasn't sure who'd done it or when, but the front door was wide open.

"I—" Kara forgot how to use words. How to breathe. "What does, what are you even saying?"

Luke spoke, not looking for her. "Backpack's for you. There's money in there, your ID, a new cellphone with a ticket on it for a flight back to Chicago. A taxi's on its way."

Micah's voice shook. She'd never heard him like this. "Chris is locked away, and so are his brothers. You're safe now."

Oh god.

"If you don't leave now, you'll miss your ride," he continued.

"And you're not coming with me?"

Conor jerked his head again, a clear no.

Oh god oh god oh god.

Her voice broke, "So you don't love me, not anymore."

"Kara, we're doing this because we love you."

She wanted them, she knew she loved them—but the open door beckoned to her. If she didn't take this chance, she knew she'd never get it again.

Her feet carried her forward. Took the shoes from Lucas.

"Will you please look at me?" she asked Luke.

"If I look at you, I won't be able to do this," he said.

One shoe on, then two. When she grabbed his thigh to steady herself, he jerked away.

Okay, so. It was like this.

Go? Stay?

Backpack now. Micah wouldn't release it, not at first, but with a heaving breath he gave it to her. She reached for him. He allowed her to place her hand over his heart. It was pounding. Except for when he was inside her, fucking her, his heart was always steady.

With the hand not holding Conor back, he gently removed her hand from his chest and wrapped her fingers around the backpack.

Finally, Conor.

She couldn't find words, couldn't touch him. He was stiff as a statue. For what felt like hours, they just stared at each other.

His voice was choked with tears. "For so long, all I wanted was you. It mattered more than anything. But what I want most, now, is for you to be happy. And you won't be happy with us."

He lowered his head to hers, kissed her forehead.

"Go. Before I change my mind. Before—"

Kara moved away from them. The mountains outside beckoned.

They were frozen in time, a tableau of pain and determination.

Her voice broke.

"I love—"

"Don't you fucking say it."

Well. Then.

One foot through the threshold, the other. The air felt different, cold and crisp and it was like she'd forgotten what it was like to breathe it fresh. Absurd, really. She was outside all the time.

Somewhere, a taxi honked.

Time to go.

She ran down the road, which stretched along, scary and endless, trees dark and foreboding because suddenly it was nighttime. Something inside her broke. She'd always thought Orpheus was so stupid for looking back at Euridice when he led her through the underworld. He could have stayed facing forward, could have saved her from becoming a pillar of salt.

She'd thought wrong. In the distance, behind her, she heard a roar of pure anguish. And when she turned, she saw Conor sink to the floor of the house, his roar shaking the trees as the door swung shut.

This was all she had wanted, and it hurt so much she could scream.

She kept running.

5

For the first time since she'd been taken by Chris and his henchmen, Kara woke up alone.

It was disorienting—doubly so, after the nightmare she'd had. Usually, there was an arm or a hairy leg thrown over her. Sometimes she was face first on the bed with a large body fully covering her so she was practically suffocated by the pillow. When her men had kidnapped her six weeks ago and taken her to the cabin, she'd hated it—or at least she'd told herself she'd hated it. Now, being caught up in their arms was as natural to her as breathing. And not having them surrounding her felt like someone had cut out her heart and tossed it off the side of a mountain.

Sitting up, she glanced around the room for Micah. He wasn't in the small dark room that smelled of old water and mold and stale cigarettes. She wasn't surprised he hadn't slept; he was probably searching for a lead. Climbing out of the bed, she opened the door to the bathroom. An empty, dark, stain-covered room the size of a closet greeted her.

Her gut clenched. Even if he were awake, he wouldn't have gone far. Not when he was so worried about her, and she was being so weak. She hated what the panic attacks had done to her, making her feel fragile and useless.

Where was he?

Making her way across the motel room, she discovered her dress, dry and mostly clean, and pulled it back on over her head, before unlocking and opening the door to the outdoor walkway, even though Micah had made her swear not to unlock the door, ever. Maybe he'd gone out for provisions or was making a phone call. Neither of them had phones currently; Micah's had fallen out when they'd escaped the sinking car, and Kara hadn't touched a phone since she'd called Lola that night in Wyoming. What was that, about two weeks ago? Kara hadn't needed a phone since, and there hadn't been time to get one, but she wanted one now. Wanted to text him, and receive the reassurance that he was coming back soon.

But, since she wasn't an idiot, she wasn't entirely surprised to see a folded piece of paper on the chipped desk.

Baby, I'm sorry...

Anger and fear filled her. Sure, he'd left a note this time, but that didn't make up for the fact that he was going to leave her. That he didn't even bother to say goodbye.

Likely because he knew she'd be pissed and didn't want to face the argument.

Would she ever see him again? Had she saved their lives for nothing? Was she destined to be protected in a gilded cage?

She slammed outside the room, hoping to catch her manipulative jackass of a lover, but almost knocking into Billy instead.

"You," she accused.

Billy lifted his chin in acknowledgment. There was a

sharp, jagged scar running down his throat. She'd never noticed it before.

"Me."

Her manipulative jackass of a lover had left her.

"He's gone, isn't he?"

Billy lifted his chin again. "I have orders to protect you, with my life if necessary. I'm taking you back to Marcus's. You'll be safe there."

Safe. That word had so many meanings. Once upon a time, physical safety never registered. Her entire focus had been on keeping her heart safe. But once upon a time was gone, and she'd risked her heart for three men she might never see again. *Fuck, that hurt.* She'd tried to keep her heart safe from them at first—and it had been easy, when she'd felt like nothing more than a toy—but they'd proven to her how much she meant to them, and she'd begun to fall.

She should've known she'd hit skull-breaking cement on the way down.

Not because she thought they didn't care about her—she knew they did—but because she didn't think she'd survive losing them. She couldn't go sit in Marcus's house and twiddle her thumbs while she waited like a good damsel for Micah to rescue the others. She'd proven she was capable, damn it. Wasn't she the one who'd deepthroated a gun for a distraction and then killed a man? Wasn't she the one who'd talked down their contact at Vixen? Who'd gotten them out of the car as it sunk? Hadn't she survived Chris's torture? She was strong enough to help now. But she wasn't sure she was strong enough to be left behind.

He's just protecting you, her inner voice pointed out. *He wants to keep you safe.*

But Kara was sick of being protected. She wanted her men. Her *family.*

"Billy, what would it take to convince you to take me to wherever Micah went?" she asked.

He shook his head. "There's nothing. And I'm not easily manipulated, even by women as beautiful as you."

She straightened, shocked. "Are you hitting on me?"

He shook his head. "Nah, darling. I know better than that. Like my head where it's at."

"If you don't take me to Micah, I'm telling him you hit on me. He'll believe me."

"No, you won't."

"Billy..."

"I have my orders. Made a promise. Don't believe on going back on my word."

The thing about manipulating someone, Kara had learned, was that you had to know where that hole was in their heart.

Everyone had something missing from their life, something they wanted so desperately it was like a festering wound. Find the wound, and you could press on it in ways that could change the trajectory of their lives. Micah was the master at it. Kara was a novice, but she was learning.

But she hadn't spent enough time with Billy to know what his was.

"Come on," he said. "We've got a long drive ahead of us."

Kara let him lead her to the car. A physical altercation wouldn't get her anywhere with him. No, she'd have to bide her time, get to know him a little better to know which buttons to push, and keep an eye out for the exact right moment to escape—once she'd gotten Micah's plans and location from him. She snorted.

Here she was again, being taken somewhere against her will, having to be patient and smart to find a way to escape and get what she wanted. What had she done in a past life to deserve this? This was the very definition of insanity.

"What's so funny?" Billy asked, an eyebrow raised, as he opened the door to the passenger seat.

"Just can't believe I'm being kidnapped again."

"I prefer 'involuntary relocation.'"

The good thing was, she'd learned from the other times she'd been 'involuntarily relocated.' Namely, that she had to tread lightly when she was hunting for information, manipulate wounds with defter fingers. She'd also learned something else valuable: she had good instincts for when to make her move.

So she leaned her head against the window, staring straight ahead of her as the dark, northern California highway passed them.

"Where are we headed?" she asked.

"Marcus's plane is at a private airport about two hours north of here." Billy glanced over at her. His bald head shone in the highway lights. Lola loved bald men. She'd be all over Billy.

Lola. When was the last time Kara had thought about her friend? She hadn't even reached out after being rescued by Micah and Conor. Lola was probably sick with worry; the last she'd spoken to Kara was right before Chris's henchmen had taken her. Just another sin to add to her list.

"Can I use your phone?"

"No."

"I need to call my best friend and let her know I'm okay."

Billy shook his head. "Did your men not tell you? The reason Chris found you in the first place was because they intercepted your call to her last time. They're probably still monitoring her phone calls."

Fear gripped Kara. "Is she safe?"

Billy smiled. "I think your friend is good at keeping herself safe, no matter the circumstances."

"What does that mean?"

Billy didn't answer her.

"Billy, what aren't you telling me?"

"Not for me to tell."

Kara wracked her brain. There was no way she was going to be able to commandeer the car from him, even if she was enough of a bitch to leave him on the side of the road. Bribery hadn't worked.

Maybe vulnerability would.

Kara swallowed. "Have you ever cared about someone, Billy? I mean deeply."

He glanced at her briefly before gazing back at the road. "Yes. In fact, I *love* two people."

Huh. "And what would you do if they ditched you to go do something dangerous? Would you let them?"

He chuckled.

"Darlin', I do the dangerous stuff. I don't get left behind. You and I are not the same."

Kara rolled her eyes. "Yes, yes, you're a big strong man and I'm a helpless little lady. What I'm asking is, if the people you loved left you behind to protect you, would you let them?"

His laughter stilled. "Love?"

She caught his gaze in the rearview mirror. "Yes. Love."

It was the first time she'd said the word out loud. She hadn't even admitted it to herself before this. Saying it to Billy instead of to her men made her some form of chicken-shit, but once she got to Micah, once they saved Luke and Conor, she'd have all the time in the world to tell them.

She wished she'd told them earlier, though. Wish she'd realized it earlier.

Billy whistled. "Damn, they worked fast."

Kara laughed, despite herself. "I don't know if two years counts as fast."

"Darlin', the last time I saw you, you seemed like you could barely stand the three of them. It's been what, a week? And you've changed your tune completely."

Kara nodded. "I stopped lying to myself. And now I can't be left behind. Billy, what would you do if you were me?"

He groaned. "I'm not answering that."

"Billy..."

"I'd do exactly this. Prey on my new bodyguard's feelings and empathy, so that he'd do something stupid, something he wasn't supposed to do."

He put on his blinker and exited the highway.

Kara sat up straight. "Where are we going now?"

"To intercept your man. But, Kara, darlin', you're going to owe me for this. And even though I don't call in markers the way Marcus does, you still don't want to owe me."

Kara laughed, relieved for the first time since Luke and Conor had been taken.

"I'm willing to take that risk," she said.

Something like approval filled his eyes. "Good girl."

The two words sending a pang through her chest, so sharp she almost cried out from the pain of it. "Only Conor's allowed to call me that."

Billy made a U-turn, entering the highway again, this time headed in the other direction.

"Noted," he said. "Now, let's go get me in trouble."

6

————

t least Kara and Micah were safe.

Conor repeated the words to himself, again, and again, and again.

He thought them while he watched her and Micah sink below the depths of the shallows, when he and Luke had fought the Johnathans' men to create a distraction so Kara and Micah could get away safely. They echoed in his head when he and Luke, by unspoken agreement, had let the other men win the fight and drag them onto the helicopter. They played on repeat on the interminable flight in the chopper to the airstrip, when they were loaded onto this military cargo plane, and he recited them in his head over and over on the even more interminable flight to god knew what hellscape they were being taken to.

They were safe. They were safe. They were safe. Micah would keep Kara safe.

Conor only wished Luke wasn't with him; that he'd thought to force his lover to leave him behind. It was a futile wish; Luke would never have abandoned him. But when one of their captors handcuffed Luke to the metal seat frame, and then punched him in the throat, Conor had roared his outrage. It had only been the warning in Luke's eyes that had stopped him from ripping his own goddamned handcuffs apart and punishing the guard for hurting the man he loved.

Right.

The man he loved.

If Micah were there, he'd point out that Conor was a fool, and had loved Luke for years. But Micah wasn't there, and Conor, fool that he was, had only admitted that he loved Luke—and Micah, and Kara—to himself when Chris Johnathan's fucking soldier had shoved a gun in Kara's mouth and Conor's entire fucking life had flashed before his eyes. Conor was not a man who let himself feel feelings, and suddenly he was swamped by the goddamned things.

Not particularly helpful at a time like this, when he needed to be focused on getting himself and Luke out of here.

But how? There were ten men on the cargo plane, not including the two pilots. Conor was strong, but these men were trained, and what's more, they clearly had nothing to lose.

Whereas Conor had everything to lose.

All ten men sat across from them, silent and impassive. Conor needed to make a plan with Luke, but there was no way that was going to happen if they couldn't talk alone. They had a mental connection, but they couldn't actually talk to each other in their minds.

As if he'd heard him, and completely negating Conor's previous thought, Luke coughed. Once, twice, three times. Four.

Conor remembered back to a mission about four years ago, when they'd been captured, and Micah had whispered to them that coughing four times meant *ask for a piss break and use it to knock these fuckers out.*

Conor coughed back, twice.

It's too soon.

Luke coughed again, four times, this time louder.

Fucking fuck it. Luke said he wanted to lead for once, to plan: Conor loved the asshole, so he had to trust him.

"Yo, is there a bathroom somewhere on this plane?" Conor called out to their captors.

Yo. He sounded like a goddamned idiot, but then that was the point, wasn't it?

One of his captors rolled his eyes. "You aren't using the bathroom. You've gotta piss? Piss your pants, we don't give a shit."

"That's the problem, though," Conor called back. "I have to shit."

Next to him, Luke choked on a laugh.

Conor continued. "As uncomfortable as it's going to be, I'm really thinking of y'all. It's going to stink like literal shit, and what, we've got at least three more hours on this flight? Four? Do you really want to sit in the stench? I'm telling you, it's a bad one."

Luke couldn't hold back his laugh anymore. Under his breath, he murmured, "You're overselling it."

But the soldiers looked at each other, quietly conferring. Finally, one spoke.

"You can take a shit, but you try anything, and I shoot your friend in the head."

Well, that sobered Conor and Luke right up.

Conor waited as two of the soldiers approached them. They wore nondescript camo that resembled military uniforms but were clearly knockoffs. Even so, the similarity to the way Conor used to dress made him swallow in sharp pain. He didn't miss the military; it had destroyed his life, had turned him into a man he didn't like much. But it reminded him of a time when he'd been softer, gentler, kinder. A good man, if a naive one.

One who deserved the love of the people in his life.

Ah, fuck. Now was not the time for this maudlin bullshit.

"Don't do anything stupid," one of the guards warned him as he reached over to unlock Conor's cuffs, the other guard training his gun on Luke's face.

Luke coughed again, just once.

Game time.

Conor pulled his arms apart, as wide as they could go. The links between handcuffs strained in resistance before breaking with a loud snap and ping as one flew across the room and hit the metal floor of the plane. A second snap followed the first one as Luke broke his own cuff free from the chair.

Before the second soldier could pull the trigger, Conor shoved Luke out of the way. The gun fired, the bullet speeding through the air and lodging itself into the wall.

"We should've just hijacked the goddamned helicopter," Luke grunted as he slammed his knee into the first soldier's crotch and grabbed his gun.

"Good point," Conor conceded as they took out another five guards, leaving three, who were firing back at them. If they weren't careful, they'd shoot one too many holes in the fuselage, and they'd fuck up the pressurization system and lose cabin pressure.

Another shot fired, and next to Conor, Luke groaned.

"Fuck," he said. Blood bloomed on his left shoulder. The one Kara hadn't shot.

And Conor briefly lost the ability to breathe.

He wasn't on the plane anymore, fighting for their lives.

He was back in the cabin, watching the Doctor perform surgery on Luke on the table after Kara shot him. Back in his guilt and regret, knowing he'd fucked up and because of it, Luke had suffered.

Just like Luke was suffering now.

"Conor. Conor! Wake the fuck up." Luke was calling his name, bringing Conor back to the present.

Funny that, from all the trauma Conor had experienced, from all the fucked-up shit he'd seen and done, it was that moment in the kitchen his memory dragged him back to.

Love was destroying him—from the inside, out.

Unfortunately, he'd mentally checked out for too long, and the other guards were on them. Conor punched one guard in his face, but it was futile; they'd lost the upper hand. And Luke was struggling to stay upright, his face going pale from blood loss.

This time, zip ties were brought out and tied tightly around their wrists—too tight to manage to get out of them.

"What the fuck, you're just going to let him die?" Conor growled, panicked.

"We'll be landing soon," one of the soldiers said.

"I'm fine," Luke said through gritted teeth. "It's just a flesh wound."

He sounded angry, confused. Hurt. Like Conor had really let him down when he'd had his brief episode.

Because Conor had let him down.

He'd let all of them down.

The plane began to rumble on its descent. Fuck, they didn't have enough time, they were caught, and they had no plan. Conor could only hope that wherever they'd been taken had a medical wing and doctor, and that the Johnathans would be willing to remove the bullet and stitch Luke up. As it was, he could only watch the blood drip from his lover's shoulder and remind himself, again, and again...

At least Micah and Kara are safe.

At least Micah and Kara are safe.

Strangely, the words no longer made him feel better. Not if he couldn't keep Luke safe, too. And how did he even know if Micah and Kara were okay? He wasn't an idiot. As much as he wanted to believe Micah had followed his orders and was on the run or in hiding with Kara, Micah wouldn't give up on them that easily, which meant Micah had probably tried to stash Kara away somewhere safely. Tried, and failed, because there was no way Conor's brave, reckless, rebellious girl would let Micah lock her up in another cage, whether or not it was for her own safety.

So Conor, who wasn't religious, didn't believe in god or any higher power, and rarely prayed, prayed once again to his dead father to keep the people he loved safe.

And he promised himself, then and there, that he'd do anything to save Luke's life.

No matter what it meant for his own.

"Conor, baby...what's going on?" Luke asked.

Conor cleared his throat. "I'm glad you're conscious."

Luke laughed hoarsely. "This isn't my first shoulder wound, remember? I'm practically a pro by now. What the hell happened back there?"

"Had a flashback. To the last time you got shot. Lost track of reality for a second."

"Fuck," Luke muttered. "Great timing."

Conor shrugged, unable to deny it.

"We should've hijacked the damn helicopter," Luke repeated.

"Yup," Conor said, and the humor in Luke's voice momentarily buoyed him.

"Boss, I need you with me, so we can get our asses out of here," Luke told him. "You with me?"

Conor nodded. "I'm with you."

But part of him doubted if he were telling the truth—something Luke would hate.

With a teeth-jarring bump, the plane landed on a rough runway, rumbling down the airstrip. Conor wished for a window, so he could know what kind of terrain they were dealing with.

The plane rolled to a stop. The hold was reinforced, so even though he strained his ears, he couldn't tell if anyone was coming for them. But they would, soon. And then the rear of the plane opened, revealing a group of at least twenty men in fatigues, guns aimed at them.

"We need a plan," Luke said quietly.

But Conor didn't have a plan. He wasn't sure there was one that would get them out of there.

"Boss, come on," Luke asked, desperation raising the pitch of his voice. "We don't have much time."

"Mr. O'Connell knows this is a fool's attempt," a voice called. The soldiers—if you could call them soldiers—parted, and a slender, nondescript man walked through them.

Conor had never seen a picture of the professor, or heard his voice, but his gut churned in recognition. This was the man who had almost destroyed Kara once, and then tortured her a second time. Who tried to break her. If he'd had a gun, he would have shot him. He eyed the soldiers holding them. The zip ties were an issue, but...

"I wouldn't even consider it," the professor said. "I'm sure it would feel good to overpower one of my men and shoot me, especially knowing I've been deep inside your whore on numerous occasions—and will be again soon, I'm sure. But if you kill me, your lover is dead."

His words froze Conor before he could even move.

"He needs medical attention," Conor told the professor. "He was shot."

"Oh?" His enemy cocked his head. "And why would I be driven to give him medical attention?"

"Because if you don't, he'll die. And I doubt we're of much use to you dead."

At least not yet.

The professor—Christopher, although Conor hated acknowledging his name, since it only made him more real —nodded. "Alright."

Conor and Luke were lifted to their feet and marched out of the plane and into the blinding sunshine.

And as they walked toward an unknown destination, Conor once again promised himself he'd get Luke out of here.

He'd die to make sure of it.

As they were marched down a steep island path, Conor briefly soothed himself with thoughts of what Kara was doing right now. Micah had probably left her at one of Marcus's many homes. He hoped the Jackson Hole compound, so at least she could see the Tetons every day.

Conor felt himself smile, sad and small. She'd hate that, hate being cooped up again, and this time without the promise of good sparring and great sex. But it wouldn't last long. She'd find a way to escape, just like she had in the past.

She was resourceful as hell, one of the many things he loved about her, and she'd find a way to him.

But he didn't want that for her. He wanted better for her, a new life. A happy one. He wanted better, and yet he'd done everything in his power to keep her from it.

"Why the hell are you smiling, asshole?" Luke growled at him, but it was weak. He needed medical help.

Conor would also drop to his knees and offer almost anything to save Luke from his fate. But the only thing he had to offer was Kara's likely location, and that was non-negotiable.

He was fucked between a rock and a hard place, wasn't he. He couldn't give up one to save the other. Plus, he wasn't a naive dipshit—Kara's location just guaranteed Luke a quicker death.

Jesus, he almost missed the fucking days when he felt nothing but lust and rage and the need for revenge. When he'd known he was evil, and therefore didn't care what harm he created as long as it got him what it wanted. And while he'd still create any and all harm to keep his family safe, he felt pain again. Kara—and his deeper bond with Micah and Luke, thanks to her—had given him back his heart, and it ached.

It was no less than he deserved. He *should* feel this pain, after everything he'd done. It wasn't even about orphaning those young boys, not anymore. No, by now he'd done far worse. Kidnapping Kara, taking her agency, making her feel used and meaningless and small. Dragging her into the darkness with him, turning her into someone who killed without remorse. Stealing her away from a nice, quiet, happy life. Would she be able to go back to it now?

She'd been better off without them, hadn't she? Without *him.* Even though everything in him railed against the idea of not having her, he couldn't deny that he had led her down the path to destruction. Just like he was leading Luke down a path to his own.

They were guided down cement stairs and into what seemed like an underground bunker but really was an underground prison. They walked down a long hallway, Conor noting the empty cells, until they reached one at the end of the hallway. It was empty, no bed, no chairs, no rations, no toilet. As good a home as any.

"Sorry our accommodations aren't very hospitable, but after you destroyed my last torture site, I had to be more flexible. You understand." The professor was almost giddy with his triumph, although he was trying to seem calm and in control.

Conor could've told him it didn't matter. He could feel as triumphant as he wanted, it didn't bother Conor at all. Nothing did, except knowing he'd never see Kara's face again, and that he'd taken that away from his partners, too. God, he would go back, wouldn't he? Knock on Kara's door, with two bouquets in his hands, one of strawflowers and one of bee balm. And he'd beg her for a date. Demand one, probably, knowing him. Give her the power for once so she could choose to give it back to him.

But there was no sense in thinking about that, now.

"Can someone look at Luke's shoulder?"

Conor could hear the desperation in his voice. Usually, he'd hate it, but he couldn't deny the truth of the sound. So what if he seemed weak, if it saved his lover and friend?

"If you give me Kara's location, I'll make sure he's patched up and good as new. In fact, I'll spare you both. Clear your names, drop you off back at home. Isn't that what you always wanted?"

Once. Once Conor thought he had. Now, all he wanted was to be free and safe and happy with his family.

Neither he nor Luke spoke.

"Well. Guess we better get to it, then," the professor said.

He motioned to two of the guards behind them—tall assholes with square jaws and dead eyes—who came forward. Conor immediately lost his inertia, jumping in to defend Luke, but four men wrestled him to the ground and chained him to the floor, then forced his face forward so he had no choice but to watch them land blow after blow. Luke held out for a while—he was a big, strong man—but when three, four, five, six men descended on him, he couldn't hold up any longer. Between that and the blood loss, he was no match for them. Kick after kick landed on his ribs. Conor heard them crack. Someone pressed on Luke's shoulder where the wound was, and Luke grunted.

It may as well have been a scream.

And Conor was forced to observe all of it. They were going to kill his best friend and the person he jockeyed the most with for power and loved so completely it threatened to destroy him. And all he could do was watch. He'd seen Luke tortured before, but he'd never worried about their survival before...because he'd never admitted his feelings before.

If Conor could shoot his feelings in the fucking face, he would.

"Conor, there's a reason why I chose Luke first. See, I think you know that this whole...situation...was your fault from the moment you asked your friends to watch Kara instead of letting her pass through your life the way she wanted. It's been your fault this whole time, and what happens next? It's your fault, as well. I hope you know I plan to keep you alive for a long time...because when I do catch

Kara and your other lover, I'll make you watch as I do the same to them. And you know what?" The professor cocked his head. "That will be your fault, too."

And as Conor was forced to watch the man he loved get beaten and tortured, he knew it was the truth.

It had only been a few hours, and Micah already missed her. He made it an unbroken habit to never let himself feel regret or self-doubt—that way lay paralysis, and as a SEAL, and then a hitman, paralysis meant death. This was one more thing Kara had thrown into complete chaos, just like the rest of his life.

And yet he still loved her. Loved her *for it*, even.

Micah glanced at the gas gage on the dashboard. Damn it. He was only about forty minutes out from the airport, but he'd been so caught up in his thoughts, he hadn't realized he was near empty.

He'd have to stop.

He pulled into a gas station, got out of the car, filled up his tank. Checked his phone to see if he'd heard anything from Billy. His silence was concerning.

Kara okay? he texted on his burner.

She's fine. Spitting mad, but fine, came the reply.

Micah chuckled. Sounded about right.

No matter what happened, she'd be angry. And no matter what happened, she'd be fine. He had to believe that.

She was strong, she'd make it through. He was just going to do everything in his power to make sure they all made it through together.

As the tank filled, Micah briefly left the car at the pump, going into the gas station to buy water and some snacks with the credit card Billy had given him. The cashier gave him a strange look when she handed him his receipt—a look that sent his senses pinging.

Something was up.

Outside of the building, he grabbed his gun and slowly made his way back to the car, praying that he didn't have to blow someone's head off at the pump and run the risk of blowing up the entire station—and himself.

As he reached the pump, he lowered the gun and shook his head.

"How'd you get away from Billy?"

Kara stood, her now-purple hair lit by the glow of the gas station lights and the quiet TV. The woman on the screen was reading out lottery numbers.

"Told him I knew the perfect woman for him, and I'd give him her number if he let me take the car and his phone," she said.

"Lola's going to be pissed," he commented, damning the relief and elation that filled him at seeing her, not just safe and whole, but here. With him. He couldn't decide if he should punish her, or kiss her. After all, her presence proved how much she cared, more than even her words would.

"How'd you really get away?" he asked.

"Turns out you highly trained criminals are suckers for an emotionally vulnerable woman," she said.

He whistled, low. "I'm impressed. Billy's not a sucker for just anyone."

"Fuck that," she exploded. "I can't believe you were just going to leave me there with him!"

There was murder in her eyes, and behind that a deep, unrelenting pain. It was the pain that stabbed him in the chest.

"What the hell, Micah," she continued, getting more and more worked up as she went on. "And I know what you're going to say. I'm a hindrance, you'll be too worried about my safety to do what you need to do to bring Luke and Conor home. And I know it's selfish of me to say this, but I know that you aren't sure you'll make it back alive, and I'm terrified if I take my eyes off you again, you'll disappear for good. And Micah, I'm not sure I'll survive that." She swallowed, the next words clearly hard for her. "I need you, and I need to be with you. I need all of you, and I need to save them too, or die trying."

"No one's going to die." He could barely control himself at the thought of something happening to her, to *any* of them, but he forced his voice to remain even.

"You think you are," she said.

"You can't risk losing me, baby? I can't risk losing you. I need to know you're safe." His voice cracked.

"And you'll know that with me out of your sight, out of touching distance? Chris got me once—what's to say he couldn't do it again? Do you really trust Billy to keep that from happening? Do you really think I'm safer with Marcus? Think about it, I've only been out of your sight once in the past two years. Even when you left me in that Airbnb in New Orleans on Christmas Eve, you made sure you still had eyes on me—Luke's eyes. And that one time you didn't have me in your sight..." she trailed off.

He'd almost lost her. Forever.

Reading his mind, she nodded. But there was no triumph in her gaze, just sadness.

"Please, Micah. I've helped in the past. I came with all three of you on the run. I created a distraction and shot that man, and I was the one who figured out where Jean Pierre's wife is. I can help you now. Don't hide me away behind protective glass like a trophy. Make me your partner. Take me with you, so we can keep each other safe."

Fuck. He'd been wrong earlier that night when he'd left her in the motel room. It wasn't make plans and god laughs. It was make plans, and the woman you love cries.

He watched her for a moment. He'd hurt her, and he hated he hurt her. So when she joined him, he immediately pulled her into his arms, squeezing her tight and burying his head in her neck, breathing her in.

She hugged him tighter, her arms wrapped around his back. They held each other like that, neither speaking, just sharing warmth and safety, unspoken love and a promise to see this thing through, no matter where it took them.

Finally he pulled back, brushing sexy purple hair—if he did say so himself—behind her ear.

"I'm a little impressed with your manipulation tactics," he admitted.

"I learned from the mastermind."

He shook his head. Fuck, he loved her. "I'd be proud, if I didn't want to spank your ass for it."

Tears filled her eyes, but she squared her shoulders. "That's Luke's job."

"Exactly," he said. "So let's go get him."

And then, because he couldn't resist it—could never resist it—he kissed her. It was soft, and heartbreakingly sweet, and so consuming he forgot for a moment that they were out in the open at an empty gas station off the highway, in the middle of the night, sitting ducks for whoever came after them. He didn't give a shit in that moment, focused on the feel of her gentle, needy lips on his, her tongue deep in his mouth, circling and driving him higher and higher, with no end in sight. Ever since the kidnapping, Kara hadn't initiated kissing. Something had changed. He'd claimed her, again and again, but this was her claiming him, marking him as hers with her lips and teeth and tongue.

And he fucking reveled in it.

He wanted to kiss her forever. He wanted to find a soft surface and love her the way she deserved. Fuck that, he wanted to bend her over this damn car—or the one she'd abandoned in a shadowy corner of the gas station beneath the trees—and fuck her hard, so she remembered that as much as he was hers, she was his, too.

But he couldn't risk it. He couldn't waste the time.

As if she'd heard his thoughts, she pulled away, pressing one last kiss to his lips, a gentle promise.

"Let's go get our guys," she said, going around to the passenger seat.

"Yeah," he said, buckling her in, unable to resist the assurance it gave him. He placed a kiss on her forehead, memorizing the smell of her. Just in case.

Just in case.

"Let's go save them," he repeated, more promise than wish, and got in the car.

Of all the places Kara thought she'd return to one day with Micah, Vixen, Marcus's sex club for the wealthiest of the wealthy, was not it. The last time she'd been here, the whole club had been blown up—yet here it was, new but not particularly improved. The nondescript stone entryway, the gleaming walnut walls, the large, scarred security guards: none of it had changed. No, she'd never thought she'd see it again. Yet here she was, the night after her confrontation and reunion with Micah, in a tight leather skirt and matching leather bustier, and short chunky-heeled biker girl boots, his hand at her back, standing at the entrance as the hostess looked them over warily.

"You don't have a reservation, Mr. Feldman."

He straightened, winking at her. "I don't need one. You know that, Annabelle."

She blushed prettily. "Of course, Mr. Feldman."

Kara, who had much more important things to be worried about than a little hostess who had a crush on her lover, was possessed by the urge to drag the woman away from Micah by her hair, and maybe bang her head against the reception desk just to get the point across. She didn't love that she had such violently possessive thoughts, but damn it, he was hers, and flirting with other people outside of their closed polycule and being flirted with? That was off limits.

So Kara turned to Micah and fussed with his collar. He grinned at her, leaning in to whisper in her ear.

"Jealous?"

"Damn right I am," she whispered back. "The rule is they can look but can't touch, remember? Well, she wants to touch."

He kissed her lightly. "No one's touching me tonight but you."

Annabelle straightened, clearing her throat, all business again. "Right this way, Mr. Feldman. And..."

"You don't need to know my name," Kara said. They hadn't bothered to come up with a new identity for her—she'd been made as Maya—so she was going incognito for now.

"Of course, ma'am." Annabelle lifted one delicate shoulder. "I'm sure you know the rules. No photos, and no weapons. Otherwise, anything goes."

Of course.

As Annabelle led them through the club to the main dining room, Kara glanced around at the naked people fucking in restaurant booths and on the burgundy leather chesterfields. A man was on his hands and knees on an Aubusson rug, sucking one man's cock while a third man fucked him in the ass. On a table in one of the restaurant booths, a woman played with her nipples while a man thrust into her mouth. Last time, the sex vibes had been overwhelming, this time, she was more or less numb to them. Eye on the prize, and all that.

"Doesn't Marcus realize that bare hardwoods would mean a cheaper cleaning bill?" she asked Micah.

Micah chuckled. "I'm sure he thinks the rugs and carpets are an essential part of the décor."

They reached a booth, and Kara slid in. Micah followed her.

"I'll go get your server," Annabelle said, and then departed.

Micah nipped Kara's neck. "I know it's terrible timing, but being here is giving me some fucking hot flashbacks, baby."

"Yeah." Kara inhaled, remembering crawling under a gleaming table just like this, and had to cross her legs to stifle the way her pussy pulsed. "But it feels wrong."

Micah raised an eyebrow. "Why?"

"Because our men are suffering, and—"

"I'm glad you call them *our* men now," he remarked.

Kara dismissed that with a wave of her hand. They were her men, she'd acknowledged that to herself a long time ago. Around the time she was locked in a cell, convinced she was going to die without seeing them again. Although damn, did Micah not know? Had she not made her feelings clear? No wonder he took so much pleasure in seeing her jealous. Or was he manipulating her into sharing her feelings more openly?

And why did she find that endearing?

She softened, letting herself be vulnerable. "They are our men. You're my man, too."

"Yours?" he asked.

"Mine."

As a reward, he kissed her, long and hot and distracting.

"Micah..."

"In response to your question, I know they're suffering, but guilt keeping you from being with me isn't right, either. We're here, waiting, and I miss your sweet pussy. I miss owning it. Neither Luke nor Conor would hold it against me if I bent you over this table and fucked your sweet holes right now. You know, when you were missing, and Luke was passed out on our kitchen island from blood loss and surgery without anesthesia, I got down on my knees and sucked Conor's cock until he came down my throat."

"What?!"

She was hot all over, partly out of anger, but mostly from the picture he painted. She could see it now, couldn't she? Conor sitting in a stool at Luke's side, Micah kneeling before him, big hands on bigger thighs, opening his throat wide and swallowing Conor's thick cock down, down...

"Hmm," Micah said.

"I mean..." she trailed off.

"We were thinking of you. We missed you. Were terrified for you. But we needed each other, and the comfort of knowing we had each other. Don't deny yourself that, don't deny me that because you feel guilty, baby."

Before she could answer, someone cleared their throat.

Kara looked up to see Marcus standing over them, an unimpressed smirk on his face. Now that she knew his true relationship to Micah, she tried to find similarities between the half-brothers. Nothing in their facial features, build, or mannerisms were similar...except for their piercing blue eyes. She'd never noticed before.

"You know, a smarter man wouldn't let the people who destroyed his club back inside," he said.

"Well, it's good you're not a smarter man, isn't it?" Kara

said. She still wasn't sure if she liked him. She certainly didn't trust him.

Micah glanced over at her, amused. But he addressed his words to Marcus. "We promise we won't get your club blown up again."

"Good," Marcus said. "I only just finished rebuilding and redecorating it."

"Fast," Kara observed.

"It's amazing what an endless supply of money and power will get you," Marcus said. To Micah he said: "By the way, I've heard through the grapevine that Jack is...causing trouble at his university."

"Yacob?" Micah asked sharply.

Kara leaned in, curious—and worried. Micah never spoke sharply. Whoever Jack was, he clearly had made an impact.

"I know you have no contact with him—" Marcus began.

"I haven't seen him since he was eight years old," Micah said, his voice still sharp. "I have no influence over his life. I doubt he wants anything to do with me."

Marcus raised a shoulder, seemingly casual, but Kara caught the way his jaw ticked. "Be that as it may, he needs interference, or he's going to burn his life to the ground. Over some girl," he added, disgusted. "I tried to talk to him, but he wants nothing to do with me. You...he always looked up to you."

Oh. One of Micah's brothers. No wonder he was upset.

"I'll keep it in mind," Micah said smoothly, back to his normal, contained self.

Kara placed her hand on Micah's thigh as she eyed Marcus. "Are you telling him this because you're really concerned? Or are you trying to distract him?"

Marcus grinned, a flash of teeth. At that moment, the debonair billionaire reminded Kara of a wolf.

Fortunately, she was no sheep.

"You don't trust me, do you?" he said.

Kara caught his eyes. "I've learned to be wary of most wealthy men. You're one of the wealthiest. Ergo..."

Micah chuckled.

Marcus tsked. "You know, I've done you several favors. You wouldn't be alive if it weren't for me. I deserve a little gratitude for that instead of animosity, don't you think?"

"When we're all safe, I'll consider it. You may be my partner's brother, Marcus, but that doesn't make you family."

"You might be surprised how connected we become," he murmured, his gaze faraway. Before Kara could puzzle out the cryptic statement, he cleared his throat and straightened the right cuff on his bespoke suit. "I know you have a meeting shortly. Be careful with this one...his demands are usually a bit...unprofessional in nature."

With one final nod at each other, Marcus left them, a sense of foreboding remaining in the air.

"You didn't have to do that," Micah said. "Marcus isn't someone you want as an enemy."

Kara waved this off with one hand, rubbing Micah's thigh with the other. "I have a lot of enemies, what's one more? More importantly, are you okay?"

Micah's smile didn't reach his eyes, but he took Kara's hand, flipped it, and threaded their fingers together. "We can only solve one problem at a time. And rescuing Luke and Conor is more pressing."

Kara shook her head. She wasn't going to let him avoid this conversation so easily. "Jack—Yacob—is another one of your brothers, isn't he?"

Micah released a sigh, long suffering and worried. "We don't have a relationship anymore, but I'm worried he's following in my footsteps—with less successful results." He smiled faintly. "I'm not sure how to help him."

"Following in your footsteps? You mean the military? Or..."

Micah gave her a meaningful look. "Or."

"Oh." Kara digested this, deciding if she was okay with being a "successful result." Well, she didn't love the wording, but it was the truth.

"I didn't realize kidnapping was a family tradition," she teased.

Micah leaned over, kissing her forehead. "Stalking, I think."

"Well, we did decide it was sexy," she said.

So long ago, at that restaurant in New Orleans. God, so much had changed between them.

"It's the only family tradition I like." He cleared his throat, changing the subject. "Okay, let's go over the plan again."

"When Victor shows up, I play dumb, like I don't know he's planning on playing us. Marcus pays him his money, he gives us the coordinates, we hope no one sets off a bomb like last time, right?"

They'd gone over the plan on the short flight here. Victor von Truc was a friend and colleague of the Johnathans—and the CEO of the international commercial building company that the Johnathans had hired to build the facilities on all their illegal torture sites. Micah had intercepted a call between Victor and Elliot Johnathan discussing the recent use of one of their sites, but they hadn't shared a location. If anyone knew where Luke and Conor were being held, it was Victor.

Micah nodded grimly. "It's essential that he thinks I'm the only one who suspects him of anything."

There was a stone in her stomach. "So there's definitely a trap."

Micah nodded. "Yes, but trust me. No matter what this weasel does, we can handle it together."

We.

His sincerity softened her, eroding the stone in her stomach until it was nothing but sand, and then gone. In the past, she would've been left out. Now, they were a team—even if they couldn't let Victor see that.

She ran her free hand through his hair.

"Okay," Kara said. "I trust you."

His blue eyes brightened, like sunlight shimmering over the ocean. His approval wrapped around her, safety and belonging a buffer between her and a world that wanted to hurt them.

"I'm glad to hear that, baby," he said with so much tenderness. "And for what it's worth, I trust you, too. We can do this."

I trust you, too.

He'd never put so much faith in her. Had never made them a team before. He had now. As his words spread through her, something clicked into place for Kara—at the least helpful time possible, because Micah spotted something. He straightened and stood, releasing her hand.

"Showtime," he said.

A man approached, tall, gym-built, with an orange tan that spoke of garish amounts of money and a disinterest in authenticity. His outfit told the rest of the story. If Marcus's suits, watches, and haircuts whispered absurd wealthy, this man's ensemble screamed it.

Kara loathed him on sight. She'd never really been one to believe in vibes, but the vibes were off.

His demands are unprofessional in nature, Marcus had said. Kara could only imagine what that meant.

But did they have another option? They'd hit a brick wall with Jean Pierre's young widow, who had died of a "heart attack" only the day before. The Johnathans doing, of course. Marcus had dug deep to find Victor and had bribed him to show up. If he wanted some "unprofessional" icing on the bribery cake, so be it. She'd do anything to get Luke and Conor back, safe and whole.

Kara wasn't sure exactly when, but they—and Micah—had become everything to her. It wasn't even worth pinpointing it, and it wasn't worth her time fighting it anymore. She'd accepted it, and now she'd sacrifice everything to get them back. Including herself, if that's what it came down to.

"Well, she's even more beautiful than Christopher said. What a rare jewel you are, Ms. Blum, even with that horrible dye job."

Her heart thumped fast, like a rabbit on the run. The man knew exactly who she was and had been talking to Chris about her.

But then of course he had.

Trap, her brain screamed. She'd already known it, but she wasn't sure what kind, and the unknown rose over her like a tidal wave, threatening to drown her.

No. She wasn't going to have a panic attack. She owed it to her men to keep it together. She didn't need Micah to keep her calm. She could do it herself. *All I have to do is breathe*, she told herself, using Luke's calming language. She breathed, slowly, and slowly, the wave shrank until it was gone.

Both men had been watching her; Micah approving, Victor curious.

"Thank you," Kara said. "I didn't catch your name."

"I'm sorry, I should introduce myself. I'm Victor von Truc."

He held out a hand to Kara. Kara didn't take it.

Micah, for his part, didn't seem concerned at all—on the surface. He leaned further back in his seat, crossing his thick arms over his chest, flexing the tiniest bit. But the threat was clear.

"Marcus promised me my safety," Victor informed them.

"And Marcus always keeps his promises," Micah confirmed, uncrossing his arms to slip a hand through Kara's hair before catching it in his hand and tugging gently —a warning. "But I believe you've promised us information."

"Yes, of course," Victor demurred. "If you'll follow me, I reserved one of the rooms for more privacy."

Kara leaned over to whisper in Micah's ear, making sure Victor could hear her. "I don't want to go into a room alone with him."

Micah nodded. "I'm more comfortable if we speak here," he said to Victor.

Victor shrugged and checked his watch. "Well then, I guess I'll have my driver come back around. It was nice meeting you, Kara."

"Wait," Kara said, and her desperation wasn't entirely faked.

Victor turned back. "Yes?"

"Show us this room you rented. We can talk there."

A sly grin appeared on Victor's face, a gleam in his eyes.

And something else that made that rabbit start running in her chest again.

But with that anxiety came satisfaction. Because Victor thought he had won. Was already underestimating her.

Got him, she thought.

"Well, I do have some time still." He held out a hand to her. And this time, wanting to at least seem acquiescent, Kara took it.

Micah followed behind her—close behind—his breath on her neck, his big body warming hers. Knowing he refused to let her out of his sight eased some of her tension. Superhero or supervillain, she was safe with him. Whatever Victor's trap was, they'd manage it. Together.

I trust you, he'd said.

We, he'd said.

The large, old-world restaurant gave way to a long, dark hallway. Heavy walnut doors with old fashioned brass knobs lined each wall, with names above them: Ravage. Pillage. Provoke. Submit.

Sex dens. These were private rooms for people to fuck in who didn't want an audience.

Trap, her brain insisted. And still an unknown one.

No choice, she told it.

Finally, they stopped in front of a door that said Sacrifice. Victor withdrew a small brass key that matched the knob and inserted it into a small lock, turning it to the right. Kara swallowed but squared her shoulders.

"After you, my dear," he said, holding out his arm.

"I think you'll go first," Micah said pleasantly.

Although Victor tried not to show it, he stiffened slightly, likely out of fear. He didn't reply as he entered the room.

Kara followed, Micah barely a foot behind her.

The room was small, and if the materials used to decorate it hadn't been so expensive, it would have looked tacky. As it was, it was grossly ostentatious.

The walls were a dark brown leather, upholstered like a Chesterfield couch. Three of them, at least: The fourth was one long mirror, like a dance studio. The rest of the room was bare—no BDSM or sex club accoutrements like sawhorses or St. Andrews' crosses, things Kara had never tried out with the guys and honestly, they didn't need them for the sex to be hot and raw and perfect, because the sex was hot and raw and perfect, and god, how she wished that Luke and Conor were here instead of this man. They could make use of the large, four poster bed with its gawdy red satin comforter and gold percale sheets.

"A room fit for a king!" Victor announced, triumph in his eyes.

"And who's the king?" Kara murmured, even though she knew better.

Micah shook his head at her, and Victor's eyes flashed. But he decided to laugh it off, as if she'd said the most hilarious thing in the world instead of a softly lobbed insult.

"Victor, I think it's time you cut the bullshit and tell us what you want from us for your information," Micah said.

This wasn't like him. His face was tense, his hands deceptively casual in his pockets, but bullshit was Micah's middle name. Something was setting him off. What was he sensing that she was missing?

She had to continue to play her part, though.

"Micah," she pretended to chide.

"Alright," Victor said, a bit huffily. "So you have to understand, I've been doing business with the Johnathans for years. Christopher is one of my dearest friends. But they've of course, done awful things, and I couldn't sleep at night without setting things right. I'd sleep better knowing I helped free innocent men, and allowed a group of lovers to live their lives without the specter of constant danger."

"For a price," Kara said.

He nodded. "For a price."

"From what I understand, Marcus already paid you."

"Yes, yes." Victor waved this off. "I have all the money I need. But there's something a man like me needs...more. You see, Ms. Blum, all I heard from Christopher was how this woman was driving him to distraction. One of his students, you see. Brilliant. A redhead. Desperately in love with him. Nothing out of the ordinary for Chris's conquests. But there was something about this one...when she 'destroyed his life' and left, he was still obsessed. At first, I thought it was revenge, but when he targeted her other lovers, it became clear this was not about revenge. No, this was about an almost manic need to possess her again."

Her stomach roiled. Micah wrapped an arm around her waist, settling her once again. *We're in this together*, his arm seemed to say.

"Now, I was surprised, and curious. Christopher has never felt particularly passionate about anything beyond his own ego. So, this woman, well, she had to be something special. I was even more sure of this when I learned three of the strongest, smartest, most disciplined men in the world had lost their own minds over her as well. And well, I decided it was time to see for myself."

Kara's face was burning. She had to force her breathing to stay slow. Not out of panic, but rage. She didn't want to be known this way, as nothing more than some siren leading men to their destruction. She was more than her sex appeal and her goddamned vagina. How was she back here?

As if he heard her thought, Micah stroked her hip. He

might as well have said it out loud: *You are more than a femme fatale to us. You have worth beyond sex. You are everything to us, remember?*

She remembered.

And she loved him for it.

She felt him kiss her neck, as if in confirmation.

"Well, now you've seen," she said. "Here I am. We'd like their location now."

"Ah," he said, removing his suit jacket and draping it on a chair. "You see, it's not only that I wanted to see for myself. I decided I needed to experience her for myself. After all, how could a man like me pass up the cunt that felled four men and possibly more?"

"You want to be very careful, Victor," Micah warned. "I'm not usually one to lose my temper, but you're about to trip a wire you'd be smart to step away from."

Victor shook his head. "I don't think so. See, I think you care too much about your loved ones to risk it all on beating me to a pulp, just because I happen to admire the pussy you're so protective over. It's simple, really. I fuck Ms. Blum here, and you get your location and move on to rescuing those two men of yours. It's much more humane than having you carry out a hit for me. This way, no one gets hurt...much."

He winked at Kara, who was having a hard time controlling her breathing.

So not a physical trap. An emotional one. Victor wasn't there to kill them, he wanted to break their bond for his own amusement, likely because he was bored in his own manicured, overly tanned, rich fucker life.

No.

She didn't want to touch him.

She didn't want to touch anyone who wasn't one of her

men. Ever. The very idea made her want to hurl, to scream, to rage. She could feel her body trembling in rejection of the very idea. She wanted to kill Victor for thinking he could negotiate for her body. It wasn't on the table. It didn't belong to him. It belonged to her, to Micah, to Conor, to Luke.

And at that thought, she froze.

Conor and Luke.

She wanted, *needed*, them safe.

Exhaling slowly, she forced her body to still, squaring her shoulders. She could do this. She hated it, but she could do it.

If her bond with Micah could withstand him seemingly abandoning her for a year and a half only to stalk her, kidnap her, and fuck with her head, if it survived her shooting his best friend and him having to rescue her from a tiny torture cell, then it could withstand one vomit-triggering fuck with this weasel. If her relationships with Luke and Conor could stay strong after everything they'd been through, everything they'd done to each other, it would survive this.

Kara was disgusted, beyond disgusted. Fucking someone else was the absolute last thing she wanted to do. But she'd fuck a million disgusting men if it meant bringing Luke and Conor back home.

She could see them in her mind, wounded and bleeding, empty eyes staring. No more being called various types of "girl" depending on Conor's mood, no more being Luke's sweetheart.

No.

She would never let that happen.

What would you sacrifice?

Anything. She'd sacrifice anything.

"Excuse us for a moment," she told Victor, taking Micah's arm and guiding him away.

"We're leaving," Micah said.

Kara shook her head. "No, we're not."

"What are you saying? Kara, he's trying to coerce you into fucking him."

She just gave him a look. Micah inhaled through his teeth.

"I'm not saying I'm better than him."

She interrupted him. "You're a million times better than him. Haven't we covered this?"

He nodded. "Fine. I'm still not going to let you get hurt this way."

God, he needed to listen. She lowered her voice. "I don't want this, you *know* I don't. The very idea of letting anyone else touch me makes me want to die."

"So then don't do it," Micah argued.

She held a hand up. "But I'm willing to, if it means getting their location and getting them free. I told you I need to help. Let me *help*."

He shook his head. "This isn't me being possessive and territorial, Kara. This is me keeping you safe. What was the point of their sacrifice, if I can't keep you safe?"

This time, Kara wanted to inhale through her teeth. Micah, usually the most reasonable one of them, was being completely unreasonable.

"If there were any other way, I'd jump at the option. But I can't not do this. I can't not do anything. I'll never forgive myself, if something happens to them, knowing I had a way to save them but didn't do it. What is it worth, you all promising to keep me safe, if I can't keep you safe, too?" she asked.

"So I'm supposed to what, stand here and watch?"

There was something working behind his storm-cloud eyes, something she couldn't quite read. It wasn't jealousy, or possession, or even protectiveness. No, he wanted something from her. Something she wasn't giving him.

But she *needed* this from him.

"No. You help me. You help me by following through on your words and actually trusting me. For once, I need you to follow *my* lead."

He eyed her. "Give me something, then. Why are you doing this?"

"What?" She gaped at him. What the hell was he talking about?

"Do you want to save Luke and Conor because you feel responsible for them?"

"You know it's more than that. I'd do anything to save them, to keep them safe. You, too."

He wrapped his hands around her face, tilting it up toward his, so his next words were a breath away from her lips.

"I need the words, Kara."

She swallowed. There was no reason for her to keep it back, not anymore. Even though they had an audience. "You *know*. You know why I'd do anything to keep you all safe, why I can't bear the thought of you hurt, why imagining what's happening to them right now..." she trailed off, her stomach churning. "It makes me sick. If the words help, I love you. I love all three of you. I didn't think I was capable of loving anyone again, but it turns out I didn't love Chris, I was infatuated. This is what love feels like, like I can't breathe until they're safe, and we're all together again."

That same thing behind his eyes was working, double time. And she knew what it was:

longing.

He didn't want the words from her, he couldn't exist without them.

The realization galvanized her. "I've been running and running my entire life, afraid my guilt and regret would catch up with me," she said, softly. "It never occurred to me to run toward something. Turns out, I needed you all to catch me. I love you."

It was funny, almost: for so long, she'd buried those words—from them, from herself. When she'd admitted her feelings to Billy, she felt lighter. But now she'd said them directly to Micah, it was like the weight was finally lifted.

Like she was...free.

And then Micah was kissing her and kissing her, devouring her with sweetness and promises and need. She surrendered to it, to him, letting him catch her and keep her heart safe. The room seemed to spin around her, everything, including Victor, disappearing, until they could have been anywhere and nowhere all at once. It didn't matter, as long as she had him.

Finally, he pulled away, dropping a kiss on her forehead. "Sweet baby girl, I could say a million words about how much I love you, and they still wouldn't be enough. When you sent me that note that Christmas Eve, you changed my life in ways I couldn't fathom, and I never want to go back. I love you, Kara."

Before she could kiss him again, Victor coughed. She looked over at him. Even from a short distance, she could see his eyes gleaming. He'd overheard their moment together, and instead of being annoyed he'd lost their attention, he reveled in it. Found some sick sort of glee in it. He didn't just want to fuck her for the sake of fucking her, or because he had some weird FOMO, or even just because he hated women and reducing her to no more than her parts made him feel powerful. No, he thought he could destroy their bond.

Too bad it was indestructible.

"Kara, I trust you. I'll follow your lead," Micah said. "It'll kill me to watch him touch you, but I'll do it."

An idea occurred to her. "What if he's not only touching me? What if you're not just watching?"

A grim smile formed on Micah's face. He nodded, releasing her face from where he'd cradled it in his hands, and turned to look at Victor.

"How about a two-for-one?"

Victor rubbed his eerily smooth hands together, considering. He wore a wedding ring, because of course he did. For a moment, she felt sorry for his wife. Not because he was cheating on her, but because being with a man like him must steal bits of your soul. Kara was incredibly lucky; she'd found devoted men who gave more than they took. She'd never take them for granted, ever again.

So when Victor began to remove his tie, she lowered her voice, making it sultry, breathy, like she couldn't wait for him to touch her.

"Here, let me."

Swaying toward him, she emphasized her breasts, her hips. His eyes tracked her movements, filling her with anxiety. And when the familiar panic reared its ugly head, she told it to fuck off. She was more than her pussy. She was more than her panic. Her men had taught her that.

Finally reaching him, she gently unknotted his tie and removed it from his neck, starting in on unbuttoning his starched dress shirt. Button after button, she reminded herself why she was doing this. And she made another promise to herself, one she intended to keep: after this, she'd never touch another man's chest again. The only pecs and abs she'd scrape with her nails would belong to the men she loved—because she belonged to them, and they belonged to her.

As she unbuttoned his shirt, he snuck a hand down and gripped her ass through her sheer dress. Faking a moan, she leaned over and kissed the smooth chest. His smell disgusted her. His taste disgusted her. But when he began to breathe heavily, she felt the tiniest bit of triumph, which in turn, reinforced her determination to see this through.

Micah joined her, his hands on her hips, comforting and steadying. "You're doing great, baby," he whispered in her ear, and although she'd always been a terrible actress, his approval made her believe this was working.

Making a decision, she directed Micah: "Move behind him."

"I thought you were submissive," Victor observed. "I signed on for a little doll I got to push around and have my way with. That's what you are to *them*, aren't you?"

A low growl emanated from Micah's chest. It was unnecessary; she only submitted to three men, and that was because she wasn't their doll. She was theirs. Period.

"You'll like this better," she murmured. "Trust me."

And before she could overthink it, she trailed a hand down his pants to his hard dick, and gently squeezed it through the fabric. He groaned in response.

"Yes," he groaned.

At her look, Micah moved behind Victor and started kissing his neck with one hand as he undid Victor's belt with the other. Kara unzipped his pants, tempted to catch his dick with the zipper teeth, but she knew better. They needed the location.

Together, they eased off their target's pants and briefs,

until his entirely unappealing penis was pressed between them, leaving a trail of precum on Kara's dress.

Don't vomit. Whatever you do, don't vomit.

Oh god, she was going to vomit. She could taste it in her mouth, feel the threat of more. But she forced herself to swallow it down. To keep going.

Taking his penis in her hand, she started to work it, back and forth. He was close, and moments before he was going to come, she stopped, squeezing it tight.

"Why'd you stop?" Victor panted.

"She doesn't finish you until you give us exact coordinates," Micah crooned. "And that big dick needs to come, doesn't it?"

"Fine, fuck, fuck, but I want her on her knees," Victor gasped, his hips jerking. Micah had done something to him that must have felt good.

She traded a look with Micah. *Trust me*, she mouthed.

Behind Victor, he nodded.

Kara kneeled in front of Victor, hating every second of this. *Conor, Luke*, she reminded herself.

She played lightly with his hard length and breathed on it. He jerked again, then reached down to fist a hand in her hair.

Micah took a step back, taking Victor with him.

"Coordinates," he crooned again, wrapping an arm around Victor's neck. "You want to be a good boy and get your cock sucked, don't you? Want to see how hot and perfect her mouth is? Want to feel the power of making the most powerful woman in the world submit to you? Then answer us."

"14.2910 degrees south by 171.1577 degrees west," Victor whimpered. "The Johnathans own a private island in the South Pacific. It's not on any maps."

"Such a good boy," Kara said, leaning in, her eyes on Micah's. *I love you,* she mouthed. *Now.*

His eyes flashed. And so fast she almost didn't see it, he grabbed the top of Victor's head with his other hand and wrenched it to the side, snapping the billionaire's neck.

Kara exhaled, hands on her knees. Even though she'd felt bad for Victor's wife when she'd touched him, she no longer felt bad for her, now that she was a widow. Hopefully he'd left all his money to her.

Releasing the dead body with a thud, Micah came around and helped a shaky Kara up.

"You never kneel for anyone but the three of us," he stated. "You don't give your power to anyone but us, you hear me? Never."

"Never," she echoed, as he lifted her into his arms and carried her across the room, shoving her against a wall. Her feet dangled off the floor.

"You never touch another man again who isn't us," he growled, unknowingly echoing her own thought earlier.

"Never," she said. "I only want to touch the three of you, ever."

She meant it. That had been horrific, but it was over.

"You're not a doll to us," he continued, sounding almost desperate.

And although she already knew it, hearing the words out loud began to settle the trembling inside her at what she'd almost just done. She hadn't felt used like that since she'd been with Christopher—even though she hadn't realized it at the time. She hated the girl she'd been; Micah, Luke, and Conor had helped her become the woman she was now.

"I know," she said. "I know what I am."

"What?" he asked, his eyes a raging storm.

"Everything," she said, repeating his word back to him—a word he'd used back in the cabin, when they were opponents, not teammates.

"That's right, baby," Micah said, and this time, his growl sounded satisfied. "You're mine."

She was his.

And.

"You're mine," she countered, with the same intensity. It was an admission, a claiming, but it was also a promise. One that soothed her. Victor was dead, he couldn't hurt them, and she was where she belonged.

"Yours," he agreed, smothering her in a territorial kiss. Keeping her lifted with one arm, he used his other hand to rip her panties off. Then he was unzipping his own slacks and shoving into her without warning.

"Micah!" she cried. It hurt at first, because she was dry and unprepared, but her body, knowing its master, relaxed, her pussy lubricating from the feeling of him inside her, owning her.

"You good?" he asked.

"Yes," she gasped.

He grunted in affirmation, then began bouncing her hard on his cock. He'd never been quite so caveman with her before, but then he'd never had to watch her touch someone outside their polycule. And she fucking loved it. Loved how he claimed her, loved how he made her his again, loved how, with each slide of his cock inside her pussy, he erased the horror of the last ten minutes. She forgot the dead body cooling on the floor as he fucked her hard, then harder, hitting the perfect spot on every thrust, his hands squeezing her ass, a thumb rimming her back hole, until she was spiraling higher and higher, tighter and tighter, Micah's grunts and growls pushing her closer and closer to the edge.

The door opened. Marcus stood there, flanked by two beefy guards.

"Damn it, you two," Marcus swore. "You promised no more dead bodies. How am I going to explain another dead billionaire?"

"Get the fuck out," Micah growled. "Busy."

"I can see that," Marcus remarked, sighing. "Get the body."

Before Kara could join the non-conversation, Micah shoved a finger in her ass and she tightened around him, so close, so close, so close...

"Don't you dare come when he can hear and see you," Micah said. The man who was okay with others looking but not touching was gone, leaving someone just as possessive as Conor and Luke in his place. He stayed inside her, but stirred his hips around, so his cock, already so girthy it filled every part of her, pressed against everything inside her, rubbing against her walls and setting every cell in her body aflame.

"Micah," she whined.

"No. Not yet. Fuck. You feel so good." He bit her neck, gripping on with his teeth, a complete claiming. "Tell me again," he ordered.

"I love you," she said immediately.

"Again."

"I love you!" she cried.

"Good. I love you, baby."

He thrust into her again as a reward, but his words were reward enough.

"Okay, we're done," Marcus called. "Feel free to continue."

"Out," Micah barked.

"Since you're obviously in a different mindset than usual, I'll let your tone slide this once. It won't happen again," Marcus said. "And you owe me—"

"A favor. Yes. GET OUT."

Nothing else was said. The door opened and closed again, and everyone else—living or dead—was gone.

Micah used that moment to pull out and then shove his cock and finger back inside her holes, setting his teeth back where they'd been. That's all it took. Kara catapulted over the edge, shaking, almost blacking out as she came. With a roar against her shoulder, Micah followed her over, filling her with his come. And Kara, desperate to claim him too, bit him right back.

She loved him. He knew now. They had the coordinates, they had each other, and soon...soon...they'd have Luke and Conor back as well.

She'd make sure of it.

9

────────

You don't get to play the martyr. You don't get to die. You're not my hero, you never have been. Don't start acting all gallant and sacrificial now.

Laying on his back across from a silent Conor, his left arm cuffed to the steel wall, Luke had replayed Kara's final words so many times, they were burned into his brain. He heard them, over and over, as Christopher's men kicked him in the ribs, pulled his fingers backward until one of them snapped, and shoved their fingers in his small wound where the bullet had grazed him. None of it had broken him. Luke had been trained to withstand pain. They taught SEALs meditation and self-hypnosis, so the SEALs in turn were able to handle torture by distancing themselves from it, as if they were somewhere else, just observing it, not experiencing or participating at all. And Christopher's men had gone easy on him. For now. Luke didn't kid himself: he knew that was just the prelude.

But then, he'd been prepared for torture when he'd taken Micah's place.

He pulled on his restraints. They were reinforced this time; Christopher and his men weren't taking any chances.

You're not my hero.

Kara's words should've hurt. Instead, they proved Kara desperately wanted him to be a villain because she didn't want to lose him. Villains, after all, didn't sacrifice themselves for the greater good. Villains burned down the world to save the people they loved.

Especially when they had a plan.

This wasn't the first time Luke had been taken by the enemy. He'd been trained to withstand dehydration and discomfort and even torture, to be willing to die for "the greater good." But he'd never been trained to be the one with the escape plan. That was—had been—Micah's role in their threesome. Things had changed when they'd taken Kara, and Luke was glad for it. He only hoped he could do his absent partner proud.

But first he had to check in on his other partner, who was busy imitating a large boulder. Conor had always been stoic, but this was frightening.

He glanced over at Conor, taken aback by his other lover's dead-eyed, thousand-mile stare.

"Boss, I don't know where your head's at right now, but you need to snap out of it so we can come up with a gameplan."

Conor laughed.

"Gameplan. Right."

Jesus.

Eyes on the door to their cell, Luke decided to outline his plan, hoping to wake Conor up. "We wait until they come next, overpower them, take Christopher hostage, find the plane, and get our asses out of here and home. Sound good?"

Silence.

"Boss, what are your thoughts? What should we change?"

More silence.

"Conor," Luke said, equally frustrated and desperate. "I need you to help stress test the plan. You're my leader. Lead."

Conor wiped a hand over his face, leaving a streak of dirt from the floor they sat on. "I haven't led you anywhere good. It won't work, Luke. The second we try to overpower them, they'll shoot us. Shoot you. You think they aren't prepared for us to fight back? And I'm sorry, because I know it's coming, but I'm selfish and not ready to see you die."

"Die? What the fuck are you talking about?" What was going on with him?

"I'm prepared to die," Conor continued, like he hadn't heard Luke. "But I'm not prepared for you to die with me. I'm sorry, I wish you weren't here. I wish I had made you go with Micah and Kara. The only comfort I have is that they're safe."

"Holy shit, man." Luke tried to keep his voice even. "You cannot give up so easily. We're SEALs, we can handle a simple escape. I'll get us out of here, I just need you to have my back."

"We're not SEALs anymore," Conor said.

Luke had never heard Conor sound like that before. Flat, toneless, like nothing mattered. It freaked Luke the fuck out. He couldn't be strong and smart for the two of them. What was he going to do, how were they supposed to survive, if Conor had given up on living?

"Boss, Kara needs you. She needs both of us. We owe it to her to work on getting back to her safe and whole."

Closing his eyes, Conor's next words turned Luke's heart into stone.

"She doesn't need me. I owed her a life, and that's what I got for her. I'm just sorry she's losing you. It should've just been me."

Luke's abandonment issues ran deep. They were part of what had driven him to take part in Kara's kidnapping and subsequent test, ignoring his moral compass. He didn't regret that, not anymore—it had brought her back to them. But it didn't mean they didn't get triggered at vastly inopportune times, like right now.

"Conor, you can share your regrets with me until you're goddamned blue, but you resigning yourself to both our deaths is a slap in the face, you fucking asshole. I'm glad Kara matters. Nice to know I don't, or you'd fucking help me."

Conor flinched. Point scored. But he didn't change his mind. "You matter more than you will ever know. But I can't rewrite the past. My mistakes dragged you down with me, and all I can hope now is that they kill me first. Or maybe they only kill me."

The stone that had been Luke's heart dropped to his feet. That had been the wrong tactic to take. So he forced himself to be vulnerable, to let his desperation through. Being strong and macho wasn't going to get him anywhere.

"Conor, baby...I cannot do this alone. I love you. Don't leave me like this."

Conor groaned, a deeply painful sound that burned Luke's ears. "You can't say that now. Not now."

"Why not now? Especially if you're right, and this is all the time we have. I'm supposed to what, shut up? Not share my feelings? Abandon you here? Fuck that. I'm going to share my feelings until it shakes you out of this—whatever the hell it is—because we are both getting out of here. I'm not letting you die, and I'm not dying either, so get that shit out of your screwed up head, man. Wake. The. Fuck. Up."

Conor blinked, and his eyes looked like they had life in them again. Not a lot, but it was enough. He opened his mouth to speak when the door opened.

Chris entered with two of his guards, a third wheeling a cart covered in torture implements.

"Let's try this again," Chris said jovially. "You tell me where Kara and Micah are hiding, or where they might be going, and I won't have my men treat Conor to the special of the day."

"Don't you dare fucking touch him," Luke warned, stiffening.

Conor spoke up above him. "Don't listen to him. You want to hurt me, don't you, professor? After all, I was the first one who got inside Kara's sweet pussy after she left you. I broke that seal, didn't I? Fuck, that must burn—"

The professor grabbed a knife from the table and stabbed it into Conor's left side, below his ribs. Conor grunted as the blood welled, spilling out onto his abs and down over his hip. If Luke could have done something, he would. He even found the strength somewhere inside to fight at the shackle holding him from reaching his friend and lover. But the shackle held, and all he could do was watch as Chris got his temper back under control.

"You know, Luke, it's interesting to see proof of who you care about more. Kara matters most to you, doesn't she? If she didn't, if you cared about Conor here even half as much, you'd at least consider giving up her location to make him safe. After all, she shot you, didn't she? Does she even return your affection, your devotion? Does she deserve this love you have for her?"

His words did what they intended to, slicing deep into Luke's skin. He loved Conor, he wanted to save him, but he couldn't give Kara and Micah up for him. It wasn't selfish, or choosing Kara over Conor. It was right.

Conor looked at him, sharing the same thought.

So Luke spoke. "I don't think you understand how something like this works, Chris. I don't know where Kara is, and even if I did, I wouldn't tell you—neither of us will. You can beat us and torture us and threaten to kill us and, hell, actually kill us. You can destroy us in front of each other, but we will not bend, and we will not break. Because giving them up to save each other? Would only be betraying each other. Our first duty to her and Micah and each other is to keep them safe."

Conor's voice rang out in the room. "You fucked up, professor. You treated Kara like a toy you were bored of and tried to break her. But Kara can't be broken, and she found her way forward—to us. You let a good thing go, and you'll pay more of a price than we ever will."

"Broken, huh?" Chris asked. "You may both think you're strong and tough Navy SEALs, or hitmen, or vigilantes, or whatever you've decided you are. But at the end of the day, you're just little boys playing dress up. I'll break you both, in ways you can't even begin to imagine."

He turned to his minions. "His left arm, first."

Luke strained at his restraint again, desperate to reach Conor, only to realize that Christopher was talking about him. They grabbed his free arm, twisted it, and then there was a pop and pain so sharp, a weaker man would've blacked out.

Luke was not a weaker man.

"Don't fucking hurt him." There was desperation in Conor's voice, and suddenly Luke understood.

The point of the torture wasn't to break Luke.

It was to break Conor.

"You see," Christopher started again, reaching out to stroke Conor's face. Conor snapped his teeth, and Christopher jumped back. "You see," he repeated, trying to regain control, "I am not at fault here, Mr. O'Connell. You are. I am merely the conduit for the consequences of your actions. Mr. James here is also not at fault, but he's going to suffer for what you did."

"Don't listen to him," Luke said, as he inhaled deeply to distance himself from the pain. "No one's at fault but him. Stay with me, boss. Don't fall for his shit."

"Luke," was all Conor said. It seemed like it was all he could say.

It was enough. The words carried so much weight. And as fucked up and morbid as it was, seeing Conor suffer from observing Luke's pain fortified him. For so long, Luke had questioned his place in their threesome-turned-foursome, convinced that if he was gone, they wouldn't care. Especially Conor. They fought so much, wouldn't it be a relief?

This proved otherwise. And even though Luke desperately wanted to close his eyes so he could float above the hell they were putting his body through, he was all that Conor had, and he refused to leave him, there. So he caught his partner's—*lover's*—eyes, and held them.

And Conor, who was suffering so much guilt and so much emotional pain, stared straight back. They remained that way, as Luke's physical pain grew worse and Conor's anguish matched it. But although Luke wished Conor wasn't here, wasn't suffering, the fact that they were together brought back the lessons from his past. Reminded him of the man his grandma had wanted him to be. The man Kara wanted him to be.

He was not a hero.

He was more.

They held each other's gazes. They held fast, and they held strong.

Until they couldn't anymore.

10

─────

Luke hadn't moved in hours.

He was breathing. Conor reminded himself of that, over and over, watching Luke's chest raise and lower. They hadn't killed him. For a time, it looked like they were close to it, and every time Luke, who had been trained the same as Conor to withstand brutal pain, made a sound, something had broken in Conor. Something he wasn't sure would ever mend.

Conor's wrists were covered in dried blood from how hard he'd fought to escape his shackles and save his lover. His throat stung from how yelling, first threats, then pleas, as Luke became bloodier and bloodier and less and less responsive.

Finally, the professor had grown bored and they'd dropped Luke on the floor, popped the shackle back around his good arm so he couldn't escape, and left.

Conor never cried. Not on his father's death anniversary, not when they'd found out they'd orphaned those little boys. It had taken seeing Luke in pain, and being helpless against it, to get those floodgates to open.

"Baby," Conor murmured, tears in his eyes, his throat. "Baby, baby, baby..."

Come back to me. Please, come back to me.

Finally, Luke coughed, struggling to open his left eye, which was dried shut with blood. Conor wasn't sure if he'd ever be able to open it again. He'd love him anyway, eyeless or sightless, beaten or broken. He'd love him, because he loved him. God, why hadn't he said it more, when he'd had a chance?

As if Luke read his mind, he rasped, "Please don't be maudlin right now. I'm in too much pain to beat the sentiment out of you."

Conor laughed with something like relief, still tinged with sadness. Luke was conscious, but how much longer did they have?

"I love you, you asshole. You know that, right?" he asked.

Luke tried to laugh. "Of course you do, you dumbass. Just like I love your dumb ass."

He hacked a cough, and Conor's heart sank when he saw it was speckled with blood.

"Ah shit," Luke said, noting the same thing.

"Yeah, shit," Conor echoed, because what else was there to say?

They were silent for a time, both lost to their own thoughts, Conor trying to recreate a happy Kara and Micah in his mind, the only thing that would keep him going, knowing neither he nor Luke had much time left.

"God, I miss them. I miss *her*," Luke said, surprising Conor. But then, Conor shouldn't have been surprised they were on the same wavelength. "I miss being smothered by her wild hair and listening to her snore."

Conor smiled, imagining it. "I miss her little ass sassing me."

"Or pretending she wants control when she really wants you to take it from her." Luke laughed. "I miss her little ass, period."

"All those times she surprised and scared the hell out of us, the little badass." Conor closed his eyes, picturing the time when she'd deepthroated that gun to create a distraction for him. They'd punished her for that, but he was so proud of her and of who she'd become when she finally let herself grow. The woman he'd first met, dressed in a tight black dress she kept readjusting, running from her past and from herself, desperate to hide what she truly wanted in sex and bravado? She was not the brave woman he knew now, who could stand—or crawl—naked and proud surrounded by strangers, without questioning her own worth or power. Who knew who she was, and settled in it, and liked it. Who gave of herself, vulnerably and willingly.

Who loved them.

He hoped.

Because he loved her, so fucking much.

"I never thought I'd be afraid to die," Conor admitted. "And earlier on the plane, I almost welcomed it, the guilt was eating me alive. But now, knowing I'll probably never see her or Micah again..."

"...all you want is to be with them, one more time. You can have that, Conor. *We* can have it. You just need to fight. Fight with me. Please, Conor."

Please. Luke never begged. Conor owed it to him, didn't he? What had Luke said? That he'd hurt Kara so much, he owed it to her to live and be better? Could he do it? Was he capable?

He looked at Luke, truly looked at him. Past the already-forming bruises and dried blood, past the way he was trying to pretend his injuries were nothing. Luke had always been so strong. He'd carried the weight of their missing morality even as he struggled with his own fears, and Conor didn't need to be Micah to know how badly Luke wanted, needed, to be loved. Conor might have control issues, and Micah might have trust issues, but Luke's abandonment issues were clear as day, now that Conor was paying attention.

"You know, together, the three of us, you, me, and Micah? We make one truly fucked up person."

Luke choked on a laugh, then groaned from the pain. "That is a weird fucking thought to have." He sobered. "Do you ever wonder why we were always at each other's throats? I mean, when we weren't fucking each other."

Conor shifted, feeling his skin itch from how open Luke was asking him to be. "I don't think about shit like that."

"C'mon, boss."

"Micah would say it was because we were measuring whose dick is bigger."

Luke laughed. "Mine, obviously."

"True." He'd had it in his ass enough times to know. "I think..." Conor swallowed. "I was so fucking jealous that Kara spent so long with you but left me after two nights. I kept questioning myself: What did you do, that I didn't? What did you have, that I didn't? What the hell was I missing? I was fucking resentful, so I took it out on you. And after we orphaned those boys in Frankfurt, you somehow still had your soul; I'd lost mine. But instead of confronting that painful shit, I made it about a fight for power in my head."

Luke nodded. "You took over so easily, you were in charge without question, and it meant that you always served a role. You were the boss, Micah was the brains, what was I? There was a part of me that was always sure you two would decide one day to move on without me. When you ignored what I said and took Kara, it felt like you had, in a way."

"I was desperate for her," Conor explained.

"I know."

"And it felt like I'd already done so much evil. What did one more fucked-up thing matter?"

Luke's smile was soft, accepting. "I know."

"And we almost lost her because of it," Conor admitted. "God, I almost lost you. When she shot you..."

Luke tried to laugh, but the pain was clearly becoming too much, based on the strain in his face. "She never wanted to kill me. She was pissed. And she's a good shot."

"You taught her well," Conor acknowledged.

"So did you. All I want, boss, is for us to be together again. Can you give me that? Let go of that crushing guilt for a second? You once told me we were Kara's villains. So be her villain with me. Burn the world down to get back to her. Starting with this goddamned place."

God.

Fuck.

"I love you," Conor said.

"Fuck, I love you so much," Luke swore. "When we get out of here, things will be different between us. I promise I'll never teabag you again."

Conor laughed, feeling less weighed down. "What happened to never lying? Yes, you will."

Luke smiled, his lip splitting and fresh blood welling. "Yeah, I will. But you like it."

"I do."

The other man reached out his manacled arm to brush Conor's face, only to come up short. Conor tried to pull toward him, but his manacles also held him back. Only a foot between them, but it felt like a mile. The air that should've been skin to skin hurt.

So he raised an arm again, holding up his hand as if to press it against Luke's. Luke moved his, so their hands mirrored each other. It had to be enough, for now.

Friend.

Adversary.

Brother.

Partner.

Lover.

"I promise I won't abandon you in this, Luke," Conor swore, meaning it. "I'll fight with you. I'll help you get us out of here. You just tell me what you need me to do."

"Good, because I have a plan."

As Luke quietly began to outline it, in case there were mics in the room, Conor listened. He'd follow it, to a point. When it came time, he'd give himself up to make sure Luke got out alive. Because he'd do anything, anything, to keep this man safe.

"Agreed?" Luke asked.

"Agreed," Conor said, lying to the man who hated lies.

And then the door opened and the professor entered the room.

"Turns out I don't need either of you," he said. "I found her."

Once upon a time, in a far, far away land called Denver, Colorado, Kara had decided to try something new. Kara, whose recklessness knew very few bounds, constantly dared herself to try new things back then.

As she'd once explained to Luke, Micah, and Conor, the recklessness had started as a way to get attention from her parents, and evolved into something she did, just to prove she could. Looking back, she realized that she hadn't made stupid choices because she was enjoying herself; she made them because she desperately wanted someone to grab her firmly by the shoulders and say, "stop." She had that, now, but back then, she'd been completely on her own, and starving for connection—even as she chased after physical risks to avoid emotional ones.

So, she made questionable choices: take a cross-country road trip with no destination. Pick up gorgeous strangers in bars and restaurants. And, on that fateful day in Denver, attempt to climb a wall, even though, as a born-and-bred big city girl, she'd never done such a thing before in her life.

And yet there she went, dressed in what seemed appropriate wall-climbing gear, and attempted to make her way up a wall. The problem, of course, was that like most daring perfectionists, Kara expected to get wall climbing right on the first go. The bigger problem was that, of course, she didn't.

Having to face failure, even a small one, had triggered a panic attack, the worst one thus far in her life. (Past Kara was, after all, a sweet summer child who had no idea what it was like to be kidnapped, *twice*, not to mention wake up in a car bobbing in the ocean. Past Kara didn't even know the meaning of panic attacks.)

And then, to her utter surprise, a meddling, unsolicited hero appeared, talked her down from her panic, and up the rest of the wall. And when he'd asked her if she had a fear of heights, she'd told him no, and opened up to him about her perfectionism-triggered panic attack. How frustration with her own inabilities and what that might say about her, especially after she'd fucked up so badly in her real life, made it hard to breathe sometimes. And then she'd gotten to know the man, and they'd fucked a lot, and she'd let him into her heart, and well...here she was, in an airplane, on her way to rescue him and their lover.

There was one tiny problem, though. Because if climbing a wall had triggered her fear of failure and set off a panic attack, then what she was about to do right now was like the five-alarm fire version. After all, she was now suited up and being given high stakes instructions on how to *jump out of an airplane*. Failure didn't mean not being able to climb a silly wall. Failure meant death: Hers, for sure, and possibly Micah's, Luke's, and Conor's, too. Especially if she took Micah down with her and there was no one to save Luke and Conor. Thinking about it was goddamn terrifying.

But it didn't matter, because Luke and Conor had saved her, more than once, and it was her turn to save them.

"Kara, you don't have to do this."

Kara, we don't have to do this, Conor had said so long ago.

"You can stay back with Billy and I can go in and get them on my own."

We can go to the mainland. Get fro-yo. Get to know each other.

Back then, she'd gotten angry at the implication that she would ever do something she didn't want to do. She hadn't been willing to admit to herself that physical risks were easy stand ins for emotional ones. Or that she wasn't making her choices—her inner demons were. She hadn't had anyone to say "stop."

And now that Kara had people to grab her by the shoulders and stop her from falling off a cliff, she was about to jump out of a plane, something she desperately didn't want to do. But recently, Kara had been doing a lot of things she didn't want to do, because you sacrificed for the people you loved.

Was that what love meant? Sacrifice?

Risk?

She'd learned one thing: love might be a risk, but it wasn't reckless when you were loved back.

"I'm doing this," she told Micah. "You need me for the plan, remember? I'm the bait, I'm the decoy. I'm the one who's going to take Chris down."

Micah shook his head. "Baby, you don't want to do this. I can tell. You're afraid of failing, aren't you? Panic attack afraid?"

"Goddamn it, how do you know everything?" she muttered, frustrated.

He smiled. "I don't know everything. I know *you*."

"And you're trying to manipulate me into staying on the plane," she continued.

"I am. Is it working?"

"We're doing this," she told him, resolute.

God, part of her truly didn't want to, wanted to take the escape hatch he was offering and get out of this. But there'd been a reason she'd manipulated Billy into taking her to Micah. There was a reason she'd touched another man's disgusting penis and hadn't flinched when Micah had killed him. There was a reason she was here, and it was because she wasn't letting Micah out of her sight. If something happened to him and she wasn't there, she'd never forgive herself.

But that didn't mean she couldn't be vulnerable with him, share a little honesty. "You're right, I'm fucking terrified of failing today. But I'm not going to let my fear or the panic attacks beat me. Not today."

"Little warrior," Micah murmured, pulling her into his arms and kissing her. "You amaze me with your bravery. I'm in awe of you."

"Let's do this," Kara said. "Besides, you'll be with me the entire time. I'll be strapped to you, won't I? You'll keep us safe. I have faith in you."

He kissed her again. "I will *always* keep you safe."

Billy exited the cockpit, catching Kara's eyes. They hadn't spoken when they'd met him at the private airstrip, so Kara didn't know where she stood with him.

"Hi, Billy," she said.

"Troublemaker," he greeted her.

"I'm sorry about guilting you into taking me to Micah."

He grinned. "No, you're not. But I've forgiven you for feminine wile-ing me. Micah told me you're going to make it up to me by giving me your friend's number. Seems like a good apology."

Fuck. Lola was going to kill her.

Still, Kara laughed, feeling lighter than she had since the day Luke and Conor had been taken. "I'll give it to you when we get back."

"Good." He turned to Micah, all business. "We have a slight problem."

Micah straightened. "How slight?"

Billy sighed. "The tandem parachute is broken."

Kara's lover swore. "What are our options?"

"We have two single-person parachutes on board."

"That's unacceptable," Micah said.

Billy shrugged. "I know you and your brother think you can control the universe, but this is reality. You're going to have to jump separately. Kara, let's go over the timing of deployment."

As Kara listened to Billy's directions, she felt her stomach tumble out of the plane without a parachute, only to smack hard on the ground ten thousand feet below. It was one thing to hold on while Micah handled the logistics, but to trust herself not to panic enough to be able to do it on her own...

No. She could do this. She had to do this. She'd spent a lifetime proving she was stronger than her fear. She would do it now, and this time, she wouldn't panic at the sight of failure...because she wouldn't fail.

Taking deep breaths, she centered herself, hearing Luke in the back of her mind, like they were on that climbing wall all over again.

Can you do me a favor? Just humor me and breathe with me. You don't have to do anything or worry about anything—I'll keep you safe. All you need to do is inhale and exhale.

That's all?

That's all.

He had kept her safe, that day. And she was going to return the favor.

Calm and centered—or as calm and centered as someone could be when they were about to jump out of a fucking airplane—she followed Billy's and Micah's instructions, repeating it back to them over and over, until Micah was satisfied.

"It really is simple," Billy said. "You're going to sit on the side of the plane, push off, and slowly count down from fifty. Then pull this thing here," he showed her where on the contraption she'd been strapped into, "and the parachute will deploy. After that, it's smooth sailing on the way down. We sent drones down and it's mostly an open field down there with some trees. Easy peasy."

"You sure about this?" Micah said.

"No," Kara told him truthfully. "But the longer we wait, the more unsure I'll be. And I'm sure I want to be down there with you. So."

Micah nodded. "I love you."

"I love you," she told him back.

"You're going first, troublemaker," Billy said cheerfully.

Oh, *god*. Was she really doing this?

She closed her eyes, picturing Conor and Luke in her head. Conor's clenched jaw, Luke's soft eyes.

She was really doing this.

She sat, leaned forward, and pushed off.

The first few moments were exhilaratingly quiet. The air swept past her, buoying her up and caressing her body like a lover. Down below, the Pacific Ocean was nothing more than a large piece of bright blue construction paper, interrupted by small green and brown stickers: islands. As she drifted, the stickers began to grow larger, white and green ridges appearing: mountains, forests, and volcanoes. The air shushed her as it rushed by, cradling her in its arms. Crisp clean air—like mountain air but on steroids—filled her nose, her lungs. She'd bottle that smell if she could.

She'd stay here forever if she could.

As she counted down from fifty, she embraced the peace and freedom of it all. She was fucking flying. She was trusting in the universe, and the universe was protecting that trust. Some feet above her, Micah—who had pushed off while she'd been busy just *being*—hovered in the air in a matching helmet and goggles, eyes on hers. He grinned, and she grinned back.

Five, four, three, two, one—

She pulled the tab for the parachute, expecting a loud sound as it popped open. Instead, the air seemed to speed up around her.

That couldn't be right.

She pulled it again.

Nothing happened.

She couldn't see Micah's face, but it was as if she could *feel* his horror. He was mouthing her name, probably screaming it, and she was sure she was screaming, too, because everything was not okay and she should not have trusted the goddamned universe, she knew better than that, and she was going to die before she ever saw Luke or Conor again and was able to tell them she loved them.

It was amazing, the clarity being so close to death brought you. It had happened that time she'd been beaten and bloody on the floor and she'd realized she cared about Luke, Micah, and Conor, and they cared about her. This time, watching Micah's face as the earth grew closer and closer to her, she knew there was only one thing she could do.

I love you, she mouthed. *So much. Tell them I love them too.*

And even though the wind was too loud to hear anything, she swore she heard Micah's roar.

12

———

"**I** found her," Chris repeated. "I found both of them."

Luke, who was already having trouble breathing after those fuckers fractured his ribs with their boots, lost the ability completely. What the fuck had been the point of any of this, if Micah had let them be found so easily? Were they here? Could he reconfigure the plan to get them out, too?

He knew better than to ask, though. If Chris were lying, Luke would just play directly into his hands.

He did his best to blink his left eye open. The world, blurry at first, cleared. Mostly. There was crusted blood blocking some of his vision, but he could see that Conor's whole body was hulking out, like he hadn't been stabbed in his left side hours earlier. Veins had popped out everywhere as he tried to break his shackles. But it hadn't worked earlier when Luke was getting the shit kicked out of him. It wasn't going to work now.

"Unfortunately, I did not find them alive," Chris continued. "We did, however, collect their bodies for you. Do you want to see?"

Conor dropped to his knees, an anguished moan leaving his mouth. Luke tried to reach out to him, to argue. They weren't dead. They couldn't be. If Kara and Micah were dead, he'd know. He'd fucking *know*. They were a part of him, he'd feel it deep in his soul. Unless when he'd been beaten and tortured, he'd lost that part of himself. Was that even possible?

"Do you want to see their bodies?" Chris said conversationally. "Of course, we can't transport them here, but we will show them to you. And, because I'm not a complete monster, I'll make sure they both get a Jewish funeral and get buried in a Jewish cemetery, together. I'll even tell you both where it is so you can go visit them there. All you need to do is tell me the coordinates of your mountain cabin, and we'll let you go."

"Go?" Luke asked, as his brain whirred, circling around this information again and again. Something Chris had said was off, but he couldn't figure out what.

"Yes. I don't need you anymore, do I? My brothers feel a bit differently, of course," Chris waved his hand, "but I can handle my brothers."

"They're not dead," Conor growled from the floor.

"Oh yes, here, let me show you," Chris said, and a TV monitor turned on. Two bodies lay in a morgue, a curvy woman with dyed-black hair, like Kara's had been when Luke had last seen her, and a large, blond man who looked like Micah. Sheets were pulled up to their shoulders, so Luke couldn't be sure...

Conor yelled, in a voice that would haunt Luke for the rest of his life, no matter how long it lasted.

...but there was no tattoo.

Buried in a Jewish cemetery.

But you couldn't be buried in a Jewish cemetery if you had a voluntary tattoo.

Which Micah hadn't gotten until after they'd been court martialed.

Luke inhaled, breath returning to his lungs. It hurt, but in a way that felt sweet with relief. He stared at Conor, tried to communicate it to him, because he couldn't say anything in front of Chris. This was it, their element of surprise. The Johnathans had no plans to let them go. But if Chris thought that Luke and Conor believed him, he wouldn't suspect the hand Luke and Conor were about to play.

He needed to wait. Chris would leave at some point.

Except then the chains came loose, and he was being dragged out before he could do anything about it.

"I think it would be good to give you both time to yourselves to decide what you want to do. I know they say misery loves company, but. . ." Chris shrugged an elegant shoulder. "While my misery likes a party, I'm sensitive to realize yours may not."

Oh, fuck. Fuck, fuck, fuck.

He couldn't leave Conor like this. Not believing Kara and Micah were dead. Conor wasn't a complete idiot, but he was too lost in his grief to see straight. And if Luke weren't with him, Conor wouldn't know Micah and Kara were alive, and they couldn't enact their escape plan.

Luke's mind was blank. Maybe he'd been wrong, maybe he wasn't up for this. Maybe he couldn't be a leader, a plotter. Maybe he'd only been good as the third wheel.

No, that was defeatist shit, right there. He wouldn't fall for it.

But what the fuck was he going to do?

13

———

Micah had only felt true fear a few times in his life. He regularly went on missions with the two men he loved most while knowing that as good as they were at their jobs, they were still risking their lives. And yet he was calm. He *embodied* calm.

Because Micah was always calm. He cultivated it internally, so externally he could create chaos. But just like she'd upended everything else, Kara had destroyed Micah's calm.

And right now, he was feeling more fear than he'd ever felt in his entire life.

Because Kara's goddamned fucking parachute wasn't deploying, and there wasn't a goddamned fucking thing he could do. He was at least ten feet above her, and she was falling, fast.

Did he have even a chance of saving her?

As he quickly weighed his options, he watched her mouth *I love you.* A roar burst out from his lungs, a complete negation of the reality he was facing.

She couldn't die.

She wouldn't die.

Making a snap decision, he didn't even bother deploying his parachute, but put his arms out as gravity did its job. And he prayed to the god he no longer believed in, for the first time in over a decade, to save her.

Kara was falling, faster.

Faster.

Micah started stroking through the air like he was swimming so he could get closer to her. The air fought him, not liking someone who was trying to change the way gravity and air flow worked, but he didn't give a fuck.

And finally, finally, as his heart hammered in his chest and ears, her hand was within holding distance. He motioned to her, and, eyes wide, she reached for him.

He grabbed her hand.

And tugged.

She span directly into his arms, which he wrapped tight around her. Oh, the air didn't like that. It wanted her back. It had plans for her. But Micah had his own goddamned fucking plans, and they didn't include the woman he loved dying today.

"Wrap your arms around me," he tried to yell.

He doubted she could hear him, but she either understood or instinct was working, because she wrapped her arms around his neck. He couldn't see her eyes through her goggles, but he leaned his head against hers, praying again as he tugged the ripcord, not knowing if his parachute was also jammed.

Nothing but wind.

Fuck.

He tugged again.

This time, with a whomp, the parachute deployed, tugging him straight up in the air as it caught the wind and pulled them backward. A normal man would have lost hold of Kara at that point—and a normal woman would have lost hold of him—but Micah was a former SEAL and Kara was determined. And besides, they fucking loved each other too much to let go.

They loved each other. That meant he'd always catch her before she fell, and as long as she held on, she'd be safe.

The world went quiet again as they sank toward the ground. It was funny how air could feel and sound like water, the same rushing quiet. How this reminded him of when their car had begun to sink into the depths of the ocean and Kara had fought to get them all out.

We're always saving each other, aren't we? he tried to say, but the words were carried away by the silent wind.

She gripped him harder.

Turning his head, he took stock of where they were. The problem was, since he'd delayed pulling his parachute, they'd been pulled off course. Instead of landing on a flat field, which had its own problems since Kara had no parachute of her own, they were going to smack straight into a bunch of trees.

Fuck. He had no idea how he was going to pull this off, but he better figure it out fast.

The ground sped closer to him, he gripped her tighter, time went into overdrive, and god, god, god, please god, let him time this right, let time be on his side...

As they passed over the trees, he spotted a small clearing...

And released her, prying her hands from his neck.

She held tighter, unsure of what he was doing.

"Trust me," he said, and thank god, she must have heard him, because she loosened her arms...

And fell to the ground.

She seemed mostly unharmed from where he could see

her, which was good, because moments later he smacked directly into a tree and his parachute got trapped in the branches and almost choked the life out of him.

But they'd made it, and he had to believe they were safe.

"Micah? Micah!"

She was standing underneath him, staring up at him in shock.

"Hi, baby," he called as he began to untangle the straps trying to kill him.

"Hold on, I'm coming to help you," she called, and then she was shimmying up the tree, much more confident than she must have been that day with Luke. He'd taught her well.

She reached him, sitting on a branch, and reached an arm forward. Together, they untangled him, he unsnapped the backpack that held the trapped parachute, and jumped down to the forest floor.

She jumped down after him and he caught her before she touched ground. Of course, she knocked the wind out of him and they tumbled over onto the ground, so she was straddling him.

And laughing, a little wildly.

"I don't, I can't," she was saying, breathless. "How..."

He grabbed her, pulling off her helmet and goggles and then his own. Then he pulled her down to him, ignoring how his head ached. "I don't know. I don't care. All I know is I could've lost you, and here you are, in my arms. I'm not about to fucking question how fate worked out, I'm just going to be goddamned grateful it did."

"Baby," was all she said, stroking his hair back from his face.

Fuck. They were alive. *She* was alive.

He'd almost lost her. He could accept any reality, but not

that one. He'd drag the god he didn't have faith in into the hell he'd been raised not to believe in for that crime. Except instead, he'd prayed to god, and while he still didn't believe in anything, here she was, alive, straddling him, as his cock hardened beneath her.

Because if he had faith in anything, it was her.

"I love you, baby," he told her.

"You caught me," she said, her voice still shaking with wonder and shock.

"I did. And I'm never, ever, letting you go."

He was going to show her exactly how serious he was. He rolled them over, unclipping her from her harness, getting rid of his own. He dragged his clothes off his body as she stared at him, a little woozy, a little out of it, a little enraptured.

It was okay. He'd snap her back to reality. Starting with getting to work on having his favorite meal in the world.

He pulled off her pants and panties, not even bothering to warm her up when he dove in to get a taste. And even though she always tasted perfect to him, raw and sweet and salty and just so fucking real and his, right now, she tasted better than she ever had. She tasted alive. She cried out, thrashing and writhing below his hungry mouth, so he grabbed her hips in a firm hold.

"You stay still, baby," he said. "You stay still and let me eat until you come all over my fucking face. That's your only job right now, alright?" Not waiting for her to respond, not bothering to tease her or work her up slowly, not even caring about her pleasure so much for her sake as for his own, he engulfed her pussy with his mouth and devoured her, thrusting his tongue inside her again and again, and then licking and nipping her clit until she'd drenched his face. Her thighs squeezed his head in a vise, making him go a little lightheaded, and his cock got even harder.

She froze, then shook beneath him as she screamed into the trees, and the birds among them screamed back, flying away.

Lifting his mouth from her pussy, he crawled up her body, dragging her legs apart, and slowly thrust inside her, determined to feel every perfect, wet, hot inch.

"Fuck baby, no one feels as good as you. Do you realize that?" he pulled back, then slowly slid back in. "Your pussy was made for our cocks, your heart for ours, your soul for ours. If I could, I'd keep my cock in you all the time, use your little pussy like a personal heater, and carry you around everywhere I went. So when I felt like coming, I could. If I felt like breeding you, I could."

Her eyes flashed at this last, and he kissed her before she could reject his statement.

He pulled back again to say against her lips, "You think you don't want that, but I just felt you clench around me and drench me again. You love that idea, don't you? The three of us filling you up with our come, again and again, making you our perfect little beautiful breeding slut? Using your holes whenever we wanted, baby?"

She clenched around him again, whimpering affirmation and agreement. "Yes," she gasped.

He smothered her with another kiss, sliding in and out of her soaked cunt, needing to say the next. She'd wanted to hate them, back at the cabin, for making her feel used.

"You want us to use your holes, treat you like our little cockwarmer, because you know we love you and we'll take care of you, don't you, baby? Know you're everything to us, including our perfect little fucktoy? That we'd die for you? That we want to live for you?"

"Yes," she cried again.

Good. With her acknowledgment between them, he pulled back his hips and shoved his cock in hard, satisfaction filling him as his woman came around him, clenching and writhing and screaming more, the greatest testament to her being alive that existed in the entire goddamned universe.

Alive, and his.

Theirs.

Part of him was aware that the whole point of parachuting in was to launch a surprise attack on the Johnathans. Fucking Kara in the middle of the island made them easy targets if they got caught. But with her cunt gripping his cock and flexing around him as he fucked into her, again and again, tension building inside him as he tried not to come, not yet, he realized he almost didn't fucking care. He needed this, and so did she, and the world could go fuck itself for a while.

"Kara, baby, tell me you love me," he demanded.

"I love you," she cried out immediately.

"Tell me you love all of us."

"I love all of you," she said.

"And you'll never leave us," he said, his voice tight with command.

"I'll never leave you!" she came again with a scream, and her words sent Micah over as he filled her cunt with everything he had.

14

———————

There was only one place Chris could be holding them on the entire island. When Billy and Micah had studied the island's topography, and searched for any heat signatures, they only found one spot. They couldn't even be positive that's where Luke and Conor were being held; there was no building there, and it just looked like a patch of ground. But it was the only thing they had to go on, and Kara's gut told her that's where her men were.

Of course, it was on the other side of the island, which meant a day of trekking through the forest and rocky terrain to get there. Kara wasn't a bad hiker, by any means, but she knew Micah could probably run the entire length of the ten-mile island without breaking a sweat. She was holding him back. It was a real concern, especially considering Luke and Conor had been taken three days ago; god knew what had happened to them in that time. Just thinking about it made Kara want to scream. She missed them; she needed them safe; she needed them whole.

But it was too late to turn back now. And not only would

Micah not leave her by herself, their plan required her complete participation. So she walked as fast as she could, trailing him, ignoring the way her calves burned and knees ached, shoving away the pain of the blisters forming on her heels and ankles from the brand new hiking boots, because it wasn't like they'd been able to go get her broken-in ones from her apartment in Chicago. Even though she was thirsty, even though her stomach growled with hunger, she kept going. Kept going, as the forest turned to dirt and thick, sharp grass and open sky.

"Do you need to stop, baby?" he'd asked multiple times, and her only answer was to shake her head, chug a little more water, and plow on.

He'd shake his head, knowing she was lying, but giving her what she needed, and she was grateful to him for it. She'd just jumped off a plane and almost died, she could handle a ten-mile hike, no matter how hot it was or how her lungs burned from the exertion as they headed up a steep hill under the sweltering sun.

Finally, he stopped, grabbing her by her hips. Gracefully sitting on the ground, he guided her onto his lap.

"Micah…"

"Baby, no," he said. "You've been going for hours and I'm proud of you, and I didn't want to stop you from doing what you needed to do. But if you don't take a break and eat something, you'll faint. I'm not going to allow that."

Sighing, she opened her hand for the protein bar he'd grabbed from his pack. Holding it out of reach, he unwrapped it.

"Open," he coaxed her.

"Micah, now is not a good time for sex," she protested.

He rolled his eyes, shaking his head. "Feeding you is not

only something that turns me on. It's an imperative for me. When I know you're hungry and thirsty, and I haven't fed you, my whole body feels off, like something is wrong and I'm not doing my job. Taking care of you *is* my job. It's the most important thing I do. Don't take that from me, not now."

As Kara digested his words, something finally clicked. "Your love language is feeding people, isn't it?"

It explained why he was so obsessed with feeding her, even back at the cabin. Why he'd made himself their foursome's cook.

He cracked a smile. "I figured you knew that already."

"I think I did, but I didn't put it together."

"Hmm. Those weeks on the streets, after my family kicked me out, I was so hungry. I became obsessed with food. Not with feeding myself, but with feeding other people. I think in another life..." he hesitated. "I would've been a chef. But that's not the life I have now, and I've made my peace with that."

"Do you feed Conor and Luke by hand?"

He chuckled. "They'd probably beat my ass for it. Besides, *that* particular compulsion only comes up with you. Now, open your mouth, baby."

She complied, and he broke off a piece of protein bar, placing it on her tongue. She chewed and swallowed, ignoring the chalky taste and dry texture. He fed her another piece, and another, until it was all gone, her stomach had stopped grumbling, and Micah seemed satisfied.

"What about you?"

His eyes twinkled in amusement. "You want to feed me by hand?"

Kara brushed this off. "If you want me to, sure."

He shook his head.

"You should eat something," she insisted.

"I will. I needed to make sure you were taken care of, first."

He fed her, cared for her, like he fucked her, didn't he? Always making sure she'd gotten off at least a few times before he let himself come—unless he was withholding her orgasm to punish or test her. Despite herself, Kara clenched her thighs, wanting him again.

But they didn't have time, and she didn't have the energy. Still, it was more proof that she was more than a set of holes. That whatever, whoever she'd been in a past life to other men, it didn't carry over to *her* men. No matter how they'd started, or how much they fucked, they wanted her for *her*, no matter how messy she was.

"Baby," he said, reading her. "When this is all over, I'm going to feed and fuck you so much, you're going to be begging me to stop. Prove to you, again and again, how necessary you are to me. But if you're feeling better, we should keep moving. We're too exposed."

"I'm good," she told him, even though it was partly a lie. The food had helped but she was still exhausted. It didn't matter. Between exhaustion and determination, determination won every time when the goal was important enough.

Luke. Conor.

They were so close to getting them back.

He placed an approving kiss on her neck, then pushed her to standing before following her up. As they began to walk, he took her hand in his, rubbing her knuckles with his thumb.

Surprised, she turned to look at him. Micah was affectionate, but she'd figured he'd be too focused to put attention into settling her nerves.

"Why?" she started.

He looked at her, his eyes bright. "Just in case, I want to make sure I get every last moment that I can."

Oh, god. Tears filled her eyes, blurring the forest in front of her. Losing her footing, she almost tripped, but he caught her.

"Oh, baby, don't cry. I won't let you die, I promise."

"But you still think you might."

He nodded. "It's a distinct possibility. On every mission, I take a deep breath and make peace with my death. I've lived a good life, Kara. And the past couple of months have been better than I could form words to describe. I don't want to give it up, I'm not going to give it up. But if I have to...I can be at peace with it, knowing every second of it was worth it, even the worst ones, because they led me to you."

She swallowed the sob before it could escape her lips. He didn't need to hear her cry. Instead, she said, "That's hero talk."

"No, it isn't. Hero talk would be if I was sacrificing myself for some greater good. I'm not, I'm too selfish for that. I'd kill every last person, burn down the whole world, if it meant the four of us were together forever. But I will not *ever* let you die. And Kara, if you can do one thing to make me happy, promise me that you won't do something stupid and heroic and try sacrificing yourself for us. If you do that, Kara? I will rise from the dead, burn down the heavens and the earth, just to get you back—and then beat your little ass for it forever."

The warning, as hypocritical as it was, tore a hole in her fabric heart, then repaired it with indestructible steel. *This,* here, was love. Micah had been right. It didn't matter if they were bad men or good men, if she'd fucked up in the past or not. It mattered that for the four of them, they came first. And for the little girl who'd been all but abandoned by her parents and ostracized as an adult for her choices, who'd insisted on never having bonds with anyone out of fear that no one would want to tie her to them...for that little girl, knowing *just* how much she was loved was all she'd never known she needed.

Not that she'd ever let him sacrifice himself.

"Kara," he said sharply. "I want a promise from you."

She didn't want to promise something she would renege on, so she took a page out of his book and crafted her response carefully. "I promise I won't be stupid, or heroic."

He'd said it himself. This wasn't heroic, it was pure self-ishness, wanting the people you loved to live on, even without you. But Kara had never had an issue with being selfish.

Accepting that, he nodded, and they continued along the hike, going downhill now. The terrain had changed again, and Kara was careful not to trip over rocks or fallen branches as they followed the steep decline toward where their men were. It was too treacherous to hold hands, and Kara missed the comfort of skin touching skin.

They were silent for a while, then she asked, "So what happens, after we rescue them and destroy the Johnathans?"

Micah cleared his throat. "You tell me what happens."

The problem was, she didn't know. She didn't know what a happily ever after looked like for her, if those even existed. "What will our lives look like?"

He stopped suddenly, turning back to her, and she fell against him. But he was strong and solid, and he caught her without tumbling backwards, thank god. "*Our*?"

She swallowed. "Yes. *Our*."

His smile lit up like a sunrise. "They'll look like whatever we want them to look like. I mean it, Kara, we want you to be happy, to find something that gives you purpose and meaning and joy, regardless of what it is. We'll make it happen. You know that by now, don't you?"

She did. Oh, she did. "But what about you?"

Micah shrugged. "It doesn't matter, as long as I don't let my skills get rusty. I've never really cared about what I was doing, all I care about is who I'm with. Whatever you all want, I'll be happy with."

"What do you think they want?" Did they still need absolution? Did they like this life in the darkness, or did they want to return to the light?

More importantly, did she?

Micah sighed. "That's not a question I feel like I can answer. But we'll get the chance to ask them soon, won't we?"

They'd reached the bottom of the hill. Before them stretched nothing but dirt. It was silent, not a bird, not a brush of wind. Foreboding filled her.

Micah took out some gadget and held it out in front of them.

"There," he pointed.

She squared her shoulders. Panic threatened to over-whelm her, knowing what she had to do next, but panic didn't matter now. All she had to do was breathe, and then continue on.

Micah glanced sharply at her. "Kara, baby, breathe."

She forced a smile. "I'm fine. I'm already breathing."

"I want you to know," he told her as he checked a gun and handed it to her, "I hate this. If I could think of any other option, I never would have involved you this way. I just hope we're all alive long enough for Luke and Conor to kill me for it later, because they're not going to forgive me using you this way."

"Micah." She drew close to him, tugging on his backpack straps to bring him against her, then wrapped her arms around his neck. "Remember what I asked you, back at Vixen? I need you to help me, and you do that by trusting me. Have faith that I can do this, baby."

He groaned, wrapping a hand around her neck, not tight but steadying, a clear gesture of dominance and control. The only control right now he probably felt he had.

"I love you so much. You remember what you promised me. You stay safe. You stay alive. You hear me, baby? Do *not* change course. Do *not* let what's happening in front of you make you change the plan," he said.

She swallowed back the lie, and just kissed him. He immediately took control of the kiss, too, overwhelming her with everything that was him, making her briefly forget her promise to herself. He gave her all of him in the heat of that kiss, the bite of it, and she gave it all back.

"Ours," he growled against her mouth.

"Yours," she agreed.

Finally, he released her, only to stroke a hand down her cheek. He was memorizing her, but she couldn't blame him for it: she was doing the same.

Just in case.

"Ready?" he asked.

"Yes, sir," she told him.

He nodded, face impassive, cold and hard, focused on the mission and the mission alone. He walked a few feet, bent over, and, muscles straining, lifted a steel and cement hatch in the ground. Kara approached, looking down into a dark abyss, and when he cracked open a glow stick and tossed it down, a ladder appeared, barely visible.

It was a long way down.

Just like they'd discussed, she waited for him to descend, then followed him, not bothering to close the hatch.

Down they went, down, down, down.

Outside, it began to rain.

15

When Conor's dad died, Conor had been eleven and enraged at the world—and especially at his father for leaving him, first slowly as his health declined from the cancer, and then suddenly when he was just gone. Hank O'Connell had been a hero, just like Conor was going to be one day. And heroes never deserted their families, no matter what.

He'd acted out at school, getting into fights and talking back to teachers. Finally, his mom sat him down, and explained that his father didn't choose to leave, would never have left Conor behind, if he'd had a choice. She'd pulled Conor onto her lap, kissed his hair, and told him that his father would always be with him. Forever. And even though Conor hadn't believed her at first, he pretended he felt his father with him, and after a while, it had started to feel true. And then it *was* true, until that fateful day in Frankfurt, when Hank O'Connell wouldn't have wanted to know his son, not anymore.

His dad had died twenty years ago. Conor had long since forgotten how to pretend. So now, as he sat alone in the bunker, numb to every sensation, while Luke was hell knew where suffering through hell knew what, he couldn't even comfort himself with pretending that Kara and Micah were with him.

And what kind of comfort would that be, anyway? He didn't want to be haunted by Kara's vengeful ghost. Or seek guidance from Micah's. All he wanted was to die, so he could join them. Heaven or hell, he'd beat down the door until he could hold them in his arms again, until he could apologize and tell Kara how fucking much he loved her, had always loved her. How sorry he was. If they were in heaven, he'd crawl across glass to make himself worthy to be near her. And if they were in hell, he'd cover her body with his, protect her from whatever torture might be doled out to her. Take every lash, every burn, just to keep her safe.

God, he hadn't kept her safe. He'd promised her, long ago in that hotel room, that he'd always keep her safe. She'd challenged him recently, pointed out that he was falling down on the job, and he'd gotten angry. She'd been right, because here he was, alive, and there she was, a cold body in a morgue.

He hadn't saved her. Hadn't saved either of them. And so he was ready to be done with all of this.

But that left Luke. Luke, who deserved to live.

Fuck, it was freezing in here.

The door opened, and the professor appeared. Flanked by guards, of course. Even though Conor was restrained, the professor had enough self-preservation to know better than to be alone with him. Conor had expected him to gloat, look triumphant, but there was a sad, thoughtful look in Chris's eyes. They were red-rimmed, like he'd been crying.

Mourning.

Fuck this man. He had no right to mourn Kara's death. He'd killed her.

But hadn't Conor, too?

"I miss her," the professor told him. "I've missed her for years, so I didn't expect this to hurt so bad, but losing her like this…"

Conor refused to listen to this. "You didn't lose her. You *killed* her."

The professor nodded. "I did."

"Why?" It was less of a question and more of wail.

"Because I am a selfish man, Mr. O'Connell. I didn't love her, in the way she wanted to be loved. I wanted to own her, and I refused to let her live a life without me. I would've saved her, killed Mr. Feldman, Mr. James, and you, but she would never let that happen. In the end, she sacrificed herself to save Mr. Feldman, taking the bullet meant for him. Mr. Feldman attacked my guards, losing his legendary cool in his grief and rage, and got himself killed in the process." He examined his tie. "They were here to rescue you, you know," he added. "I guess in the end, she did love you, like she never loved me."

A moan, or a sob, or maybe a severed roar, broke through Conor's chest and teeth. The pain was too much. He understood now why Jewish people tore their clothes when they were mourning. He wanted to rip his clothes, his skin, his heart out of his chest.

"You know," the professor said, "I think I always hated you most. Not because she was with you, first, but because you and I are the most similar. Yes, I have some of Mr. Feldman's scheming in me, and I suppose there have been times where I possessed Mr. James' purity of spirit, but at the end of the day, I am as selfish and intractable as you."

"We're nothing alike." Conor slashed his head to the side in negation.

His enemy raised an eyebrow. "Aren't we? You, too, stopped at nothing to have Kara in your keeping. You'd have killed me in a heartbeat, had you had the chance."

"To keep her safe," Conor growled.

He'd only ever wanted her safe.

The professor shook his head, sympathy in his eyes. "To get rid of the competition. You didn't want your other lovers to have her in the beginning either, did you? Came around to it, because of how close you all are. But if you could have had her to yourself, you would've. If she'd wanted to be with me, would you have let her go?"

"I wouldn't have killed her." Just kept her, forever.

The professor's eyes flashed. "I do not—" he cut himself off. "I did not plan on killing her." He rose to his feet and with a motion to his guards, walked toward the door. "You are like me, Mr. O'Connell, because you would never have set her free."

Anguish burned like a fire in Conor's chest. He wanted to roar and rail that it wasn't true. But wasn't it? If Kara were alive, if she wanted to leave him, leave *them,* for someone else? He'd never have let her go. What if she had another lover? What if she'd jumped in front of the bullet to save another man?

He would've loved her anyway.

He hadn't always wanted her to be happy. He'd only wanted that for himself. But as they'd grown closer over the past month, he'd realized how badly he needed that for her.

And now that she was gone...

"Wait."

The professor turned back.

"Luke," Conor said.

"What about him?"

"I want to make a deal. Let him go," Conor said.

The professor shook his head. "I don't see what benefit that is for me. See, I am also a sadistic man, and I am an angry and vengeful one. Since I cannot hurt your friend Mr. Feldman for his part in Kara's death, I can hurt the two of you for your role in it, forever."

"I'll give you whatever you want," Conor said. "I'll be your little torture puppy, let you and your brothers experiment on me with whatever drugs they're dreaming up, be your personal hitman and kill all your enemies without question. You can do whatever you want to me, take out your sadistic needs or your practical ones. Just let Luke go free, and I'll do any of it. I'll do it all."

There was a strange light in the professor's eyes. One that Conor should've thought more about, questioned. But what did it matter? All that mattered was his grief, and Luke's freedom. Yes, the professor could renege, but it was Conor's only chance. Luke's only chance.

"Mr. James won't like this," the professor pointed out.

Conor shrugged. "Doesn't fucking matter."

"And how do I know, when I let him go, that you'll keep your side of the bargain?"

Conor looked the other man dead in the eye. "Because I always keep my promises."

"Yes," the professor murmured. "I suppose you do."

16

Luke had finally assembled some semblance of a backup plan when the door to his new cell opened. Chris Johnathan stood there, freshly showered, hair damp, his hands tucked in his pockets.

And he was alone.

Luke smelled the trap immediately. He didn't know what type of trap it was, just that it existed. He'd been sure something was off when they'd never chained him up this time, just left in there to think.

"Mr. James."

Luke said nothing.

"Mr. James, I know you're mourning. But I have some good news...you're free to leave."

Luke closed his eyes. Not only because it was clearly a trick, but because he didn't want Chris to know Luke had already figured out the man's other trick. If he looked at Christopher for too long, the truth—that Luke knew Kara and Micah were still alive—would be obvious. He wasn't distraught enough, he didn't seem like he was grieving. Luke didn't just hate lying; he was a terrible actor. And he needed him to think that Luke hadn't noticed the lack of tattoo and was still in the dark, so he would let his guard down around him.

"Aren't you going to ask why?" Chris sounded...curious.

"I'm assuming it's not out of the goodness of your heart."

The slender man chuckled. "No, I won't pretend as much. Mr. O'Connell made me a promise I couldn't pass up. The trade was for your freedom. At first, I thought he'd finally exhibited some selflessness, but then I realized it still came from a selfish place—his inability to watch you suffer more. And, well, torturing you stopped being fun, now that I have the balm of his grief over Kara's and Mr. Feldman's deaths." He swept his hand forward. "So you're free to go."

Luke ran through his plan, again. He'd have to change a few elements of it, like pretend he really was leaving, but this could work in his favor. Even though he was still unsteady on his feet, his left arm was useless, and his left eye was still crusted over, he could handle this on his own.

Struggling to his feet, Luke crossed to Christopher and loomed over the man, who stepped back in fear before recovering.

"Mr. James, I recommend you don't try to harm me," he said softly. "If you do, my guards have orders to kill Mr. O'Connell immediately."

"Isn't that your plan, regardless?"

Chris shook his head, a small smile on his face. "He has more use to me alive."

Well, that was sickening. But he was right, killing him wouldn't help.

Yet.

"It's straight down this hallway. There's a back exit, hidden. Not the one down the ladder we originally took you through. It's usually locked and only a retinal scan will unlock it, but we overrode it for the next fifteen minutes. So, I suggest you get moving. No time for any fond farewells, I'm afraid."

That was fine. Luke wouldn't be needing a farewell. Still, he had to say something.

"Where are you burying Kara and Micah? I want to go see them—their bodies—when I'm free." He coughed multiple times, like he was trying to cover a sob.

There. That should do it.

Christopher sighed. "The Jewish cemetery in Skokie, Illinois. You're welcome to visit their graves whenever you like, and you can arrange the Yartzheit ceremony."

"Why Skokie?"

Christopher sighed, unable to fully hide the smirk on his lips. "Because there's not a Jewish cemetery near the Tetons."

Luke froze for a moment. Kara would want to be buried near the Tetons. What if Luke was wrong? What if they'd removed Micah's tattoo, or he'd looked at the video too quickly, or he'd just seen what he wanted to see? What if they were truly dead? But his heart rebelled at that. They weren't dead. He would know. Besides, Micah would've dyed Kara's hair again; it wouldn't still be black.

They weren't dead.

He would find them once he and Conor were free.

He walked quickly down the hallway. It was empty of guards. Chris really had taken a risk, believing that Luke wouldn't kill him.

There was, however, blood on the ground.

Whose blood? Conor's?

Finally, he reached the end of the hallway. There was the steel enforced door with the retinal scan Chris had told him about. And there were guards, one positioned on either side, rifles at the ready, both wearing face shields, like they knew he was going to try something.

"It's been real guys," Luke said, not even bothering to catch their gazes as he stumbled to the door and pushed it open with his good arm, stepping through toward his freedom.

The guards relaxed, lowering their rifles.

And Luke spun around and grabbed the rifle of the guard on the left with one hand, headbutting him with it. The guard went down, and as the other raised his own rifle, Luke shot him through the chest. The guard was wearing a bulletproof vest—they both were—but it was enough to knock him over so Luke could grab him and snap his neck, then his colleague's. He'd never snapped a neck one-armed, but there was a first time for everything. He grabbed the second rifle and waited, cradling both, expecting the shots to alert the other guards. But after a few minutes, none came.

Uneasy, Luke headed down the hallway to the right, back to the bunker where it all began.

Back to Conor.

Luke was probably free by now.

Conor stared at the grey cement wall, covered in dark stains. Blood stains, obviously. He wasn't the Johnathans' first torture victim, and he doubted he'd be the last. Because at some point, Chris would get bored, decide he'd outlived his usefulness, and kill him. Conor had only just made this deal, but he already couldn't wait for that day. His future stretched before him, full of pain and horror and misery, and he wanted nothing to do with any of it. He thought he'd hear Kara or Micah by now, in his head, chastising him and coaxing him to live, but they were silent.

Because they knew the truth: Even though the remaining moments of his life would be hell, every fucking second would be worth it, now that Luke was free.

Please, fuck, let Luke be free.

The door to his cell opened.

"I didn't realize we were getting started so soon," he remarked. "What's it going to be, more torture? Or do you already have a job lined up for me?"

"Torture and capitalism aren't my kinks," Luke said from the doorway.

Conor's heart thudded to a halt. This, here, was his nightmare. What was the point, of any of it? Of all of this? He and Luke had sacrificed themselves so Kara and Micah could be safe, and they were dead. He'd sacrificed himself *again* so Luke could be free, and the motherfucker hadn't left. Helpless rage filled him. He was going to have to watch Luke die. He'd never be free. He'd been ready to shut himself off, turn into nothing more than a machine, and he could've done it if he were alone. But Luke was determined to be the hero, wasn't he?

"You were supposed to go free. That was the deal I made. Why are you here?"

"Yeah, we're going to be talking about that later." Luke glanced around. "But we don't have time right now. We need to get our asses out of here before they figure out what I did. We've got like, five fucking minutes, and I only have one good arm."

Conor rose to his feet, looking up at the taller man, unsure if he wanted to kiss him or throttle him.

"You were supposed to leave me behind!"

Luke drew close to him, wrapping an arm around Conor's back and pulling him tight, so they were chest to chest.

"I will never, *ever*, leave you behind. You hear me? Never," he said, before capturing Conor's lips in a fierce kiss. "Ever," he said, then kissed him again.

And in the darkness that was Conor's mind, heart, and soul, a light appeared. Faint, but there.

It glowed brighter when Luke pulled back to add, "We need to get the fuck out of here. I brought you boots." He bent, helping Conor lace them up, then looked up, his eyes bright. "Kara and Micah aren't dead. It was a trick to shut us both down, and because Chris is a cruel, evil, shit-for-brains asshole. I didn't say anything because I needed that extra element of surprise against him."

Alive?

Alive.

Only for the flame to flicker out and die.

He so badly wanted to believe it. Everything in him yearned for it. Except Conor had seen their bodies with his own eyes. Had heard the remorse from the professor's lips. He couldn't believe it, he refused to. It would hurt too much when they both woke up and realized it was nothing more than a dream. Or worse, Luke was pulling a Micah and using this to incite Conor into escaping.

Conor shook his head.

Luke's eyes widened. "Really, Conor? You said you'd have faith in me. And yet here you are, not having faith in me. Does nothing ever change with you?"

"We need to get going," Conor said. "Lead the way."

Luke's jaw worked, but he didn't say anything, just handed Conor a rifle and limped back out the door, Conor following close behind. There were surprisingly few guards, but fresh blood on the ground.

"Yours?" he asked Luke.

"I thought it was yours."

What the fuck was going on?

As they continued down the hallway, Luke's frustration emanating off him in waves, Conor said, "It's not that I don't have faith in you. I want to believe you, man. I do. You have no idea how much. But are you positive you haven't convinced yourself they're alive because you can't deal with the alternative?"

"Micah's tattoo wasn't there," Luke pointed out.

"The sheet was covering his arm, it could've been below it," Conor suggested. As much as it hurt to destroy Luke's hope, better now than later.

"And Chris was talking about burying them in a Jewish cemetery. He couldn't do that, with Micah's tattoo. Remember when Micah made the choice, and said to hell with a Jewish cemetery, because he wanted to be buried with the two of us, anyway?"

"The professor may not know about the Jewish cemetery tattoo thing." It was as simple an explanation as any.

Luke was about to respond when they heard the thump of boots on a cement floor. Luke looked at Conor, who nodded. In this, he'd follow Luke's lead.

Backing up against the wall, they waited for the guard to come past them. As he approached, Conor stepped into the hallway and waved. "Hey there."

Jerking in shock, the guard raised his rifle to shoot him, but Luke was already there behind him, snapping his neck and then lowering the now dead man to the floor. Conor grabbed his rifle and as they continued down the hallway, Luke spoke.

"I know hope isn't an easy thing for you, Conor. But I'm begging you, believe me. Have faith in me, in this. And don't go doing anything stupid and heroic. Remember?"

Despite himself, Conor cracked a smile. "Because we're not her heroes."

"Never were."

Luke came to an L in the hallway, paused for a second, then said, "You know what, we're not going through the back door, even if it's unlocked. I don't trust it, so we're going to go out the way we came in."

"Lead the way, boss," Conor said.

He started to follow Luke, then froze, as clapping echoed down the hallway.

The professor sauntered down the hallway, followed by guards—six of them.

Luke groaned. "My dumb, fucking ass," he muttered. To Conor he said, "I'm sorry, I fucking led you straight into a trap."

"Oh, don't be so hard on yourself," the professor said, almost kindly. "It was a well-thought-out plan, faking out my guards, and then deciding to escape another way. Unfortunately, I have cameras everywhere, so all we had to do was follow you. It was easier than sending my guards after you when you didn't go through the door, Mr. James."

Conor moved to block Luke from the professor, his guards, and the six guns that were trained on them. His life would be worth it, if he saved Luke. "We made a deal."

"Yes." The professor tsked. "And it seems you reneged."

Conor stared at him.

"Or," the professor considered, rubbing his chin, "was this all a ploy to get Mr. James here to leave, and then you were going to come running back in to distract us while he escaped, dying in a symphony of useless bullets?" He shook his head. "It seems you both were playing each other. Mr. James here believed you wanted to live, and you started to believe in his lie that Mr. Feldman and Kara are alive."

"Luke doesn't lie," Conor said automatically, then wanted to slap himself.

"Ah, yes, that," the professor said. "It seems you were hiding something from me as well, Mr. James. No matter, although unfortunately, your theory was wrong. We removed Mr. Feldman's tattoo after he died as a courtesy so we *could* bury him in a Jewish cemetery. I wish you had asked—it would save you enormous amounts of pain now."

"You're lying," Luke said, raising his rifle, his eyes an almost incandescent green, lit with hope and rage. "They aren't dead. She's *not* dead."

The professor chuckled. "Oh, they're very, very dead. Micah Feldman is dead. Kara Blum is dead. Now, which of you two heroes is next?"

Conor pushed Luke against the wall, but Luke shoved him out of the way. "You don't get to die," he said fiercely.

"I quite agree," the professor said. "I think I prefer that Mr. James goes first."

The guns were all pointed at Luke now. Conor moved to cover him, but Luke stepped out of the way.

He heard the guns cock.

"Please," Conor begged, weeping. "Please."

I love you, Luke mouthed at him.

It couldn't end like this. Not like this.

Behind them, a woman's throat cleared.

"Just one problem, professor. I'm not dead," said Kara. "But I don't know if you can say the same for long."

---

17

*W*here the fuck was Micah?

As Kara glared at Chris, she worked to keep her face calm and body alert but relaxed. She was surrounded by masked, armed guards, dressed in military fatigues and holding guns. They were at the end of a long, dark corridor that split off into another perpendicular hallway. The whole place was grey and musty; cement dust and dirt everywhere. It reminded Kara of where she'd been held the last time she'd seen Christopher. The guards clustered in a semi-circle around Chris, Luke and Conor across from them, perfectly situated to be target practice.

Chris glared at her from the center, angry, but not worried. Understandable, given his backup, but he wouldn't feel that way for long.

Luke and Conor had both whipped around to look at her. The utter relief on Luke's face quickly turned to terror when he took stock of the situation. And the disbelief and love shining from Conor's eyes, the way his hand shook as he raised it to brush her cheek, almost broke her resolve. All she wanted to do was turn into their arms, check them over to really prove they were alive. They both looked worse for wear: Luke cradling his left arm, dried blood crusted over one eye, cuts and bruises everywhere. Conor, dirt and blood smeared on his left side, didn't look much better. Both were thinner, muscles and bones more pronounced. Had they even been fed? But at least they were there, standing, breathing. Alive.

She was determined to keep it that way.

"Sweetheart, run," Luke ordered.

"Kara..." Conor trailed off, like he'd seen a ghost, and he wanted her to haunt him forever.

Good. She was going to.

"I'm not going to run," Kara said. "I'm done running."

"That's a beautiful sentiment, sweetheart, but we didn't sacrifice ourselves just so you could get yourself killed or taken again. We're blocking the guards, go," Luke said.

"No. I'm not letting either of you die."

Conor growled. "Get the fuck out of here, brave girl. What the hell happened to following orders?"

"And where the hell is Micah?" Luke added.

"The whole point of this was to keep you safe," Conor said.

Kara shook her head, making sure to look into Conor's dark eyes and then Luke's green ones, not letting herself get lost in either. "I'll let you boss me around for the rest of our lives, I'll submit to you whenever you make me, but not this. I won't leave you behind, and I won't ever give you up. I'm not heroic, either, boys. I'm fucking selfish and vindictive and I refuse to lose the men I love, especially to this asshole."

Conor choked. "The men you..."

Before he could finish, the true villain interrupted. "As much as I hate to break up this little lovefest," he sneered, "I feel it behooves me to point out that none of you are going anywhere. It seems you're on a fool's errand, Ms. Blum. A quite entertaining one to watch, but a fool's errand all the same."

Oh, this motherfucker. She couldn't fucking wait to kill him.

"A fool's errand? Do you know that as we stand here, your brothers are currently being held for treason and espionage? Seems that even though you killed Jean Pierre's widow, you didn't get rid of all the evidence. She left a USB in a safety deposit box at Johnathan Bank. Kind of like the irony of that." Kara laughed, shaking her head, shocked at how much she was enjoying this. "Anyway, *on* the USB were files upon files of evidence, including a conversation between you and your brothers about the Frankfurt mission. They're, of course, about to cut a deal with the DOJ that their fancy lawyer arranged for them. Turns out brotherly love only goes so far."

Chris's face turned a very satisfying red, and then grew redder. Kara used his shock to begin unzipping her jumpsuit.

Confusion filled her men's eyes, but she shook her head, stepping away from them so she was between them and Chris and his guards, directly in the center of the melee.

"It's not possible," Chris scoffed. "My brothers and I destroyed all the evidence of the Frankfurt mission after we had the widow killed. There's no trail connecting any of us to it, or evidence that we bribed the military to send Conor, Luke, and Micah there in the first place. You're the same little lying bitch you—"

Kara pulled the gun out from beneath her unzipped jumpsuit and fired a shot. The blast sounded, followed by a scream—Chris's scream.

"Sorry, did you need that knee?" she asked. "Piss me off again, and I'll shoot the other one."

A rifle was shoved in her face. Well, she'd been expecting that.

She inhaled, then exhaled. It was funny; it wasn't long ago that a gun in her face would have spiraled her directly into a panic attack—and probably one of the worse ones. Now, a gun in her face *steadied* her. As if the actual risk of danger convinced her body that a panic attack was not only unnecessary, but unhelpful—and her body listened.

Something worth considering later.

"Don't shoot," Chris groaned from the floor. "Don't kill her, I want to play with her first."

Behind her, Luke and Conor growled, and then she was being dragged to the side and shoved behind their broad backs.

"Damn it, boys," she muttered.

Were they not going to let her have any fun?

"You aren't fucking going to be playing with anything but your detached dick," Conor said.

"He won't have hands to play with anything," Luke added.

"Boys, you're ruining my moment," she complained. She appreciated the care, the protectiveness, but she didn't *need* it. Not right now. She was going to have to convince them of that, though, because they ignored her.

She took a step backward, only to feel a gun press against her back.

Fuck. Fuck, fuck, fuck.

Maybe she could use their protection. Where was Micah when you needed him?

"Ah," Chris said from the ground, as one of his masked guards helped him up to his feet, supporting him. He grimaced, speaking through gritted teeth. "I hope you enjoyed your little show, Ms. Blum. I'll have plenty for all three of you to participate in going forward." To the guard behind her holding the gun at her back, he said, "You. Start the show now."

The gun that was pressed into her back moved around her waist, and down, down, only to press over her pussy and tease over her clit. Fear filled her, and with it, desire. She felt herself growing wet from the pressure—and the heat of the body at her back.

What the hell, was she turned on by this random guard and his gun play?

Oh.

Understanding her response, she relaxed against him.

"I don't mind if you shoot another hole into her," Chris said conversationally. "Just one more place for me to stick my *attached* dick into. And you, gentlemen, will get to watch."

Luke and Conor both roared, Luke in anguish, Conor in desperation.

"Don't you fucking touch her."

"Don't hurt her! It's us you want. We'll give you anything. Please."

"Oh, Chris," Kara said. "You've always been a fucking idiot."

Luke turned his head to look at her, confused, as Kara grabbed the gun out of Micah's hand and lifted it, firing off both guns, one in each hand. Moments later, two of Chris's guards fell with thuds. The rest watched, temporarily shocked that Chris's untrained "whore" had suddenly become a DC Comics character.

"My little badass baby," Micah murmured from behind

her, then he shoved her out of the way and lifted his other gun, shooting the remaining guards.

Luke and Conor, who had finally caught up to the program, grabbed the dead guards' guns.

"I did a good job teaching you how to shoot," Luke said, aiming and taking a shot.

Four, three, two, one. Down the rest of Chris's men went, until he was the last one alive, cowering on the ground.

"You didn't shoot his dick, Supergirl," Conor said.

Kara laughed, elated with the feeling of her own power, the thrill of fulfilled vengeance, and the love that she saw in his eyes. "Got to save something for later. By the way, *professor,*" she added, "You were right, your brothers weren't detained, and there wasn't any evidence—until now." She patted Micah's chest. "We hacked into your security and recorded the whole thing. Pays to be in love with the world's greatest tech geek."

Micah pressed a kiss to her cheek. "I'm so proud of you."

"I'm not," Luke growled. "Both you *and* Conor are getting your asses belted when we get home. Micah, too, for including you in this goddamned rescue mission. What happened to not being a martyr?"

"I'm not a martyr," Kara said, blowing a kiss at him, practically giddy. "I'm a—"

A shot rang out, interrupting her.

"No!" Conor roared, jumping in front of her.

Chris was still on the ground, holding a gun aimed at her. A gun that had gone off.

So then why wasn't she bleeding? Why wasn't she in pain? Why—

Conor fell to his knees, the thud echoing through the long hall.

He'd taken the bullet for her.

"Conor!" she dropped to her knees beside him, barely aware of Luke disarming a cackling Chris, while Micah tried to staunch Conor's blood with his shirt. She attempted to help, but there was just so much of it, welling from his chest.

"Hit an artery," Micah muttered. "Fuck. Fuck!"

Kara stood, fumbling with her jumpsuit's zipper and stripping out of it before kneeling back down on the cement ground and pressing the fabric against the bullet wound.

Beneath them, Conor groaned.

"Don't you dare die on me," she ordered.

"Wouldn't dream of it, baby girl," he said, choking on a laugh. "My brave girl. I love you. You know that, right?"

"Conor," she warned.

"He's bleeding too much," Micah said, and Luke was there, gently pushing her to the side.

"Kara, sweetheart, let me work on him."

She shifted over, lifting Conor's head into her lap and stroking his hair.

"I love you," she told him. "But I'm not kidding, don't fucking die or I will *follow* you wherever you go and beat the shit out of you for leaving me."

He groaned, his words so faint she could barely hear him.

"Worth it."

"What?"

"All of this. Worth it. Just to hear you say you love me. Live for me, good girl," he said on a sigh, his eyes closing.

"Conor?"

No answer.

"He's gone into shock," Luke was saying to Micah. "I think we need to..."

Boots pounded behind them.

"Drop your weapons!" a gruff voice in camo and swat gear commanded.

"Aha," said Christopher. "The cavalry has arrived."

Kara ignored him. Ignored the fact that they were surrounded by Christopher's backup team, that apparently Christopher *had* a backup team, that Luke and Micah were lowering their guns to the ground and raising their hands, that they were doing that because there was a gun pushing against her left ear, that somehow Christopher had gotten the upper hand back. At the moment, she only cared about one thing.

"Conor!" she screamed.

Conor didn't reply.

18

———

s a young SEAL, nervous about his potential death but too cocky to show it, Conor spent a lot of his free time picturing what the afterlife would be like. But of all the ways that Conor had imagined it, it was never like this: opening his eyes to a pale-yellow glow that illuminated the dark shadows lining another concrete cell, this one bigger than the last, the sound of Luke's and Micah's murmurs, soft, feminine snores, the copper scent of blood, and with it, the devastating smell of bee balm. Sharp, intense pain radiated through his chest to the rest of his body. And beside him was Kara, curled up on the cold ground, purple hair covering her face, her hand holding his free one, even in sleep.

Because his other hand was chained to the wall.

So, either he'd been sent to hell, and hell was another version of the professor's bunker with the woman he loved forced to endure eternity beside him... or he wasn't dead.

Based on the pain in his chest, he guessed he wasn't dead.

He cared less about that and more that Kara was alive.

For now.

He tried to swallow and ease the dryness in his throat, but it stuck together like sandpaper.

"What happened?" He managed to croak the words. "Is Kara okay?"

Luke and Micah, both shirtless, hands zip tied behind their backs, covered in filth and grime and what looked like fresh blood, looked over at him.

"Oh, thank fuck, you're awake," Micah said.

Luke didn't speak. His eyes were a dark, angry forest, promising retribution.

"Luke, man..." Conor started.

Luke shook his head. "I don't want to hear it. You're alive, the rest can wait."

There was an unusual awkward silence between them, as Conor struggled with what to say. "What happened? Why is Kara asleep?"

Micah spoke, his voice low. "She's fine. Ish. Had a horrible panic attack while you were in surgery, cried for hours after. She finally passed out, which is a relief." He cleared his throat. "You took the bullet meant for her. The bullet hit you about an inch from your heart, so you were almost—" He broke off. If Conor wasn't wrong, Micah's eyes were wet. But then, it was hard to tell for sure in the dim light of the bare lightbulb overhead. "You almost didn't make it. Fortunately, Christopher has a surgeon on staff, and a penchant for sadism and torture that makes Luke look like a teddy bear. He said that—"

"Fortunately?" Luke interrupted. "You think anything about this situation is fortunate?"

"Of course not," Micah snapped, his calm gone. "But losing our shit over it isn't the answer. We've been in worse situations."

"Yeah, the three of us have. Not with Kara. You were supposed to keep her safe."

Micah gritted his teeth. "I fucking tried, okay? We talked about this already."

Conor wanted to talk about that part, more. But first he needed the rest of the story. "What did the professor say?"

"*Christopher* said that it was a waste, letting you die from a bullet wound. That he had other plans for the four of us, and so 'out of the goodness of his heart' he was going to save your life."

"For now," Luke muttered. "He's going to save your life *for now.*"

Micah shrugged. Or tried to. "It's another day that we're alive. I'll take as many as we can get." Micah returned to his story. "You were under the knife for a while; fortunately, they were able to get the bullet out, give you a blood transfusion, patch you up."

"And don't worry, because he 'won't hurt us until you fully recover,'" Luke added. "He says he's saving it for the 'grand finale.'" Luke snorted, but there was no humor in it. "Real saint, that guy."

Luke's arm was broken; having it twisted behind his back had to be causing him an incredible amount of pain. But did it matter? If they were still trapped there, then they were all going to be in incredible amounts of pain soon.

Even Kara.

Oh, god. Kara.

"I still don't understand," Conor said, trying to piece it together. "He was down. Kara shot him. All his men were down. So how are we here?"

"Seems like there's a whole second underground level to this bunker. Or research facility. Or whatever it is. And there was a second team of Christopher's soldiers. Back up, in case of emergency. *We* were the emergency. I'm sorry," Micah said, shaking his head. "It's my fault. I got distracted by you being shot and didn't move fast enough."

Conor could picture it in his head: him, bleeding on the floor, Kara screaming his name, Luke and Micah too worried to move until it was too late and they were surrounded by a new group of guards and there was a gun shoved in Kara's face. And Chris, laughing hysterically, even in pain, knowing he'd won.

"It wouldn't have mattered," Luke said, sighing, as if he'd heard Conor's thoughts. "They had us surrounded, they had a gun on Kara, and we couldn't have saved her in time without her getting shot."

"Oh, so you aren't pissed at me anymore?" Micah raised an eyebrow.

"Oh, I'm still pissed at you," Luke said. "I'm pissed at both of you. *You,*" he jerked his head toward Conor, "tried to sacrifice your damn ass to save me, even though I begged you not to, even though you promised me you wouldn't. Refused to even believe me when I told you Kara and Micah were alive. And *you,*" he turned his head to glare at Micah, "were supposed to protect her. You were supposed to be *safe.* What the hell was the point of any of this, of us splitting up and sacrificing ourselves, if we were all going to end up here, anyway?"

Conor wasn't the type to make wishes or fantasize. But for a moment, he wished that everything had gone differently, and that all of them were safe.

This was his worst nightmare. This was exactly what he'd been trying to avoid.

But saying that, sharing how hopeless he felt, helped none of them.

"How long have I been out?" he asked.

"Three days," Luke said, glaring again. "For two of them, we weren't even sure you were going to ever wake up."

"Man—" Conor began.

Luke raised his hand. "Still don't want to hear it."

Micah glanced at them, then rolled his eyes. "The two of you were locked up together alone for three days, and you're still bitching at each other. Kara and I worked our shit out, don't tell me you didn't."

"Apparently," Luke muttered. "Since she's here."

"Luke, please," Micah groaned, sounding like he was in pain.

Luke shut his eyes for a moment. "Fine." He answered Micah's earlier question. "No, we settled the pissing contest, finally. That's not why I'm angry. I'm angry because—"

Conor cut him off. There was a frog in his throat. "—because I got lost in my own guilt and decided it wasn't worth it for me to live. And sacrificed myself, so you would. I'm sorry."

Luke jerked, surprised. Conor almost smiled; he hadn't managed to surprise either of them since he'd first met and fell for Kara. But it wasn't funny, was it? Maybe if they'd all managed to escape, it would be.

"What are you sorry for?" Luke asked, so quietly his words could barely be heard over the quiet rhythm of Kara's snores.

Conor carefully moved Kara's hand to his chest, then immediately winced in pain.

"Fuck, that was a mistake."

"Take it easy," Luke ordered, worry in his voice.

Conor ignored that, reaching out his hand to Luke, only to come up short. Conor was still on his back, Luke kneeling near him. He wasn't quite used to this position. Unless they were fucking, he was usually the one in the dominant position, no matter how much taller Luke was.

"What are you sorry for?" Luke repeated.

"I'm sorry for giving up so easily and abandoning you. I'm sorry for not having faith in you like you needed. I promise, I'll be better." Shockingly, as he said the words, the frog began to disappear.

Luke's eyes flashed. "That's all your sorry for?"

Conor tried to nod. "I'm not sorry for making that deal with the professor. I'm not sorry for sacrificing myself to save your life. I'd do it again, over and over. You know me, I'm a selfish bastard, and I refuse to live in a world that doesn't have you in it."

Although that might come true, soon. The only comfort Conor had, no matter how small, was that Conor would likely be killed soon after.

Where and how had he gone so wrong?

Luke interrupted his painful thought. "You think I could live in a world that you weren't in? Or knowing you were out there somewhere, suffering? You fucking dumbass, I swear to god. I'm a selfish bastard, too, you know."

The tightness in Conor's chest loosened. Luke had told him he loved him, back in the cell. But hearing it was like breathing clean air for the first time. This was what it was like, to be so openly loved—and to feel safe enough to love them back.

"I love you," he told Luke, softly, again.

"I know, boss," Luke said. "You said already. I just wish you loved yourself better."

"Well," Micah said, closing his eyes, and Conor's chest went tight again. "Not much time for that."

"There's got to be a way out of here," Luke said.

But Conor knew better. And not because he was going

down some maudlin path. Because they'd lost their chance for escape. How the hell were they going to get out of there, especially if Conor was healing from a bullet wound?

Except.

"Marcus," he said. "I'm assuming that's how you got here?" he asked Micah.

Micah nodded. "Billy, actually. And he has the coordinates. If we don't come back soon, they'll come looking for us."

"So." Hope, dim as the lightbulb above their heads, but still real, began to glow.

Especially as Kara stirred next to him. Conor wished for a bed, a blanket, something to keep her soft and warm. Not this cold, empty cell.

"Sweet girl," he murmured.

She lifted her head. "Conor? Oh, thank fucking god."

Sitting up without complaint, as if she slept in cold locked cells every day, Kara reached out a hand to stroke his face. Her arms, unlike his own, were free. The professor was still underestimating her, apparently. Sort of shocking, given that she'd shot him earlier. But then some men were so convinced of women's uselessness, they'd never understand how powerful they truly were—to their own detriment. The professor's misogyny was something they could potentially use to their advantage—if Conor was willing to let Kara risk her life or her safety any more for them than she already had.

We're the same, you and I, the man whispered in his mind.

Conor did his best to ignore it. Especially when his sweet girl swallowed, and when she leaned in close, he could see her eyes were wet. Kara, who so rarely cried, was crying for him.

"I thought we'd lost you," she told him. "When you took that bullet for me—why the hell would you do that, Conor?"

"Because without you—" he twisted his head to look and Luke and Micah, "—without all of you, my life is completely meaningless."

Luke inhaled through his teeth, before exhaling. "Same here."

"Same here, of course," Micah added, his teeth flashing for a moment.

They all lapsed into silence, contemplating their harsh reality—as cold and unforgiving as the walls of their cell.

Kara broke the silence, her voice fierce with conviction. "In case our attempted rescue didn't prove it—and you don't know half of what I did to get to you—I don't want to live a life without the three of you, either." She cleared her throat, then wiped her eyes. "I hope they have a big bed for us in heaven. Or hell."

"I thought you didn't believe in hell," Luke teased, but it sounded halfhearted.

Micah chuckled. "Fair enough. What's the saying about hell being an eternity spent stuck with your friends?"

Kara raised her hand to silence him. "Hell would be an eternity spent without you."

Conor held his breath, waiting for her to tell them she loved them again. He hadn't imagined that, had he? Dreamed it up while he'd been recovering from his bullet wound? Her silence made him wonder if it hadn't been anything more than a fantasy.

"Although I'd rather the big bed," she added, and the continuation of the bit lightened some of the fear within him.

Fuck this. What did he even have to lose at this point?

"You're supposed to add, 'because I love you,'" he demanded.

She laughed, shaking her head. Stroked his cheek. "How are you barely recovered and still this bossy?"

"Because you saying you love us was the single best moment of my life, and I want to experience it again—this time without guns pointed at us."

She rolled her eyes, trying to smile. "Like I said, so bossy."

"Kara," he warned. He didn't care how injured he was, or that there were cameras. He was going to sit up and smack her little ass until she admitted that she—

"I love you. I never meant for it to happen—I tried so hard to fight it. But you snuck into my heart the same way you snuck into my apartment and made yourself a home there. I couldn't kick you out if I wanted to. And I *don't* want to," she ended, her voice as fierce as the tears in her eyes. "I love you all, so much, and I'm keeping both of you, and that means no more martyrdom or sacrifices. We're done with that. Time to play the villains we've been all along."

Conor wasn't sure what this feeling in his chest was. He'd never felt anything like it before. Ironic that he felt this way, on their own version of death row. And still.

Still.

If he were some fool poet, he'd say it was like his slightly-damaged heart took flight. He wasn't a fool poet, so he'd never say it out loud, but he still felt that way.

"Kara, sweetest girl," he began.

"I love you," she interrupted him. "But I need to hear you say it back."

If Conor could have reared back, he would've. How was it remotely possible she didn't know how he felt?

Had he never told her?

"Kara, I know I'm a complete dumbass, but how could you not know? I think I've loved you since those two nights we had together on Coronado Beach. Fuck, earlier. I *know* I started falling for you when you commandeered the jukebox in that bar." He smiled, remembering. "And I was a complete goner for you when we got to your hotel room and you told me, point blank, that I wasn't pressuring you into fucking me, because 'no one ever makes me do anything I don't want to do.'" He quoted, transported back to that night outside her hotel room door, when he'd tried to be a gentleman for the last time in his life. "I thought it was obsession, I thought it was just this never-ending want. You have consumed almost every waking and sleeping moment, and I *couldn't* sleep without knowing if you were safe. I stole you from your life because my heart is a greedy fucking stupid bastard who refuses to be without you. I felt that way then, and I feel it now. I love you, perfect girl, and I will love you for my entire life—no matter how long it lasts—and after, too."

And yet it's your fault she's here, a small voice whispered in his mind. *Are you sure that's really love?*

The voice sounded like the professor.

"Ditto," Luke said, startling a laugh from Conor.

"Ditto?" Kara whipped her head around. "Really?"

"Romantic," Micah observed. "For what it's worth, also 'ditto.'"

She laughed, more like a hiccup, and turned back to Conor. Her smile turned her wet eyes to liquid gold. Kara, it seemed, didn't care about his similarities to Christopher Johnathan. "I knew you loved me when you threw yourself between me and that bullet," she joked. More seriously: "I just needed to hear the words."

"I'd do it again, a million times." Although the idea of

her ever being shot at again made him want to murder someone. "I'd give you the words a million times, too. But you aren't getting shot at ever again, Kara. I fucking mean it. No more heroic shit. I know you're going to want to do something to get us out of here, but all it will do is get you killed. Please don't do that to us."

Sooner, his mind told him. *Get her killed sooner.*

He shoved that thought away.

"Okay," she said.

"That doesn't sound like a promise."

"No heroic shit," she promised that time. "Just villainess shit from now on."

That didn't sound good.

"Kara," he warned.

"Nope," Luke added. "None of that."

Micah cleared his throat. "I think villainess shit sounds good, personally."

Kara beamed.

"Since when do none of you listen to me?" Conor growled.

"Since you started making bad decisions," Luke muttered.

Kara rolled her eyes, tossing her matted hair. "When have I ever listened to you?"

"Sweetheart, I will smack your ass if you do something stupid," Luke said again.

"I think she's smarter than the rest of us," Micah countered. "Even me, as much as it pains me to admit that."

For a moment, it was like everything was okay. Like they weren't locked in a small cell, facing torture and pain and their imminent demise, and probably worse. It was like they were back at the cabin on one of the better days, teasing each other in the kitchen as Micah cooked. Or, better yet, like a perfect day in the future—one that they could have, if he wished hard enough.

But wishes were for people who weren't Conor. The brief spell was shattered when the cell door slid open with a groan, revealing the professor.

19

Christopher looked the worse for wear.

Surrounded by guards, two on each side, the man's face was unnaturally pale, cheeks pulled back in a pained grimace. He leaned on a titanium cane, and the usual unhinged malice in his eyes had grown to unholy, rageful glee.

Luke took at least some satisfaction in that, knowing he was in pain—and that it was Kara who caused it.

Before Christopher appeared, Luke had been rolling Conor and Kara's conversation around in his mind. He was still pissed at the other man for his betrayal and attempt at sacrifice, but wasn't Conor right? If it had come down to it, Luke would have done the same.

"And how is my favorite doomed foursome doing?" Christopher asked, his voice amicable and easy, like they were friends meeting up for a lunch. And not like he was planning their deaths—or worse.

"Great," Kara quipped. "Although once again, our room is seriously lacking in amenities. Really, Chris, what's the point of being related to billionaires if you can't treat your guests appropriately?"

Luke desperately wanted to tell her how proud he was of her. How far she'd come from the anxious woman panicking on a climbing wall. How much he loved her.

There'd be more time for that. He hoped. She deserved more than a "ditto."

Christopher laughed. "It's nice to see your spirits so high. Will make it so much more fun when I break them."

"You can try," Kara countered, and Luke went rigid. There was being brave, and then there was provoking the man when he held their lives in his hands.

"We're the ones you want to break, though, aren't we, Christopher?" Luke said quietly. "You want to destroy our minds, our bodies, our spirits—get revenge on how we almost escaped. How we took her from you."

Kara whipped her head around to glare at him.

Micah jumped in. "And you haven't even had a chance to torture me. Wouldn't you like to hear how I scream, Chris? How I rage? What would it feel like, to defeat the man who's mentally bested you multiple times? I bet it would feel," Micah paused, licking his lips, "delicious."

"What are you doing, man?" Luke asked under his breath. The mind games were freaking him out, even though they weren't directed at him.

Micah ignored him.

"Ah, Mr. Feldman. Each time we speak, I can't help but admire your...skills," Christopher said.

Christopher and Micah had only spoken once, briefly, while Conor was in surgery.

So you'll keep him alive?

For now.

Luke shivered.

Christopher straightened his tie, briefly forgetting he needed his left hand for the cane. He stumbled but caught himself before he could fall.

Topple, motherfucker.

Brushing invisible lint off his button down, he continued. "And thank you for the offer, but no, I don't think I'll partake. I have more fun games for the four of you planned. As I said earlier, I'll give Mr. O'Connell some time to recover, and let you all spend some quality time together, before we reach the very exciting conclusion to our journey."

"Hmm," was all Micah said.

"Really?" Kara repeated. "Some big threat?"

Christopher's cheeks reddened. It was Kara who had an impact on him, Kara who could rile him up and make him lose his disturbing cool.

"Remember what I threatened last time? Well, I have more guards, and these ones are much more interested in your...parts and much more annoyed by your...whole. Or should I say they're much more interested in your holes than your whole?" He chuckled, sounding like the clever, likeable professor he pretended to be. Luke, of course, knew better. They all did.

Luke felt himself growl at Christopher's words; heard the growls coming from Micah and Conor. And when he glanced at Kara, he noticed she'd gone pale, her hand gripping Conor's free one.

It won't happen, he promised himself. *We won't let it.*

But how could they stop it if they were dead?

Micah was calm. Angry, but calm. Well, more like furious. But still: calm.

At least on the outside.

They had an ace in the hole. Marcus had promised him that if they didn't contact him for a pickup in twenty-four hours, he'd send his best people there to rescue them. Now, Micah was going to owe his half-brother more favors than he ever had before, and he wasn't particularly looking forward to paying up, but he'd rather deal with that than the alternative. If he was paying back favors, it meant he was still alive.

"Now, to me, you're used, damaged goods," Christopher was still musing. "My guards, however, don't care how soiled you've become. I have yet to make up my mind; they're just happy to find a warm, unwilling hole to destroy."

After checking in on Kara's breathing—normal, even— Micah returned to his plotting. All he needed to do was fuck with Christopher's mind enough to keep his attention on Micah and off Conor, Luke, and especially Kara. That shouldn't be too hard; even though the professor was clearly a megalomaniac, he wasn't a mastermind. All his power came from his family's wealth and his own arrogance— which would be his downfall in the end. Conor and Luke weren't the only ones who could make sacrifices.

And meanwhile, Kara's brilliant mind would get to work figuring out her "villainess shit." Micah was so proud of her. Luke and Conor were slower to recognize her power and accept that she, too, had a role to play in all of this. They were a little more...behind the times than Micah and had a harder time trusting that Kara could handle herself. Yes, she wasn't trained like they were, yes, she didn't have their physical strength or endurance, but she was cunning and flexible and quick and courageous. She was even learning to handle the panic attacks better. It wasn't that he'd let her risk herself unsupervised, but she'd made it clear to him multiple times on their journey to rescue Conor and Luke: if he—they—wanted her to be with them, they had to accept her as a full-fledged member of the team. Had to trust her.

Proving him right, Kara straightened her shoulders. "Interesting that you worked so hard to have me, only to pass me off like...oh what did you call me? 'Used goods.' I'm just not sure I believe it, Chris. It seems much more likely that you're still a little boy who's afraid of rejection. Hmm?"

"Kara," Conor said sharply.

Micah grinned to himself. His little badass.

"Afraid of rejection, huh?" the professor spat. "Do it."

Micah saw the punch coming, and ducked his head, bracing. There wasn't much he could do to fight; all he could do was endure. So he endured: the kicks, the other, more successful punches, even the later ones that included brass knuckles. The pain. The screams and roars from his family. He could withstand pain; it was harder to withstand their suffering. He just wished they understood what he did: the professor had said earlier he wanted to torture Micah mentally, not physically. Yet here he was, beating the shit out of him. Or, rather, ordering others to beat the shit out of him; the professor likely had no idea how to throw a punch.

Micah had found the crack in his shield, and all he had to do was tap on it, more and more, until it spread, and the whole thing shattered.

Kara would help with that, too. He was sure of it.

They only needed to endure until Marcus arrived.

Finally, the beating stopped. Micah's ears were ringing, but he could still hear clearly enough to understand the professor's parting words: "Oh, and if you thought your usual savior was coming for you, I have some unfortunate news. We shot down the airplane that dropped you here—and the pilot, Mr. William Lenox, is dead. Marcus is devastated from what I've heard—and angry. At you, dear Mr. Feldman. Your rescue won't be coming. Not this time. Sweet dreams."

As he turned to go, Kara spoke, with so much rage in her voice, it echoed through the small room. "Be careful, Mr. Johnathan, of a woman in love. She can move mountains if she has to. And you're no mountain."

A long silence followed her warning. Finally, without a word, Christopher left the cell.

"Micah?" Kara was at his side, lightly checking him over. "Did they break anything? I don't know what to do for you."

"He's lying," Luke said. To Kara: "Rip off part of your shirt and rinse it in the water they left for us earlier. It's the best we can do to keep his cuts from getting infected."

"He could be lying," Conor agreed. "But there's no way of knowing. And him knowing that it was Billy flying the plane? When Marcus has other pilots on staff?"

"It could be a lucky guess," Luke countered.

"Look, Boy Scout, I don't want to doubt you again. You were right last time, thank god. But I also don't want us to get our hopes up that we're going to be rescued, or plan around it. Okay?"

Micah listened distantly to their debate, but deep down, he ached—and not only from the beating he'd taken. He and Marcus might not ever display affection for each other. In fact, they usually expressed disdain in public. But his half-brother, stick-up-the-ass that he was, mattered to him.

And he knew how much Billy mattered to Marcus. Micah couldn't—and didn't want to—imagine how painful losing either Conor or Luke would be, and so he believed that, if Billy was dead, Marcus wasn't coming for them.

"Time for Plan B," he said under his breath.

Kara, who was still fussing over him, looked at him. "What was Plan A?"

He tried to smile, but it hurt too badly. "It doesn't matter now."

"Okay then, what's Plan B?"

"Do you trust me, baby?"

Her worried eyes were clear. "You know I do."

He thought about obfuscating to give her hope. Lying, to protect her. But she wanted more—deserved better.

Even if the truth hurt.

"I don't know," he said. "I can't think of anything. Not yet, anyway. But we'll think of something, together."

Conor must have caught the end of what he'd said to Kara because he nodded. "Together."

Luke was silent.

"Luke," Micah coaxed.

"I don't want any of you to die. But if you're going to, I'm glad that I'm here with you, that I can be with you until the end," he finally said.

The end. Micah closed his eyes. And prayed to the god he no longer believed in. That this wasn't their end, but a part of their rocky beginning.

20

Time took on a surreal quality for Kara after that. For all of them.

Once a day—if she could even keep track of the days anymore—the door to their cell opened, a guard slid in a tray with water and a small ration of food, changed the bandage on Conor's chest, guns pointed at Kara's head so no one tried anything, and then dragged Kara out.

The first time, she'd been taken by surprise, one moment holding Conor's hand, the next his head thudding to the cement floor as she was being lifted by her elbows and marched out the door.

Behind her, Conor, Luke, and Micah lost their minds. She turned her head, only to see Micah straining so hard against his zip ties, it looked like he was about to sprain or break his wrist. Luke and Conor were no better, fighting so hard against their restraints their wrists bled.

As she was marched down the hallway, she heard them yelling her name, as if their fury had turned them into one furious man.

"Where are you taking me? Are you taking me to Chris?" she asked the closest guard.

He didn't answer, leaving her alone to dwell in her thoughts and her fear. She didn't want to get raped. She was terrified of him putting his hands on her body, touching her. She'd promised herself no one would ever touch her again without her permission, and she was determined to keep that promise to herself.

But when she was pushed into the bathroom and told to use the bathroom and shower, she wasn't sure if she should be relieved or even more afraid. The men watched her, and their eyes on her burned her bare skin, but none of them spoke. None of them touched her.

Once she was clean and dry, they gave her sweats and marched her back to the cell, where they threw her to the ground and left.

"Kara, oh thank fuck, sweetheart."

"Baby, what did they do to you? What happened?" Micah asked urgently.

She shook her head. "Just stared at me while I showered. I didn't even see Chris."

Luke watched her, his eyes gentle on her face. "Kara, sweetheart, you don't need to lie to protect us. You don't—"

She cut him off. "Luke, I'm not lying. They didn't touch me. I think he's trying to break us down with fear and not knowing what's coming next. We can't let him."

Conor shut his eyes. "I don't want you hurt. How do we keep you from being hurt?"

"Conor, I don't want *you* hurt, either," she said. "We don't have a choice. We just need to survive, okay?"

She circled the cell, kneeling down and kissing each of her men, stroking their faces, aware that the fact that they couldn't hold her in their arms pushed them even closer to breaking.

Micah pushed his forehead against hers. "We will," he murmured.

Luke took her mouth with his, kissing her passionately, desperately, so desperately that she got lost in him for a moment and forgot where they were. "Sweetheart, I—"

"I know," she murmured. "I know."

Finally, she reached Conor, who drew her down with one arm, and she lay on the side of his chest that wasn't damaged. He was healing.

"We just need to survive," she said again.

She repeated those five words to herself every day, almost hummed them to herself when she stood under the cold water and closed her eyes, and imagined a time away from this, a time when they were happy—and Christopher Johnathan was buried six feet under.

They just needed to survive.

On the tenth day, Kara came back from the shower, her eyes full of fear.

Conor sat up immediately. The wound was healing—incredibly quickly, in fact—and besides, he didn't give a shit about his wound, he cared about the look in Kara's eyes.

"Kara," he said urgently. "Talk to me."

"No one touched me," she said immediately, and Conor believed her. "But they were talking, about how it wasn't much longer until I have to watch the three of you die." She looked at Micah. "If you have a plan, now's the time."

If Micah had a plan, he would've shared it by now. Conor searched for hope, but he found none.

Micah sighed. "Not yet. I need Christopher here to fuck with his head; his avoiding us doesn't help me. There's no escaping here without us all getting shot, but if we wait, we're still all getting shot. And for all I know, they're listening to us now, so any planning is useless. All I can ask for is patience, because the right moment will come—and then we all need to move, together." He stared at the camera when he said the last, a clear dare to whomever was watching.

"Like we used to," Luke said.

"Like we used to," Micah agreed. "Except now we have a secret weapon."

A sliver of a smile appeared on Kara's face. "I like being the secret weapon," she joked.

Conor didn't. Conor didn't want her to *have* to be the weapon, he wanted her protected in bubble wrap but also free to do whatever she wanted. To fly away, if need be.

What had they done to her? What had *he* done to her?

Kara carried out her new ritual: circling the room to kiss all of them, before choosing one of them to lie down with. She alternated, but today was Conor's, and since he was a greedy bastard, he wasn't going to complain.

She sat down and he drew her into him with his free hand, his nose in her wet hair. She no longer smelled like bee balm, and he missed the smell.

"Conor," she murmured, "will you do me a favor?"

"Anything, perfect girl," he said.

"Will you sing to me?"

Conor cleared his throat. It had been years since he'd sung anything.

"I'm shocked you even remember," he said.

"I remember everything about those nights," she said. "Leonard Cohen, remember?"

He remembered. That second night together in the hotel on the beach. He began to hum the words to "Hallelujah," the song he'd wanted to play for her, so long along ago. It felt like another life; it felt like yesterday.

I like your artsy soul. What do you play?

Guitar.

Dreams of being Led Zeppelin?

Leonard Cohen.

I think that's the sexiest thing I've ever heard.

Maybe I'll play it for you some time.

For a moment, he got lost in the lyrics. When he looked up, all three of his lovers were watching him: Luke, bemused; Micah, pensive; Kara, tender.

"I never thought I'd get a chance to hear you sing," she said, her voice quiet.

He paused his humming. "I never thought I'd get a chance to sing for you. Would be nice to have a guitar."

"Right," Luke said from across the room. "To really sell the whole emo college freshman looking to score thing."

"Hush," Kara said. "You all don't have to be macho assholes all the time. Let's have this, okay?"

Luke immediately softened, and Conor didn't blame him. "Okay, sweetheart." To Conor, he said, "I haven't heard you sing since the early days we served together. You still sound good."

Kara hummed in acknowledgment. "You don't sound like Leonard Cohen, by the way. Or Led Zeppelin, for that matter."

He laughed, even though part of him wanted to cry. It was an unfamiliar feeling, the way he had to clench his abs and squeeze his eyes to keep the tears away. He'd never cried, not until Luke had been tortured by the professor's men and Conor was forced to come to terms with his culpability in Luke's pain, in Kara's, even Micah's, for that matter.

We're the same, you and I.

He'd give anything to stop hearing the professor's voice in his head.

He cleared his throat. "So who do I sound like?"

She wrinkled her nose, thinking. "I think Damien Rice? But that's not right, either. You sound like you, and I love it."

"I love you," he told her, the words feeling suddenly, incomprehensibly urgent.

She kissed him, gently, her hand falling over his heart. Unable to help himself, Conor pulled Kara into his lap, kissing her, soft, hard, everything in between, trying to capture this moment between them because even though Conor O'Connell didn't get scared, didn't believe in fear, he was fucking terrified that soon the moment would be gone, and so would she.

"I love you, too. All of you," she said. "So much."

Conor desperately wanted their story to go differently. It had started back at that bar on Coronado Beach, with a redhead in a short black dress, a faraway look in her eyes, and sand in her shoes, who wasn't trying to find herself, but a place she could call home. The part of him unwilling to let go of hope, that didn't take no for an answer, insisted that it ended with them together. But even if they escaped, did he still deserve her? He could hear her in Marcus's airplane bathroom after they'd rescued her from the black ops site, reminding him that he'd stolen her from her life.

And what kind of life could they give her, anyway? So far, all they'd given her was blood and darkness.

As if she'd heard his train of thought, she rested her

hand on his cheek. "Who do you think you would be now, if you hadn't met me?"

He considered. "Do you mean if we hadn't met, or do you mean if the professor hadn't found out we'd met, and decided to set me up and ruin my life?"

She winced, but put on a brave face, and he wanted to kick himself for hurting her. "Both, I guess," she said.

Luke and Micah were quiet. Just listening.

"Sweet girl," he said. "Let me be clear. *You* didn't ruin my life. He did. You gave me a life, more of a purpose than I ever had in the military. I don't know who I'd be without you, and I don't care. I don't want to know that man, because that man would be sad and empty and unsure why."

Her eyes filled, and she kissed him—this woman who rarely cried, was crying for him.

He kissed her back, trying to comfort her with his lips, and then he pulled back, needing to ask, and already hating the answer.

"Who do you think you'd have been, if you had never met me? Met us?"

She was quiet for a moment, thinking.

"I like to believe I would've stopped feeling so lost, at some point, but I don't really believe that. I think I would have finally gotten that dog I wanted, but I don't think I would've stayed in one place at first. I think I would've bought a little van and tried to make it pretty and stayed on the road for as long as I could, and I guess, after a while, the pressure of society would've gotten to me and I would've settled down in a job, in a house, with a partner and some kids, just like everyone else. I think I would've felt safe, and I think I would've felt normal, for once." She shook her head, and laughed. "I think I was on my way there, to that reality, before you and Micah abducted me. Already had that sad, empty feeling. All I was missing was the boring, stable husband, and the dog."

Her eyes were focused on the wall behind him. Her voice sounded dreamy, almost wistful. Would she never get the life she wanted? No matter what it was?

The thought shook him to his core.

Conor, the old Conor, wouldn't have cared, because the old Conor didn't give a fuck about what Kara needed, only what he wanted. Wasn't that the whole point after all, that he'd been through hell and deserved one good thing, even if he had to steal it and lock it up to keep it by his side? But trying to be that old Conor was like trying to play an out of tune guitar. If he loved her, really, then what she needed mattered.

I think I was on my way to that reality...

It didn't matter now, not when she might not get a life outside of this.

He worked to settle his face, kissing her again.

"Well, thank fuck you didn't end up with anyone boring or stable," he joked, and she laughed and kissed him.

"Thank fuck for that."

She looked at him, then, but he couldn't read the thoughts in her golden eyes.

"I don't want to be that person," she said. "Not anymore."

It should have reassured him. He wanted it to reassure him. But knowing she might never get the chance to find out shook him.

We're the same, you and I, the professor whispered in his head.

Not if Conor could help it.

"Kara, are you sure?"

Her eyes cleared, and she laughed in shock. "Conor, what about me—the woman you know, the woman you love

—makes you think I want that life anymore? That I ever did? I don't want to settle for a quiet life in the suburbs with kids and a dog and a nine to five. Well, that's not true. I want the dog. And maybe kids. Someday. If, you know, we make it out of here alive."

Micah chuckled.

"I want kids," Conor said automatically. "If we make it."

Doubtful.

She raised an eyebrow. They'd grown out a bit, in the past two months since they'd first kidnapped her—a little shaggy and thicker than usual, but he liked them, how natural she seemed, how comfortable.

"That explains the breeding kink," she said, making Luke snort.

"He has a breeding kink with me too, sometimes. He thinks it's hot."

Conor nodded. "I like filling you all up with my come."

His three lovers laughed again. He didn't.

"Okay brave girl, then if you don't want a quiet, regular, easy life, if we get out of here, what do you want?"

"You," she said. "All three of you."

And once again, Conor wanted to believe her.

And once again, he couldn't.

Kara wasn't sure what exactly they were asking her, or why. She wanted them, wasn't it obvious? She could've escaped them, a dozen times. Left them behind, so many times. But she'd stayed and sacrificed so much to keep them safe. To try, anyway. How could they think she wanted anything else?

"But more than that," Micah was pressing on. "What do you want our lives to look like, together? If we could live any life—if you could live any life—*now*. What would you want it to be?"

"Oh, that's easy." She snuggled against Conor, who absently played with her wet hair.

"Yeah?" Luke asked.

"I want to be like you three."

Around her, she felt a stillness, a quietness. She couldn't make sense of it at the moment, nor did she want to.

"What do you mean by that?"

"You know." She sighed, the fantasy clear in her mind—one of vengeance and strength. One of blood. "I want to hurt people who hurt me. Who want to hurt other people, people who don't deserve it. I want to let myself be angry, be violent. Let out my rage. I don't want anyone to think they can beat me. I want to be an hitwoman—just like you."

That stillness went heavy.

It lasted for a while.

Finally, Luke broke it. "Well, you're going to need a lot more training before we get to that point."

He wasn't wrong. Although she didn't think she'd done too badly for herself. If only she could figure out a way to get them out of there. Oh, she had an idea—one Luke and Conor would hate, and Micah wouldn't like much, either—but she wasn't even sure it would work. Not yet, anyway.

"Luke, what do you want, when we get out of here?" she asked.

When, not if. She was tired of hopelessness.

"I like our lives," he admitted. "I didn't use to. I thought it was something we were stuck with, because we couldn't be heroes anymore—because we discovered we'd never been heroes in the first place. But that life doesn't hold much sway for me anymore. You were right—I don't need to be anyone's hero. I need to be your villain, as long as it means keeping you safe."

His words stabbed her in her chest, ever so sweetly.

"Luke," she began.

Luke shook his head. "You know, I used to have to be a good man. Even as I went down this path, I tried to convince myself I was still good. Like the label even mattered. But the thing I realized, when I was being tortured? I don't need to be a good man, anymore. Or anyone's hero. Because if I were one, I wouldn't have you."

Conor pushed her gently to stand. On wobbly legs, overcome by Luke's words, Kara went to him, kneeling by his side.

"I love you," she said. "And I don't want a good man. Or a bad one. I want you. I want to rock climb with you and hike with you and go to a shooting range with you and fuck you and be fucked by you, to be a brat and take my punishments, to let you finally make me go running after threatening me with it back in Denver." She took a breath. "If we get out of here—"

"When," he interrupted, echoing her word earlier.

"When we get out of here, it doesn't really matter what we do, as long as we're together."

"Oh, sweetheart," he said, his voice hushed with awe, "I love you with words that don't even exist."

She kissed him then, and he kissed her back, soft as rain drops, full of promise, and regret, because "when" was just a fantasy. They shared breath, between them, and love, and all Kara wanted to do was to curl up beside him and close her eyes and be somewhere, anywhere, else.

But she was a big girl, and she had to face facts.

"This will have to be enough," she said out loud.

"It will never be enough," Luke said fiercely.

"Eternity wouldn't be enough," Micah said. Kara turned to the last member of the group. Micah was the most open, in some ways, but also kept so much to himself. She understood him better, after the time they'd spent together trying to rescue the others. She trusted him. She got how tightly he wove his reality so nothing could disturb it. How manipulation was a survival mechanism.

But maybe he didn't need it anymore. Not with the four of them, anyway. "Micah," she said.

"Yeah, baby," he cleared his throat, and she left Luke to go stand, staring down into his blue eyes.

"What do you want our lives to look like?"

Micah considered. "I want to see you grow into the person you were meant to be. I want you to realize that even though the panic attacks will never fully go away, you know how to cope with them."

Kara's heart squeezed. He'd done so much for her, hadn't he? All of them had. "With your help," she said.

"In the beginning," he agreed, shifting around, probably to release some tension from his shoulders. She went around his back and started rubbing them. It was hard to give someone a massage when their hands were zip tied behind their back, but she could provide comfort, at the very least.

"And then?" she prompted.

"And then you learn how to do it on your own." He cleared his throat before continuing.

"I want Conor to realize he doesn't have to control everything, all the time. That it's okay to let someone else lead, every so often. And Luke—well, I think you're already getting there, baby. Realizing that the man you are is enough. Realizing that we aren't going anywhere."

Kara nodded. Luke was always so afraid of being left behind, but he hadn't seemed that way in a while. Probably in part because they were all locked up together, but mostly because they'd given him proof he could trust in their staying power. Even hers. "You're stuck with us to the bitter end, baby," she teased.

The joke fell flat, and they all grew quiet again.

Because it might be bitter.

Shaking her head as if to dislodge water, Kara continued. "And Micah, what do you need to realize?"

He smiled, a sad flash of teeth. "That I don't need to manipulate the people I love to make sure I get what I need," he said.

She kissed him in reward. He took over the kiss quickly. Even with his hands tied behind his back, even bruised, he commanded her lips with his teeth and tongue, taking and giving, giving and taking, until she was dizzy and out of breath and her thighs were clenching. She wanted him, but more than that—

"I love you," she said.

"I know, baby," he said, warmth in his tone. "And, ditto."

Laughter rang out in the cell, and a short-lived relief with it.

They all lapsed back into silence.

"I want that life," she finally said, meaning it. "Murder and mayhem, fire and blood, and all three of you by my side. Help me figure out how we get back there."

"Invincible girl," Conor began.

She cut him off. "And if we can't figure out how, then at least we died together, trying. At least we have these moments together, okay?"

Conor didn't speak, and the silence felt heavy. She didn't know what was going on in his head, but it worried her.

"Why don't I tell you what our life will look like soon?" Micah said, his deep voice casting a spell around them, protecting them from what lay outside. "Let me give you a day of it."

He cleared his throat, and then on a soft croon, began.

21

———

"We're back at the cabin. It's winter, and the snow is thick on the ground, weighing down the evergreens and topping the mountain peaks, so everything is white and shimmering with promise. Kara, you've made the not entirely wise, entirely impulsive decision to make sufganiyot for Hanukkah, and I'm supervising to make sure you don't burn yourself—or the house down."

Kara giggled, despite her sadness. "You'd never let me near hot oil."

Micah hummed. "Oh, you made it worth my while. Wandered into the kitchen barefoot, in my hoodie and nothing else, got up on your tiptoes and leaned into my back and whispered the request in my ear. And when I said absolutely not..."

He trailed off, and Kara filled in for him, picturing it— the warmth of the concrete and copper kitchen, the stillness of the snow outside. "...I dropped to my knees, pulled down your sweatpants, and sucked you and teased you until you would've promised me anything for the privilege of coming down my throat."

"Yeah," Micah said, voice husky. "That. So I teach you how to make the jelly donuts, patiently working you through the steps: how to combine the warm water and yeast so it rises, adding the eggs, oil, and sugar, the flour. Wrapping my hands around yours and showing you how to whisk properly. Forming the dough, cutting it into squares. My body behind yours, holding you close, because any excuse to have you in my arms is a good one, even if I know these are going to taste like shit."

This time, Luke chuckled. "Even with you supervising?"

She could hear the smile in Micah's voice when he said, "Even with me supervising. Because I help her make the first batch, teach her, but trust her to make the second on her own."

"Just not to burn the house down," Conor interjected, his voice a mix of pain and longing.

"Or burn that soft skin," Micah added. "I'd rather touch it, stroke it, than risk it getting harmed."

Kara inhaled sharply, not only at the sexy spell he wove around them, but at the deeper implication—the promise, the wish there. The juxtaposition between the dream he was forming for them, and the nightmare they were currently in.

"When the oil is heated and we start dropping the donuts in, Conor, you and Luke enter the house after chopping down a tree for firewood. And, of course, you leave tracks of snow all over the hardwoods because neither of you are capable of remembering to take your boots off when you come in."

"Well," Luke said, voice gruff, "We don't want to miss the show."

"You both gather around the stove, Luke teasing Kara

about her adventures in cooking and promising to eat the sufganiyot..."

"Despite how bad they're going to be," Luke interjected, his voice amused. "With a second promise that I'll punish you both later for it. Maybe with some Hanukkah candle wax play."

"Mm," Micah said, quiet for a moment, like he was also lost in the fantasy he was weaving for them.

"And what about me?" Conor asked, and although the words were light, his voice was not.

"Oh, you're still bitching that I wasn't precise enough with my chopping, but your cheeks are flushed and your cock is hard, because when you called me on it, I took it out on your ass without letting you get off," Luke murmured, a filthy, tender promise in his voice.

"You mean you didn't take it out on my ass because you were still angry at me? Or will you have gotten over it by then?" Conor asked.

Both men were quiet for a beat as they looked at each other.

Luke sighed. "I understood why you sacrificed yourself to save me, because I would have done the same for you."

Kara closed her eyes, letting their words wash over her. The peace behind them. The forgiveness. The cell disappeared, and so did her desperation, her regret.

"Right," Micah prompted. "The donuts are browning in the oil, and the whole kitchen begins to smell like fried dough and sugar. As they fry, my phone buzzes. It's another request for a hit, this one in Europe. A Christmas party, which just happens to be our anniversary, baby," he said, turning to look at her. Her hands were still on his shoulders, rubbing absently.

"Yeah," she said. "It is. Although our real anniversary is May third."

"May?" Luke asked.

"When you kidnapped me, and I woke in the cabin," she said, holding her breath, waiting for their response.

Someone sucked in a breath. Conor.

Luke's teeth flashed in a quick smile. "Yeah, I guess that's our real anniversary."

Micah, head still turned, dropped a kiss on her shoulder in reward. Kara bathed in the sensation, committing it to memory. Just in case.

And then Micah continued. "We discuss the details, the pay, decide we're going to do it..."

"Figure out who's staying back with Kara," Conor said, his tone intractable.

Kara broke in. She was determined to make this part clear. To him, to all of them. "No, no one's staying back with Kara. I'm a part of the mission. I'm the honeypot, remember? The one who keeps meetings from exploding into murder—until it's called for."

"Kara," Conor warned.

"No," she said, making sure it was *her* voice that sounded intractable. "In fact, it's my mission. I take lead with the planning."

"Our little badass queen," Micah murmured, and Kara was glad that at least he was on her side with this. That he trusted her the way she'd asked him to back at Vixen, right before they'd killed Victor.

Luke was silent.

"Luke?" she asked.

"If that's what you really want, sweetheart, then I meant what I said earlier. We'll make sure we teach you how. Just like we taught you how to shoot a gun."

Conor growled but didn't say anything.

Well, she couldn't win every battle. Not immediately, anyway.

"And then what happens?" she asked Micah.

"The donuts are done. Some of them are a little...burnt, but I was prepared for that. I get the squeeze jar of jam out of the fridge."

Kara laughed. In some ways he'd changed, in others he remained who he was. In the ways that mattered. "Because you knew I was going to ask to make them?"

"Of course I knew," he hummed. "I'm your mastermind, remember? Anyway," he continued. "We pierce little holes in the fluffy, cooked dough, and then we squeeze jam inside. Filling them up to the brim, and more...so that some juicy sweetness spills out."

"Fuck," Luke said. "I can't tell if I'm hungry, or horny."

"Both," Conor suggested, and all four of them laughed, together.

"We turn off the stove. I don't let you touch anything to clean, because I might let you cook in my kitchen, but I know it won't ever be as hygienic as it needs to be."

"Which is hypocritical," Kara says, remembering back to other times in the kitchen. "Because we've fucked in there."

"And we fuck in there now. Conor feeds you sufganiyot, then his cock, so the sugar and his precome mix together, and then his come washes it all down."

"*Fuck*," Conor said, and Kara was relieved that he'd briefly let go of what she'd declared, lost in the story with the rest of them.

"And Kara, I'm deep in your pussy, which is wet and warm and welcoming for me, because it knows it's my home, that you're my home. And pierced, by the way, because we pierced you as a way to prove our commitment to each other." He cleared his throat. "And Luke, you're deep inside Conor's ass, reveling in Conor's brief submission to you while he masters our sweet baby girl."

"Fuuuuuck," Conor said again. "If I didn't think there were cameras in here..."

"I know, baby," Micah murmured.

Kara felt the same way, but she'd been naked enough, vulnerable enough to Christopher and his men. She wouldn't share their intimacy, their love, with him.

"We fuck each other, in our kitchen, in our home, safe, and in love, and happy, don't we?" Kara said, eyeing the corner of the ceiling where she thought a camera might be. "Even though we argue, even though we squabble for power sometimes, even though you all treat me like your little fucktoy, we fight together and we fuck together and we love together, and nothing will take that away from us."

"Nothing," Micah said.

"Oh, sweetheart," Luke murmured.

"My good girl," Conor added.

And Kara, *oh god*. She wanted that future so badly for them, she wanted to be back at the cabin, she wanted to be anywhere with them, as long as it wasn't here, as long as they were together. She wasn't sure if she wanted to thank Micah for what he was giving them, however briefly, or rail at him, because it almost hurt more, seeing it, when it might get taken away.

"Don't lose hope, baby," he whispered to her, as if he didn't want the other two to hear and argue with him. "Don't let him take that away from you. Because that would take you away from us."

"I know," she murmured back, forcing the tears down. "We just need to wait for the right moment."

But what she didn't say, what she couldn't say, was that

when the right moment came, she'd give herself up, give anything up, just to make sure they had that future together.

Even if she wasn't there to share it with them.

"Do we have a Christmas tree?" Luke asked. "Because not all of us are Jewish in this room, and I like Christmas."

"A Christmas tree covered in sex toys," Conor muttered.

"Just glass dildos. So beautiful." Luke sighed.

"I can see it," Kara giggled again.

She hadn't known you could hold joy and fear in your chest at once, but maybe that's what joy was: fully participating in your own happiness, despite the darkness surrounding you. Holding love tight to your chest, and not letting despair steal it away.

The moment was shattered when the door to their cell slid open, revealing Chris, leaning on his cane, guards with guns at the ready beside him, because the coward was too weak to face them alone.

"That's a nice dream," he sneered. "Truly beautiful. But I have a prettier one I'd like to share with you—and mine, unlike yours, is going to be your reality."

22

———————

Micah could not fucking wait until this motherfucker died. He might even convince the others to keep the man's skull and place it on the mantel above their fireplace in the cabin. Or taxidermy his body and stick it on the wall, like a hunting trophy.

Well, maybe not that. That was too morbid, even for him. But the skull thing? That had possibilities.

Micah sighed at the thought.

Christopher eyed him. "Something you want to share with the class, Mr. Feldman?"

"Oh, just that one day, your skull will make a nice candle holder," Micah said lightly, relieved to draw the asshole back into his web. To turn his anger back on Micah. The beating before had hurt—and knowing his family suffered alongside him hurt more. But he'd take that over Kara being frightened in the shower. Or worse.

He was egging Christopher on. Of course he was. And the man was going to try to torture them, psychologically, to make up for it. Maybe physically. Micah needed them to be strong enough to handle it, because Christopher was going to slip up and tell them something—something that would help.

"Thank you for the idea," the professor said. "That sounds aesthetically pleasing. Maybe I'll save your skulls for Kara to look at, after you're gone."

Micah tried to hide how his ears perked up. *Scooby Doo* had gotten it right, after all: evil villains often liked to share their plans; if they didn't, how would they get the accolades and the response they wanted? Micah, too, was a villain. Not evil, but Machiavellian enough to skirt that line a bit. However, he didn't need anyone to praise his machinations, which served him better than having an ego.

Behind him, Kara was frozen solid. Micah wanted to pull her into his lap, to comfort her, but that would give too much to Christopher. Instead, he tried to telegraph strength to her.

And she must have picked up on it because she said, "And what does *our* life look like together, Chris? Me trapped in your big house, you forcing me, knowing that you'll be stuck with someone who hates you? It doesn't really matter, it's not like you could ever make me come, anyway," she scoffed. "It's going to be, well not fun, but a little satisfying, watching you live your pathetic life while your brothers have all the power and just leave you table scraps. Watch New York's literati make fun of your pretentious, stilted writing and inability to create a satisfying ending to a single novel, being known as a one-hit-wonder. The laughingstock of the book world."

Micah was torn between being proud of her and wanting to hide her. He forced himself to let go of the latter. She was showing her strength, he had to trust her.

"You know, on second thought, maybe I'll just save your

skull, Kara dear. I've always wanted to skull fuck someone, and I won't mind doing it when you're dead."

The entire cell went electric, Conor and Luke's fear and desperation and rage pulsing around them like a living thing. None of them spoke.

"Let me weave you my own story," the professor continued through gritted teeth. "After all, there's no need for an element of surprise anymore. You deserve to know how it's all going to end for the four of you. I promise you, this one does have a satisfying conclusion."

And then he began. "You see, as you all grow closer, it only makes your imminent demise that much more painful to think about, doesn't it? Especially because one day—and you won't know exactly when—I'm going to come in here with my guards, and stab all three of you men in the gut. You'll bleed out slowly while I rape your little whore's mouth in front of your eyes, and you'll be unable to do anything. And Ms. Blum, I'll make sure to switch things up and rape you from behind after, so you can see as the life leaves their eyes. You'll all be helpless to stop me, won't you? As I pound into your cunt and tear you up inside? I'll let these guards have a go at you, too. They deserve a little extra compensation for their hard work."

Luke spoke softly, and Micah was impressed at how terrifying he sounded. "Careful, Christopher. You remember we killed the others, don't you?"

"Ah, which makes them even more excited for revenge."

Micah was repulsed to see that the professor was the excited one, as the man adjusted his dick in his slacks. Repulsed, but unsurprised.

It was okay. They needed him to get lost in his fantasy, so they could hear the rest.

"And then what," Micah asked, adding fear to his own voice. "What happens after you've hurt her?"

"Ah see, I think a synchronized climax is the answer to this. My guards will wait for my signal—my own climax, you understand—and shoot you all at the same time that I snap Kara's neck." He shook his head. "A waste, in some ways. All of your deaths will be a waste. After all, you did good work for my family when you all thought you were heroes but were really killing good men."

Micah glanced at Luke, expecting this to affect him, but Luke didn't even twitch.

"A waste," the professor repeated, and his eyes gleamed as he turned his attention to Conor.

And Micah, who until this point was positive he had control of the situation, braced. Because Conor hadn't worked through his shit yet—his own need for control, his own guilt, which had come much too late in the game. And Micah couldn't work through it for him.

Whatever Christopher says next, don't fall for it, he tried to telegraph to his lover. *Don't let him manipulate you.*

"A waste of life," the professor said a third time. "Especially Ms. Blum's."

...at the same time that I snap Kara's neck.

The words sliced through Conor. He couldn't decide if that was better or worse than a life spent trapped with the professor. Oh, he knew Kara was strong, and she could overcome anything, but he didn't want her to have to, damn it. He didn't want Kara to die. He loved her. He didn't want this for her.

If they'd never taken her, would she have lived?

The professor directed his next words to Kara, but his eyes were still on Conor. Conor knew he was being manipulated, but it didn't mean there wasn't truth behind the professor's words.

Especially with what the professor said next. "See, you've changed, Ms. Blum, in ways I never could have imagined. There's a darkness in you now, and it's infected everything bright and lovely. A true waste of a brilliant brain, ruined by too much cock. The things you could've done with your life, Kara. Instead, you gave up all your potential for two meatheads and a manipulative sociopath. In some ways, maybe I'm doing you a favor."

He tsked as he hobbled forward to stroke Kara's hair. She shivered beneath his touch. In front of her, Micah's body went solid. And Conor couldn't get to her, he couldn't *get to her.*

"An assassin? Really, Kara? That's what you want from life? To waste your brain and talents on killing people, when you could have given so much to the world?"

Conor waited for Kara's reply, but she said nothing. There was fire in her eyes.

As horrible as the professor was, as much as Conor wanted to rip the man's entire body into pieces, he wasn't entirely sure the man was wrong. Maybe Kara hadn't known what she wanted before, but was a life in the shadows with them any better? Was that what she really wanted, or had she been so traumatized she no longer knew which way was up? If they lived, would he be forced to watch Kara lose every part of herself and become someone he'd created out of his own selfishness? Living a life she hadn't been meant for?

How many wrongs had he committed? How could he ever right them?

He vowed, then and there, to fix it. If he survived this, if they did, he would *fix it.*

He glanced around to see if Luke and Conor had the same reactions. Luke's eyes were intent on Kara, thoughts moving behind his eyes, too fast for Conor to catch. And Micah?

Micah looked fucking *proud.*

It stymied Conor for a moment, set up some doubt in his head. Was he wrong? But the doubt quickly turned to anger. Micah wasn't seeing this clearly; he wanted what he wanted, and he'd done what he had to in order to get it. Kara was fully invested in their life together, without any thought to what could have been if her original escape had stuck. That must be enough for him.

It had been enough for Conor, once upon a time. But now he wanted, no, needed more. For her. Conor doubted anything he'd done in a long time would make his father proud, but this—making sure Kara had a good life, the life she deserved, even though it meant giving her up—*that* would have made Hank O'Connell proud.

Now he had to convince Micah and Luke he was right.

23

Luke wasn't sure he'd ever get the feeling back in his left arm. It was already broken, and being zip tied behind his back for almost two weeks didn't help matters. It worried him; it made him feel useless, helpless— more helpless than he'd ever been. But over the past days, as Kara fussed over him, cleaning out his left eye so he could see clearly, and Micah checked in on him and made sure he ate, and Conor was gentle, even tender toward him, Luke had grown to appreciate the pain. Or rather, what it signified. That this was his family, where he belonged. He no longer felt like he was on the outside looking in. Even if they died, they'd do it together.

But god, he hoped they wouldn't die. Christopher had been right; now that he'd told them how he was planning on killing them, Luke was even more on edge, waiting for that pin to drop. He dreaded that cell door opening, and not only because Kara was going to be dragged away where he couldn't see her or protect her. He dreaded every day, worried it may be their last. And despite the pain, and the fear, he treasured every day it wasn't.

Today was another reprieve. The door to the cell opened, the guards entered. When one approached Conor, Luke rose to his knees, preparing to do something, anything to protect the other man if it came down to it, only to relax back on his heels when the guard changed the bandage on Conor's chest.

"It's looking better," the guard said. "Good news for us, bad news for you."

Shit.

"C'mon," the guard told Kara, and without fighting, Kara stood gracefully and walked out of the cell, turning at the door to stop and say, "I love you."

It had become a ritual of hers. She said it every time she left.

In case she didn't come back.

Luke desperately needed her to come back.

The moment the cell doors closed, Conor cleared his throat. Luke had dreaded this, too. The night before—or whatever passed for night in this hellhole—Conor had waited until Kara was asleep before whispering, "The next time she's gone, we need to talk."

Luke wasn't looking forward to whatever it was. Something was up with Conor. Something *had* been up with Conor since the attempted rescue. Since before that, even. And he needed to find out what was going on so he could slap some sense into him. Verbally, since he didn't currently have use of his hands.

"Okay, she's gone," Conor said.

"You know," Luke said, watching the door, "Kara's going to hate that we're having a conversation without her."

"She's going to really hate it when she realizes this conversation's about her," Micah commented from his side of the cell. He was, as per usual, calm and controlled, and like he didn't have a care in the world.

"This is wrong," Conor said, looking at Luke. "All of this is wrong."

"What's wrong, boss?" Luke asked.

"What we're doing to Kara."

Stymied, Luke gaped at him. "*We* aren't doing anything to Kara."

"No, I mean...what we've done. What we will do, if we survive this. Keeping her with us. Making her live this life in the dark with us. Keeping her from who she could be."

Luke had had a similar thought, before the car crash. He knew Kara cared about them, knew she might even love them, but he hadn't been sure if she understood what she was giving up. A life in the shadows seemed sexy, exciting, at least at first. And the life she'd lived in the light, as it were, hadn't been particularly good to her. But back then, he'd wondered: would she grow to regret their life together, and then, grow to resent them for it?

Was there a day, far off in the future, that she'd leave them? Leave him?

And this time, they'd have to let her go?

But Luke didn't feel that way anymore. Not since she'd appeared in front of him like an avenging angel, determined to save him and Conor, no matter the price. The way she'd carried herself, the fire in her eyes when she'd shot Christopher's kneecap, the confident way she faced their current hell with both strength and vulnerability...all of that told him two essential things:

One, that Kara had grown into the person she *was* meant to be.

And two, that she truly loved them, and didn't want to leave.

Luke didn't know how to get that through Conor's thick skull.

"Conor, man, listen to me. I know the guilt and shame over what we did before has caught up with you. I know you're..." Luke searched for the right words. "...mea culpa-ing all over the place. Did you ever think it's not only because you're coming to terms with your own culpability in all of this, but also because you're avoiding the real truth: you can't control everything?"

Conor looked stricken. Over the last week and a half, color had returned to his face, and the strain in his cheeks, jaw, and neck had begun to disappear. But now, it was like all that healing had never happened. As if he'd been shot in the chest all over again.

As if Luke was the one holding the gun.

"Maybe that's true," Conor said, throat thick. "Maybe I'm still trying to control everything. But that doesn't change the fact that she's different now. She always flirted with danger, but she lived in the light. She had a whole life ahead of her. And now she thinks she wants to be a hitwoman? She wants to murder people? She's okay living in the shadows with us? That's light-years away from what she told you back in the cabin. You told us, remember? She was excited for the future. She wants a basset hound, for fuck's sake."

"We can get her a damn basset hound," Luke said, both frustrated and desperate.

"Really? Really, Luke? And who's going to watch the damn dog while we're all on a hit together? What if we have to go on the run again? Did you ever think of that? She deserves a *life*. All we've given her is death."

Fuck. Luke's certainty popped like a pin in a balloon.

"Hmm," Micah said.

Luke glanced at him sharply. There was something

working behind Micah's blue eyes, but he wasn't sure what, and Micah probably wasn't willing to share. Yet.

Bullshit. They needed to be past hiding crap from each other. "What are you thinking?"

Micah blinked. "You're asking?"

"Yes," Luke said.

Micah sighed, stretching his neck, his shoulders—as best as he could, given the zip ties. "Conor, you said that was how she saw her life before us, right? Well, you're not considering one simple but important fact: she's not the same person she was before us. It doesn't matter who she would've been because that person doesn't exist. Why would she live someone else's life?"

The hole in the popped balloon closed, and the balloon began to reinflate. Micah, as always, was right.

He watched Conor, who rubbed a hand through his hair. It was longer now; hitting his ears. He desperately needed a haircut, and yet Luke liked him like this. With his hair longer, Conor no longer seemed like the impassive ex-military man who had never let go of a military haircut and the closed-off heart to go with it. No, he seemed...

...vulnerable.

Too vulnerable, physically. But emotionally, it was a good change.

"Micah's right, you know," Luke told Conor. "I mean, that would be like me asking you who *you* wanted to be before all this shit happened, and then expecting you to be that person. Our old selves would still be in the military, thinking we were doing our part to save the world when we were really being used by greedy motherfuckers. Hiding that we were *together* from a community that would pretend to accept us while being wary of us. We wouldn't be free. Do you want that?"

Conor shook his head. "No. Absolutely not. I like our lives the way they are. I like what we do. I know it makes me bad—"

Luke interrupted before Conor could keep spiraling. "I know you're having an existential crisis, but it doesn't matter if we're good or bad men. It matters that we're her men. It matters that we're each other's men."

Micah snapped his fingers.

"What?"

"Oh, I'm agreeing with and supporting you. I'm proud you've finally gotten your head there, baby."

Luke shrugged, feeling proud and, if he were honest, a little bashful. "Yeah."

To Conor, he said, "What the hell happened to you? Why did you let that fucker get so deep inside your head?"

"I'd like to know the same thing," Micah said, stroking his beard. It had grown back in over the past month, soft and sexy despite the filth of the cell. Luke forced his attention back to the matter at hand.

"The professor—"

"Chris," Micah interrupted. "You're giving him too much power over you. He's just a man."

But Conor was being stubborn. "*The professor* pointed out that everything that had happened to Kara and to Luke was my fault. And that he and I were the same, because just like him, I took her from her life, and still refuse to give her back."

Shock reverberated through Luke's body. "Conor, you— we—are not the same as Christopher Johnathan. How could you even think that?"

"How could you think differently?" Conor's voice had a desperate tinge that Luke had never heard from his lover before. "What makes us different? What makes us better for her?"

"We care about her, for one thing. The whole of her. We love her," Luke said.

"And more importantly, she loves *us*," Micah pointed out.

As Luke watched, Conor's stiff shoulders started to relax, like their points were getting through.

And Luke had one last argument. "And we want what's best for her," he said.

Conor's jaw went tight. "Do we? Is this what's best for her? Being trapped in a cell with the three of us, living under the threat of rape, of death, being mentally tortured by those fuckers every time they drag her off to take a shower without us—"

At that, Luke had to pause. Because Conor was right about that.

Conor continued, his voice breaking in ways that broke Luke, bit by bit. "What if we do get out of here, and we pick up another enemy, and then all of this happens again? But worse?"

Luke hated that he could imagine worse. Still, he had to ask. "Are you really willing to give her up?"

"If that's what it takes," Conor said. "You're right. I'm not the man I was, before we kidnapped her and brought her into all of this. I've changed. She's changed me. And the man I am now—it's a man that can't keep her locked in a gilded cage in case she ever wants to go free."

"She won't—" Micah started, then sighed.

"Can you be sure?" Luke asked.

Micah shook his head. "I've changed, too. I've learned that, as omniscient as I try to be, even I can never be sure of everything. The only person who can be sure of anything is Kara. So we need to ask *her*."

"She's going to tell us what we want to hear, and I think she's been brainwashed by us, accidentally..."

"Jesus fucking Christ, Conor!" Micah ground out. Luke was taken aback. When they'd first met Micah during BUDS, he never said "Jesus" anything, still deep in his religious past. As time went on, and they rubbed off on him, it slipped from his mouth occasionally, but not like this. Micah rarely raised his voice.

"You know, I try to lead you in the right direction. I know you're aware of it. I've been trying to coax you toward getting your head out of your damn ass, but clearly that's not working. We need a giant fucking pair of forceps to remove it." Micah was visibly shaking from anger. "You are being a complete dumbass, and I am sick of it. I know we're in a fucked-up situation, but this pity party you've been throwing yourself isn't helping. It's like you're halfway there, to understanding Kara deserves to be free —but you still don't get what freedom *means*."

As if on cue, the door to the cell slid open with a grinding sound, as bad as nails on chalkboard.

Kara walked back inside, shivering, head held high. And Luke was torn between gratitude that the walls were too thick for her to have heard them fighting, and wishing she had heard the whole thing, so they could have it out, once and for all.

She stopped, staring at them. "What's going on? What happened?" she asked.

"Did they hurt you?" he asked. Despite the interrupted argument, they needed to know, like they always needed to know.

"No. Same as always, although they did taunt me by

telling me the clock's ticking. 'Tick tock,' one of them said, and if he weren't holding a gun, I would have walked right up to him and kneed him the balls." She shook her head. "Something's happened, I can tell. Did Chris visit you? Micah, you're shaking." She walked over to Micah, and Luke —who had forced himself not to think about it—couldn't help but look at her cut up bare feet. "Someone tell me what's going on. *Now.*"

Something had changed while she'd been gone. Kara was already worried. The phrase "tick tock" had echoed in her head all the way down the hall on the march back to the cell. The one guard had even winked at her when he unlocked the door and shoved it open.

"I'll tell you, baby," Micah said, inhaling and exhaling slowly, as if he were trying to get himself back under control. That alone was cause for concern. "Conor here has the stupid fucking idea that when we get out of here, we need to let you go."

Kara's nightmare—the one where all three men told her they loved her and then sent her packing, *literally*—came back to her. She'd told herself it would never come true, and yet here they were, talking about doing the same thing.

Well, Conor was, anyway.

She tried not to blow up. Tried to calm herself down, to explain to herself that he had and was still suffering a major trauma, and it had fucked up his already fucked up brain. But when her anger at Conor's bullshit decision met her panic at being left behind, it was like a lit match to a fuse.

No. She wasn't going to have a panic attack.

She wasn't going to blow up at them.

Just breathe. You're okay. All you have to do is breathe.

Except she wasn't okay, was she?

"You dumbass," she exploded. "You complete, utter fucking dumbass." Turning away from Micah, she stomped toward Conor, who was reclined against the wall, and shoved him on his good side.

He still flinched.

Good.

"You fucking *dumbass*," she repeated, feeling her face get wet.

Crying. *Fucking great.*

Fine. He'd seen her at her worst, he could handle her angry tears. Because Kara hadn't been this angry at him since he'd first kidnapped her. In fact, she might be angrier now than she was then.

"You want to leave me?" She hated how high pitched her voice sounded.

Conor shook his head. "No, free girl. I don't want to leave you. I want to give you your life back."

Kara tried to inhale, to clear her mind, so she didn't strangle him. She failed. "What life? What life, Conor? Living alone in my bland apartment with my one friend, going to my stupid corporate job, volunteering at the farmers market as if that could bury the truth of how goddamned lonely I was, how unfulfilled I felt with my life?" Distantly, she felt her heart speeding up, anxiety keeping pace with her anger. If she weren't careful, the former would outpace the latter.

"Kara, sweetheart..." Luke said.

Kara whirled around on him. "Do you agree with this? You want to what, walk away from me, too? After everything? Haven't I fucking proven myself yet?"

Luke tilted up his head to look at her, straining at his bonds. "As long as this is what you want, then this is what I want."

Kara covered her face with her hands. "Have I not made it clear? Get it through your stupid fucking heads. All three of you. What I want is *you.*"

Luke nodded. "Okay. That's all I needed to hear."

Micah cleared his throat. "To be fair, I wasn't a part of this."

"Kara," Conor said, his tone broken, his eyes almost wild. "You think I *want* to give you up? I heard what you said. You want to be like us? You want to kill people? For money? I like our lives, now, but you could be so much more. *Have* so much more. We dragged you out of the light and into the darkness, literally kicking and screaming, and I'm sorry it took me so long to see it, but it was wrong of me. Of us. If the professor doesn't kill me, you leaving us will, but it's not about what I want anymore. It's about what you need."

It was amazing, truly. How anger could be so all-encompassing, it made her forget everything else. Forget the dirty, dank cell she was locked in. Forget the damages her lovers had suffered. Forget Damocles's sword hanging over her head, hanging on by a thread and the tick of a clock counting down the hours to her death. Until all that existed was Kara and the men who surrounded her at three corners, so she was literally the center point of their triangle. And the man she faced, who she loved, who was such a fucking idiot she could happily rip his head off.

"What I *need*? You're so sure of what I need, you didn't even think to ask me? Conor, you've read me well in the past. You knew minutes after meeting me that I needed control taken from me, sexually, and I needed to be pushed, otherwise. You figured out I was running from myself and my shame, and how unhappy I was when you kidnapped me. You know a lot, but this, you don't know. You don't know what I need, but you know how you could find out? By *asking* me. By *listening*. By trusting me when I tell you that what I fucking need is *you*."

Conor's throat worked, but he said nothing.

She wanted to kill him, for being so stupid, and breaking her heart in the process.

Inhaling—this time she succeeded—she quieted her voice. "Here's the worst part, *boss*. You're doing it *again*."

"Doing what again?" he asked.

Tears threatened to choke her, but she forced the words out anyway. "Choosing for me. Taking my decisions, my *agency*, right out of my hands."

"Kara, innocent girl," he began. "You think this is what you want, now, but I promise it isn't."

"Innocent? Who was it, who shot a man in the dick, for threatening her with rape? Who played honeypot to lock down a target? Who deepthroated a gun as a distraction? Who the hell was forced to touch a stranger to get your location before Micah killed him?"

"What the hell are you talking about?" Luke broke in, growling. "Someone made you touch them?"

"Long story, not the time," Micah commented.

"And who fucking parachuted out of a plane, even though trying new things is terrifying, and almost died, in order to save you?"

"No one told us that part," Luke interrupted again.

"Not. Now." Micah said sharply.

"Sweet girl," Conor tried again. "That's my point. You never would have had to do those things if it weren't for us."

"Oh, and that's it, huh? You only want me if I'm sweet and innocent and helpless?"

"Of course not!" Now Conor was yelling. "I want you every fucking way you are. Sweet and honest and vulnerable in my arms, tied up and helpless for my cock, fierce and brilliant as you face down an enemy. I want all of it. But—"

"But you're fucking terrified, because once again you're trying to control everything," she interrupted, glaring at him through her tears. She'd given up on trying to suppress them. God, how could anger *hurt* so much? "You know what, Conor? You might get to control me when it comes to sex, but you've gotten confused and think you control me outside of it. And until you understand that *I* am in control of my own goddamned choices, and that I choose you, you won't—"

She was cut off by the groan of the door sliding open.

No. Not now.

Everything her anger had hidden from her reappeared, including that ticking clock.

She needed more time.

"Ah, I see there's trouble in...well, maybe paradise isn't quite the word," Chris said jovially.

Kara turned her glare on him. "Did you come here to gloat?"

"No, I have an appointment with Mr. O'Connell, if you don't mind sharing him for a bit. I promise I'll return him the same way I found him. Well, I'll try to, anyway."

The fiery anger that lit her was doused by fear.

"You aren't taking him anywhere," she told Chris. "It's me you want, anyway."

"Kara!" Conor tried to struggle to his feet to block her, but was stopped by the cuff on his wrist.

"Sweetheart, stop," Luke said urgently. To Chris, he said,

"You've had your fun with him. Don't you think it's my turn?"

"Actually," Micah drawled. "I think you and I still haven't had a fulfilling enough...conversation. I'm sure you're curious, aren't you, professor?"

Two guards raised their guns in Luke's and Micah's faces, safeties off. Kara turned back to Chris, trying to use her body as a shield, not sure who to defend, or how.

"Don't you dare take him anywhere," she told Chris, the fire building back up inside her, drying up the fear. "Don't you dare hurt any of them. Or I swear to you, Chris, I will make sure you regret every second of it. Do not doubt me."

Chris stared back at her, and although he didn't tell the guards to lower their guns, there was a tic in his cheek. She waited as he seemed to consider, before he said, "The melodrama doesn't suit you, Ms. Blum. Really, you're better than that."

Ignoring her, the guards pushed her out of the way, unlocking Conor from the wall. He glanced around, as if considering fighting back, but the guns in his lovers' faces must have stopped him, because he raised his arms.

"I love you, all of you," he said. "I'm so sorry."

And then *he* was the one who was dragged out of the cell, leaving Kara staring after him, absolutely terrified.

24

The room Christopher took Conor to was nicer than anything he'd seen since San Francisco. Pale grey striped wallpaper, a large sectional, a fireplace and a TV. The room belonged far, far away from where they were.

"My quarters," the professor explained. "Please, have a seat."

As if Conor was a guest and not a prisoner. Not like Conor could forget, given the rifle poking him in the back.

He sat. Considered if this was a good time to take the professor out, for good.

As if he'd heard him, Christopher said, "I wouldn't try killing me. See, Ms. Blum is being taken back to the bathroom as we speak, and the guards that are with her have strict orders to check in with me every other minute. If I don't respond, their orders are to rape and kill Ms. Blum, and then kill Mr. Feldman and Mr. James."

"What if I don't believe you?" Conor said through gritted teeth.

Christopher lifted a shoulder in a shrug as he carefully used the cane to sit down in a large armchair facing the couch. "You can choose not to. But is it really worth the risk?"

Choose.

And until you understand that I am in control of my own goddamned choices, and that I choose you, you won't—Kara had said. Conor desperately wanted to know what she'd been about to say. What wouldn't he be able to do, or have?

And was she right?

"You know, Mr. O'Connell," Christopher began once he was situated. "I had such high hopes for you, too. We were going to achieve great things together. If only you had stuck to the plan and hadn't tried to escape with Mr. James, this whole thing could have gone very differently."

"Oh?" Conor asked, still distracted by what Kara had said to him.

"Yes. Mr. James, Ms. Blum, and Mr. Feldman would all be safe. All you had to do was sacrifice yourself for them, and they would be living easy, happy lives now. Mourning your absence, of course. But they'd be safe."

Safe. Conor focused on what the other man was saying. His gut clenched. Yes, he knew that the professor was still manipulating him, but once again, there was truth in what he was saying.

The professor rubbed his chin. "You know, Conor, I know what it's like to fuck up. After all, my preoccupation with Ms. Blum destroyed my marriage and my career, and as much as I blame Ms. Blum for that, I also recognize my fault in it. The worst part, about all of that, was that I didn't have to behave the way I did. But I was lost in what I wanted instead of what mattered. And of course, I keep making the same mistake again, because I keep being preoccupied by her." He sounded rueful.

"If you know that, then why are we here?"

"Because I can't help myself," he told Conor. "In that way, you and I are also very similar. She's my...what did Mr. James use to call her? Kryptonite pussy?"

Hearing the words come out of their enemy's mouth was like a punch directly over Conor's healing bullet wound. He had to force himself not to deck the man.

A small, sad smile appeared on the professor's face. "You, too, keep making the same mistake, and if I let you live, I believe you're doomed to keep repeating it. You and I are both so similar, except in one way—you're willing to give her up, and I' m not, and I believe that makes you the better man."

Conor was, after all, trying to be a better man.

Except what had Luke said? It didn't matter if they were good or bad, because they were hers? Each other's?

He didn't want to be like Christopher. But how could he be different, and still give Kara what she wanted?

I am in control of my own goddamned choices.

I choose you.

"Professor," Conor asked. "Since you know she's your Kryptonite, since you think I'm the better man because I'm willing to give her up, wouldn't you give Kara the choice? If she asked you to let her go, to let us live? If you are so ... preoccupied with her, wouldn't you let her choose?"

The professor chuckled. "Kara doesn't know what she wants. You heard her, didn't you? No, she needs to be given structure, have decisions made for her. You understand that."

Conor had heard her. That time, at least. How adamant

she was that he wasn't listening to what she wanted or needed. That once again, he was deciding for her, because he needed to be the one in control.

You don't know what I need, but you know how you could find out? By asking me. By listening. By trusting me when I tell you that what I fucking need is you.

Jesus, she was right. He was a fucking dumbass.

He was choosing for her, again. He was so desperate to distance himself from the man who hurt her most, to not be a man who hurt her, ever again, he was fixated on pushing her away. He hated the idea of her becoming like him, but that was nothing more than his own shame and self-loathing. He was trying to control everything, instead of realizing that in this, she had to be in control.

That's what would make him different from the professor. From Christopher. Not "giving her up," or setting her free. But letting *her* choose. That's all she wanted, to have agency and feel like an equal partner of theirs, to be a full part of their team. She wanted to decide, and even if what she decided on was a dangerous, dark life, that was her choice. If that's what she wanted? Well, then Conor would give it to her.

Or die trying.

Except not that, either. She wanted to share the darkness with him, so he owed it to her to try to live. He didn't know how the fuck they were going to figure it out, but he'd do it. For her.

For all of them.

Because he loved them too much not to.

"Christopher," he said. Not 'professor.' Because Micah was right, Christopher was just a man. No more, no less.

And men weren't invincible.

Men could die.

"Yes?" Christopher asked.

"Go to hell."

A muscle in the other man's cheek ticked. But all he said was, "Ah, I do believe I'm headed there one day. But since you'll get there first, you'll save me a seat, won't you?"

25

Luke was about to lose his fucking mind.

Oh, he'd been teetering on the edge of a mental breakdown for days. Christopher's psychological torture was effective in that way, and his still healing ribs and finger and broken arm didn't help matters. But he'd managed to pull himself back from it.

Until now.

Both Conor and Kara had been taken away, and all he and Micah could do was sit in their cramped quarters, arms literally tied behind their backs, and try to force their will on the universe to keep their loved ones safe.

The universe wasn't fucking cooperating.

"Goddamn it," Luke exploded, desperate to pound something. Ideally Christopher's fucking face.

"Yeah," Micah said. "I—fuck. Yeah."

It was unlike Micah to lack words, and it was insight into how helpless the other man felt. How truly fucked they were. Part of Luke wanted to comfort him, but it reminded Luke of something that had pissed him off earlier.

"You didn't have to bring her, you know," Luke said. "In fact, you were supposed to do the opposite."

Micah shook his head, and that small movement, head to the right, head to the left, lit a spark of anger in Luke that had lain dormant since they'd been captured again.

"That was the fucking point of all of this, wasn't it?" Luke added. God, he was angry. "Conor and I sacrificed ourselves so that you could keep her safe. And here we are, all trapped together, with Jesus fucking Christ knows what happening to her right now, all because what, you couldn't stand up to her?"

"Really, Luke?" Micah's frustration came through his voice.

It was as if their circumstances had stripped Micah of his legendary calm and his ability to hide his thoughts and emotions from the rest of them. Maybe it had taught him that manipulating the three of them wasn't the best way to cement their relationships with each other. Or that their relationship didn't need cementing anymore.

Good.

"Really," Luke said. "To be clear, I wish you hadn't come after us either—I wanted *you* safe, too."

Micah snorted. "Look at you, lying now. You may have wanted me safe, and I love you for that, but you knew that I'd come after you. Don't pretend for a second you didn't. Bullshitting yourself doesn't suit you, Boy Scout."

Okay, that was fair.

"Fine," Luke conceded. "But you didn't have to bring her, you could have left her with Marcus."

Even in the dim light, Luke could see Micah roll his eyes. "Two for two, Luke. You really think Kara would let herself be left behind? That she wouldn't fight her way to be here? She literally sweet-talked Billy into bringing her to me. And do you truly think she would have been safe with Marcus?"

"Safer than here," Luke shot back.

Micah processed this, then nodded. "Okay, let's say you're right. Would that have been fair? To abandon her, knowing we probably wouldn't have made it back? She's part of our family. Our team. She's one of us. She doesn't deserve to be put in a glass box and kept safe. She deserves to live her life the way she wants. To fight for us. With us. Why do you think she's so livid with Conor right now? Don't fall for the trap Christopher laid out for us. It does us no good."

Before Luke could respond, Micah added, "Are you really angry at me, Luke?"

Trust Micah to get to the heart of the matter. Luke was having a hard time holding onto his anger at him.

"No," Luke admitted. "But I feel helpless as fuck, and I hate that feeling more."

"You're scared," Micah said.

Fuck, he was.

And he hated it.

The last time he'd been scared was when Kara had been taken, and they didn't know how to find her. Luke had been left behind that time, recovering from his injury, and lying in a bed at Marcus' goddamned mountain castle, alone, he'd felt angry and scared and...helpless.

Yeah.

"Terrified," Luke admitted. "I'm fucking terrified, and I don't know what to do about it."

His terror wasn't over dying. No, it was having to watch his loved ones die that scared him. Somehow, he'd been able to deal with that fear when they'd been SEALs, had known how to compartmentalize the feeling so it didn't impact their missions. But back then, he'd never admitted his love to Micah and Conor. Not to them, not to himself. When they brought Kara back, she'd catalyzed an entire emotional journey that led to him here, unable to shove his love and fear and helplessness back in a box where it couldn't hurt him.

"I am, too," Micah admitted. "I'm trying to see a way out of this, but I'm failing. I thought I'd come up with something by now. I've even been doing what I can with my... usual skills," he said, only alluding to his manipulation tactics because of the mics. "But it requires more time than we may have. Fuck, I even prayed, and you know I haven't done that in a long ass fucking time. I don't know what to fucking do. Except try to love each other in the time we have left."

Luke digested this. "I love you," he said, his voice gentle. "In case I haven't told you that before."

Micah smiled sadly. "I know you do, baby. But it's good to hear you say it, anyway. I love you, too, more than I ever thought possible. For what it's worth, I wish you weren't here, either."

God, that was it, wasn't it? They all wanted to face their deaths alone, but—

"We're a team," Luke said. "Leave no man behind, and all that shit."

Micah's voice was more serious than he'd ever heard it. "I'd never leave you behind, Luke. Never leave you. Ever."

This time it was Luke's turn to say, "I know. Tell you what; this whole fucking mess has killed my abandonment issues." Then he grimaced. "Bad choice of words."

Micah chuckled. "I'm glad they're gone, bro."

"Me too."

Luke wished, desperately, that he wasn't chained to the

opposite wall from Micah. That his hands were free, so he could touch his lover, kiss him, caress him, make love to him.

As if Micah heard his thought, he said, "I wish I could touch you. Wish I could hold you. Wish I could wrap my mouth around your cock and—"

Ah, fuck. Luke interrupted him. "Please don't make me hard, when there's nothing I can do about it."

But Micah wasn't going to be deterred. "I miss you inside of me, baby. And I promise, if we get out of here, I'll let you beat my ass for bringing Kara. Just because I love you."

Luke's cock thickened at Micah's words, and the image they created. And he wanted that, so badly, not even because he wanted to fuck. No, because he missed being close to his lovers in that way, connecting with them through touch and taste, rough or gentle, fast or slow.

So he said, "You also love getting your ass beat."

Micah laughed again. "You know I do. Do you forgive me?"

Luke sighed. "I forgive you. It's hard to argue with how rational you are, sometimes."

Micah's voice was rueful. "I'll tell you what, I don't feel fucking rational right now."

"Me neither," Luke said, glad he wasn't alone.

Because no matter what happened, live or die, he'd never be alone again.

They were quiet for a bit, waiting—and, on Micah's end, probably praying—for Conor and Kara to come walking through the door.

Of all the times she'd been taken away from the cell, this had been the worst. Almost ironic, because no one forced her to strip at gunpoint and shower in freezing water while they watched. Instead, she'd been brought into the kitchen, and forced to eat. She wasn't sure where or how they'd gotten the chargrilled oysters, or the biscuits, or the halibut, but it was so similar to the meal she'd eaten with Micah that she'd wanted to vomit out of fear—no matter how fucking hungry she was.

It was a sign, wasn't it? They supposedly gave prisoners on death row their favorite foods for a last meal, too.

No one had said a word to her the entire time, but "tick tock" echoed in her head. She remembered her dream, too, from when Luke and Conor had first been taken. She'd thought it was about her fears of being abandoned by them, but maybe it had been something else. Maybe it had been a portent of the end. There were so many ways to leave people, to lose them. And now that she'd finally found where she belonged...

The thought steeled her resolve. She still didn't know how she'd get them out of this, but she wasn't giving up.

So she forced down food—she doubted it was poisoned, where would the fun in that be for Chris?—to gather her strength, and then when she was done, ignored the guards behind her and walked back to the cell, head held high.

She heard the clomping of boots coming from the other direction and turned. Conor walked, barefoot and a little unsteady. He looked no worse for the wear, thank god.

When he reached her, she reached her hand out to stroke his face. She was still angry at him, but so relieved to see him upright, alive, she pushed her frustration to the side.

"Stop," one of the guards barked, and she lowered her hand.

"Are you okay?" she asked Conor quietly.

"Fine," he said. "Kara…"

She shook her head. "Not here."

They waited, Conor a heavy presence behind her, as one of the guards walked around her to unlock the door and push it open. Luke and Micah were on their knees, facing each other, their heads twisted toward the door.

"Oh thank fuck," Micah said, surprising Kara with his tone.

Luke released a heavy breath.

Kara walked back inside, Conor trailing her. The guards chained Conor back to the wall again—this time shackling both his hands.

"See you soon," one said, before sliding the door shut, leaving their foursome trapped inside.

As she always did, Kara inspected the door, just in case it wasn't locked this time. And like always, it was.

That done, she turned to face them all. "I'm fine," she said quickly. "They fed me, they didn't hurt me." She swallowed, preparing to tell them the rest. "But they fed me what we got at that restaurant in New Orleans, Micah. It felt like…" she swallowed again, aware of all three men's eyes on her. "…like a last meal."

"Fuck," Luke said this time.

"I don't know what we do," Micah said, his voice almost inaudible. "Anyone else have ideas?"

Kara had one, but they weren't going to like it, or agree with it. So she kept it to herself.

"Not like we can talk through them, anyway," Luke said, gesturing around the room, implying what they all assumed: there were cameras and mics present.

They lapsed into silence. It was Conor who broke it.

"Kara, I'm sorry," he started.

Oh, he wanted to continue their argument from earlier, did he?

"If this is more 'mea culpa' bullshit, Conor, I swear—"

He interrupted her. "What were you going to say, before Christopher showed up? 'And until you understand that *I* am in control of my own goddamned choices, and that I choose you, you won't—'" he quoted her. "I won't what?"

Kara was temporarily taken aback by Conor calling Chris by his actual name instead of the professor. It felt like progress. Was it, though?

She forced herself to focus. "That until you understand that I'm in control of my own choices, and you're one of them, you'll never find happiness. Or peace. Not with me, not with us, not with anyone. Not even with yourself."

And she would make sure he had a chance to find both.

He nodded. "Makes sense."

She gaped at him. "'Makes sense?' Please don't placate me, Conor. Not now."

"I'm not placating you. I'm trying to apologize for being a complete dumbass. An ass, period."

Her heart leapt into her throat. "What are you saying?"

He glanced over at Micah and Luke before turning back to her. "That I was wrong. I let my delayed guilt and self-loathing get the better of me. I was so worried I was like Christopher by taking you, I did exactly what I did before. I decided for you. Once again, I didn't let you choose. Just repeated the same stupid mistakes."

His dark eyes were filled with remorse, and for once, understanding. But she needed to make sure he really got it, so she crossed the room and stood, looming over him. It was a new experience for her—he was so much taller than her, she always felt so small beside him. This time, he was the one looking up.

It made her feel powerful in a way she hadn't before.

"And what were those mistakes?"

"Not listening to you. Not trusting that you know your own mind. Trying to make decisions for you. Preemptively going down a path without your input because I was too afraid of the outcome and wanted to control it, get it over with. I get it now, wise girl. I promise. If I had to live without you, every moment, every breath would be torture. But I'd take that torture, if that's what you wanted. And if you want to be with us, then I'll gladly do that, too."

Oh, god. He was getting it. The idiot really, finally, understood. She felt tears fall from her eyes and track down her face, and Conor tried to reach out his hand this time, only to come up short.

"How did you figure this out?" Micah said from the other side of the room. "Because before..."

"Christopher, actually. He brought me into his quarters to psychologically torture me, tell me how similar he and I were—again. And I finally got it. He and I were similar—"

"No," Kara interrupted, and Luke and Micah echoed her.

But Conor wasn't done. With a hoarse voice, he said, "We *were*. Because neither of us were giving you a choice. But that's how I can be different from him. That's how I can give you the life you deserve. By giving you that choice. Whether it's to be with us, or to leave. Whatever it is, I'll accept it, even if it destroys me." He gulped, and closed his eyes for a moment, before opening them again. Kara could have gotten lost in the dark, beautiful promise in them. "You decide this time, my brave, strong, wise, extraordinary girl. You."

Lightness filled Kara, and an even firmer resolve. If this

was what it took, to get them to this point, where they could meet each other as partners, as equals, then she would take it.

She leaned down, until their lips were a hairsbreadth apart.

"I decide," she said.

"Yes."

Placing her lips to his ear, she whispered, "Good, boss. Because I already decided. I'm keeping you."

Before he could kiss her, she turned her head to look at Luke, then Micah. "I'm keeping all of you."

"Damn right, you are," Luke said.

Micah just smiled at her, nodding. Once.

Did they know she meant forever? Or did they really think she was going to let them die?

Dismissing that, she turned back to Conor.

"Kiss me," he ordered, and when she leaned back down, he captured her lips with his, demanding she open her mouth with no more than his lips. The moment she surrendered to him, he took over. But instead of the kiss turning hard, it turned soft, almost reverential. Like with each nip of his teeth, each lick of his tongue, each whispered word of love and apology and praise against her lips, he was worshipping her. Like she was a queen, and he was nothing more than a loyal subject.

She reveled in it, lost in the feeling of his mouth on hers for the first time in a long time. She forgot about the guards outside the door and the cameras. She even forgot about their deaths, looming over them, and her decision.

Conor must have remembered because he pulled away first. "The cameras," he choked, but his eyes were still on her lips.

Kara shook her head. "I don't want to worry about the

cameras. They've already seen me naked, already hurt me. What does it matter at this point? I don't want him to take this from us, too. Not anymore."

"You sure, baby?" Micah called gruffly from across the room.

She moved across the small room, kneeling down so she faced him, their eyes close together, their breath mingling. "I'm sure," she said.

Micah peppered her lips, cheeks, and jaw with kisses. Approval, affection, and agreement, all in one.

She kissed him back, their lips pressing together with a sweet solemnity that made her heart ache.

And then she pulled back and crawled across the room to Luke. His green eyes tracked her, his expression unreadable.

"I know back at Vixen, you didn't want any other man looking at me. But if this is all we have, if this is it—" because she could fail, and it could be, "—don't you want to spend it together? The way we should? As close as we can be? I don't want to..."

She trailed off, unable to say the rest.

Die without being with you all, one last time.

As if he'd heard her, Luke nodded, just once. Conor did, too.

"Of course, baby," Micah said.

Luke spoke. "If this is all we have, then I want us to spend it together. But first," he looked at Conor. "No more self-sacrifice. You don't get to die so the rest of us live." He repeated himself, making sure Micah and even Kara heard it. "You hear me? We live together, we die together. Promise me."

No one said anything.

"Promise me!" he barked.

"I promise," Conor said.

"Promise," Micah said.

"I promise," Kara said. She had no plans on dying.

But just in case she was wrong, she placed her hand on Luke's cheek and drew his face up to hers. He was so tall, that, even on his knees, she didn't have to bend far to reach his lips. She kissed him, coaxing his mouth open with hers, and he let her lead the kiss, let her explore the inside of his mouth with her tongue as if it was her first time doing so. Warmth and then heat filled her, as she tasted him and drew groans from him, as she teased him by pulling back and he chased her. Until he stopped letting her lead, and demand she follow.

Finally, he pulled away.

"Kara, take off your dress, and let us love you properly," he said against her lips.

Purposefully ignoring the cameras, she stripped out of the flimsy tank dress and underwear Chris's men had given her, until she stood naked before her men.

"Move closer," he said, still demanding.

"But you can't use your hands," Kara said. "What if—"

What if I hurt you. What if I smother you.

What if I can't?

Kara wasn't used to being the one in control, sexually. It happened so rarely.

"Good," Luke said. "You can use yours. Guide me where you want me. Show me what you want, sweetheart. You're in charge now. Use me however you want."

Kara stepped closer, until her pussy, already soaked from their kiss, brushed against his lips. She shivered from the gentle touch.

"Put your hands on his head," Conor coaxed from across the room, his voice husky. She did as he said, catching

Luke's copper hair under her hands and tugging him closer until his nose pushed against her clit as he licked her.

"There you go. Good girl," Conor added.

Luke stopped, and she wasn't sure why at first, until Micah crooned. "Guide him like he asked you, baby," and echoed, "You're in charge now."

She was in charge.

Gently, she tilted Luke's head back, until his lips met her clit.

"Lick me there," she said.

He followed her gentle order, his tongue drawing circles around her. Slowly, assuredly, patiently. Like they had all the time in the world.

Her legs began to tremble.

"Does that feel good, baby? What he's doing to you?" Micah asked. "Tell us how it feels."

"It feels..." she panted. "It feels like..."

Hot and bone-melting and as if everything inside her was drawing tight like a rubber band about to snap.

"Use your words," Conor said.

Her words? What were words?

"Like everything feels tight and hot and I'm out of control. And perfect. It's perfect." She stroked a hand through Luke's hair. "You're perfect."

"And?" Micah prompted.

"Power," she admitted on a gasp. "It feels like power."

"Good girl," Conor crooned again. "Magnificent girl."

Luke growled against her pussy, and the vibration—and Conor's words—made her moan. Her legs trembled, but she needed to stay upright, so she didn't hurt Luke.

"What do you need, baby?" Micah said. "Give him your words."

"Faster," Kara gasped.

Luke complied, licking in smaller circles, each spiraling Kara tighter and tighter. Her already shaking legs threatened to give out, but she stayed standing, suspended between pleasure and completion.

Realizing she was gripping his hair too tightly, she began to release it, but Luke growled again. So she held to him tight and rubbed her pussy against him, so close, so close.

"Are you about to come for him, baby?" Micah asked.

"For us?" Conor added.

Kara could do nothing but moan, and when Luke—lightly, gently, so, so tenderly—bit her, she came with a cry, and the only thing that kept her standing was her hands around Luke's head.

Finally, she released him, falling to her knees while she gasped.

"Was that okay?" she asked.

Luke smiled, lips glistening. "Sweetheart, it was perfect."

She glanced down. He was hard, his cock pushing against his sweatpants.

"Oh, baby," she murmured and leaned forward to pull them down. As if reading her mind, he lifted his hips so she could shimmy them down his waist to the ground. His cock jutted up, thick and long and ready.

"You're going to have to do most of the work, you know," he told her, teasing. "No more pillow princess."

She giggled. "I can make that happen." She kissed him, tasting herself on his lips. "But I don't want to be in charge. I want us—"

"To do this together?" he asked. "That we can do, sweetheart. That we can always do."

He was in awe of her.

Of all of them.

When she'd pressed herself against his mouth and taken his head in her hands, he'd never been more proud of her. Never felt more whole. And even though they weren't touching him, Conor and Micah's words had echoed in the small cell, brushing over his skin like reassuring, cock-thickening strokes. And as Kara ground her hips against him and shook, as she came, he felt more connected to his lovers than he ever had.

And they weren't done.

As Kara stood over him, gripping his cock in one hand, stroking it once, twice, and sending the sweetest pain through his cock to his whole body, Luke couldn't help but admire the queen above him. Her auburn roots were beginning to grow in, and he wanted to kiss them. To hold her forever. But he wanted her pussy to swallow his cock more.

"Sweetheart," he begged.

"Yes," she agreed, lowering herself onto his cock and sliding down, her soaked pussy easing her way. Tight perfection surrounded him, squeezing his cock with a brutal beauty he'd been afraid he'd never feel again.

"I missed you, sweetheart," he told her, raising his hips to push deeper inside her.

Kara moaned, dropping her head to his shoulder. Luke gave into his desire and twisted his head to drop a kiss on her roots. If he could forget what might be coming for them, if he could forget that he couldn't touch her, hold her, then everything about this was perfect.

"How does she feel, baby?" Micah asked.

His woman wrapped around him, her scent surrounding him, her pussy squeezing his cock in pulse after pulse as she moaned against his shoulder, knowing he had her love and she had his, with their partners watching...if he could freeze this moment, he could.

"Incredible," he groaned. "Like coming home."

"Yeah," Conor hummed from his spot across the small room. "It is."

But Luke couldn't freeze the moment, and it was good, Kara began rocking against him, circling, seeking the friction she needed. She ran her nails up and down his back, his straining arms, trailing a hand down his chest and lower, until her hand traced where they were connected.

"Feel that?" she murmured to him.

"Yes, sweetheart," he moaned again.

She raised her head, staring at him with love in her gold-brown eyes. "That's us together, Luke. That's a promise—of forever."

"Yes, sweetheart," he said, her words making his chest light and his cock impossibly harder. "Take what you need. Take me."

She did, raising and lowering, raising and lowering.

"That's it, sweetheart," he crooned to her. "You're so good, fucking me like this. Fuck me harder. I want to feel you come around my cock. Take me with you. Show me how much your pussy loves me. How much you love me."

"All of me loves you," she said on a moan, riding him faster and harder. "Come with me, Luke. I want to feel you fill me, I need—"

"Yeah," he said, shifting his hips up, and then up again, until she was bouncing on his cock. "You need me, don't you? Well, you're going to have me. All of me."

At that, she froze, clenching around him as her cries echoed off the walls.

"Fuck," Luke groaned as her tight pulsing triggered his own orgasm, long and sweet. He came inside her, filling her up, just like she wanted, and once again he wanted to freeze time.

She rested against him as they both came down from their orgasms. Dropping kisses on her shoulder, she murmured, "Mine."

"Yours," he agreed.

"Ours," Conor corrected, chuckling. And Luke caught the other man's gaze. There was so much lust there, and so much love. Open and honest, like there was no reason to hide it anymore.

"I love you," Conor said.

"Same, boss," Luke said. To Kara: "Come on, sweetheart, you have more cocks to tease."

Kara rose off his softened cock, his come slipping out of her pussy and trailing down her inner thighs. Marking her as theirs.

But Kara wasn't done. Kneeling back down, she took his softened cock in her hand and mouth, licking him clean. Then, with a final butterfly of a kiss on the tip of his cock, she redid his pants before taking shaky steps to Micah.

Micah was already hard. Watching Luke and Kara come together without any more friction between them—except for the good kind—was incredibly satisfying, and watching Kara act like the queen she so rightly was made him want to fuck her, badly. She'd grown so much, from that lost woman who thought she belonged nowhere, to this strong, powerful badass who knew she belonged with them.

And he wanted her. *Now.*

"Kara, baby," he said. He needed to taste her. Taste *them.*

She didn't make him wait. As if she'd heard him, she pulled his filthy camos off, releasing his cock, and then knelt on top of him, slipping him inside her sopping cunt. She was still dripping with Luke's come, and feeling the wetness of their combined release on his cock as she slipped down, down, down—it made him equally ecstatic and envious.

But once again, Kara was reading his mind, because she kissed him, open mouthed and hungry, sharing her taste and Luke's with him until he was drowning in their essence and fucking loving it. She continued kissing him as she began to ride him, slow and confident and completely in control.

"Baby," he broke away, gasping. "I need you to move faster."

"No," she teased, slowing her movements until she was grinding slow figure eights around his cock.

That's how she wanted it, did she? Fortunately for her, he was happy to beg.

"Please, baby, I need you to move. Fuck me, hard and fast. Make me come."

She hummed, but began to increase her pace, making Micah's cock throb. Making his heart hum with her, because no one was a better match for them than her.

"Tease him," Conor suggested. "Make him work for it."

Kara hummed again, like she hadn't quite decided yet. But she slowed back down, leaving Micah trapped between a hard place and a harder place. Every twist of her hips sent shivers of pleasure and heat into his cock, each twist of her lips made him smile right back, so glad she was with him.

Them.

Now.

Completely.

But: "Baby, please, I need you to move."

"Say the magic words." Although the words were teasing, her beautiful eyes were serious.

"I love you," he said.

In reward, she sped up her movements, until she was riding him so hard and fast, she was practically bouncing on his cock. He felt the climax building, his balls heavy with the need to come, but he held tight to his control, needing one more thing from her before he let go.

"Tell me," he urged.

"I—" she gasped, rising partway off his cock.

"Love—" she hovered above him, a whimper breaking from her lips.

"You!" And she slammed down hard, her pulsing cunt taking him with her.

He came for what felt like forever, releasing everything he wanted and everything he felt and everything he hoped inside her, heart pounding in his chest, beating against hers.

Finally, their hearts slowed. Kara kissed him, climbing off, his cock slipping out of her cunt. And even though he'd just come, he wanted more.

With a wicked wink, Kara bent down and wrapped her mouth around him. Working him with her mouth and hand, she opened her throat to take him deep.

"That's it, baby," he said roughly. "Show me how much you love me."

She hummed again, the vibration moving through his body. He hardened and thickened, more quickly than he thought possible—but then it had been a while since they'd been together like this. And despite his hope, his faith, it might be the last time. Desperation and desire—more than he could handle.

So when she swallowed around him, her tight throat caressing every part of his cock, Micah came with a shout.

Releasing him, she opened her mouth to show him his release.

Fuck.

And then she crawled across the dirty, cold floor, ass swaying.

Toward Conor.

Just as it should be.

Conor watched Kara move toward him on her hands and knees. She'd been on her hands and knees before, but never with so much strength and power she practically glowed.

Not a girl, then.

A goddess.

"I don't deserve you," he began, but she interrupted him with a finger to his lips and a shake of her head. He opened his mouth—maybe to speak, maybe just to breathe—and she pressed her open mouth to his, sharing Micah's come and love until all Conor could do was to accept it and swallow it down.

Nothing in his life had ever tasted so good as the mix of her mouth and Micah's release and a faint hint of Luke's cock. If this was his last meal, then so be it. He'd die with their taste on his tongue. He'd die with their love inside him, making him whole.

Kara licked off the bit of come that had escaped his mouth.

He needed to fuck her, to be inside of her, if she'd give that to him. Because he'd give her anything, and right now, what she wanted was control.

"Conor, you do deserve me. You almost died for me," she said. "But even if you didn't, so what? We've all done fucked up things, Conor. We'll keep doing fucked up things. What matters is that we do them together."

"Yes," he said.

Yes.

"How much does this hurt?" she gently touched the bandage above his bullet wound.

"Not much," he said.

"And this?" she slid her hand down to his heart.

"It doesn't hurt anymore," he told her. It was true. Even if they died…

His throat caught in his chest. He couldn't—wouldn't—think about that now.

Biting her lip, Kara slid her hand lower, until she was cupping his cock through his pants. "And what about this?"

"Aches," he groaned, because in that moment, it did. "Needs you." He cleared his throat, making sure she could see the love and respect in his eyes. "I love you, glorious girl."

"Sit up," she murmured.

He did.

"Raise your hips."

He did that too, eyes on hers as she slipped his pants off and then planted his feet on the floor, one after the other, so his legs were wide and knees were bent.

"What are you going to do with me?" he asked her.

"What do you want me to do?"

"Anything. Always," he promised.

A smile lit her face, brilliant as the sun and just as blinding. It brought light to the dim room.

And then she turned around so she was facing away from him, and, his cock in her hand, lowered herself onto him, so slowly he could feel every wet, warm inch of her. His heart in his throat, he leaned forward to kiss her shoulder.

"I missed this," he told her.

Kara bottomed out on top of him and rested there for a moment, letting them both just feel their connection. Turning her head, she kissed him again. "I missed you."

Yeah. "That," he said. "That the most."

She stayed there, teasing him with the ecstatic perfection of her pussy. But as he leaned over her shoulder to watch as she stroked her clit in circles, he decided she could tease him forever, as long as she stayed there.

Please, let us have forever.

"You look so good, baby, locked on his fat cock," Micah said from across the room, his eyes shifting from where Kara played with herself to Conor. He shook his head, but smiled.

"What's that look mean?" Conor tried to ask, but at that moment Kara tightened around him, so it came out as "Wha?"

"I knew it would take you a while to get here, boss," Micah said. "I'm just glad you did."

Luke cleared his throat. "Agreed." To Kara, he said, "Keep touching yourself like that, sweetheart. Let's see you come."

Kara's fingers moved faster, leaning back against Conor. Her back and neck were slick with sweat, wisps of her hair curling. Bee balm teased his nostrils. Her pussy tightened around him as she moaned.

"That feel good, gorgeous girl?" He bit her ear and she clenched around him. "Touching yourself with me inside you? Knowing I'm helpless to do anything but let you fuck me? Knowing you're in control?"

"Yes," she moaned again. The sound of her fingers

working through her slippery wetness was teasing his own control.

"You're going to make me come this way, just seated on my cock and touching yourself."

"You're so close, baby," Micah said. "We can see it."

"Smell it," Luke added.

"Still taste it."

Kara whimpered, writhing all over Conor, her legs tightening where she sat above him, her body trembling against his.

"I can't," she whimpered.

"Why?" he asked.

"I still need you to make me."

Of course she did, his goddess. She wanted control, but she still needed him to take it, too. It was that push-pull between them that connected them. She gave, he took, and vice versa.

Right now, it was his turn to take.

"You're going to come on my cock," he told her, voice thick. "You're going to come for all of us, because you want to give us everything. You're going to come around me and then I'm going to fill you up so full, fuller than you already are, until we're all so deep inside you you'll never get us out."

And then he bit her on her shoulder and shoved his hips upward, once.

That's all it took. With a scream, a cry of their names, she came around him, so fucking tight, so fucking perfect, squeezing the hell out of his cock and giving him everything so he could do the same in turn.

He heard himself shout her name, and his love, as he came inside her, the taste of all of them still on his tongue.

It tasted like a promise.

Like forever.

But forever didn't last long. It ended moments later, when the door slid open with a rough groan, revealing Christopher.

"This looks fun," he said. "Can I join?"

26

___

Chris looked like a complete mess. Gone was the affable, well-dressed, mild-mannered professor. His shirt was wrinkled, one cuff hanging loose like an afterthought. His face was mottled red, and he leaned more heavily on his cane than the last time Kara had seen him. And there was a crazed, angry look in his eyes.

Was this it? Was this the moment?

Could she use it to her advantage?

Kara kept her face impassive.

"I watched your lovely little show," he continued, taking his time to look at all of them. Slowly, he withdrew a sheathed knife from his pocket. "Exciting stuff, really. In fact, it made me realize that it was time for my show. After all, Mr. O'Connell is mostly healed."

Two of the guards grabbed a still-naked Kara, while Chris took shaky steps into the center of the cell. He grinned at her, his expression nowhere close to sane. "Ah, what I have been waiting for. Turn her around. Hold her still for me." To her, he said, "You may want to say your goodbyes now, Ms. Blum." He rubbed his hands together. "You're going to be too busy screaming after."

This motherfucker. She wasn't sure if he was referring to her pain, or he was just that delusional about possibly giving her any pleasure.

She held her breath, eyes on the knife, as Chris continued. "Oh, I know you say you don't want it, but you told your lovers that, too, didn't you? I made you come multiple times before, I can do it again. It's the least I can do before killing you."

"You won't touch her," Luke warned.

"Just watch me." Chris cocked his head. "Oh wait. You will be watching me."

"Kara, fight! Run!" Conor dragged his arms forward, tensing, trying to break the chains that held him—again. But like before, they were too tight, too strong.

Only Micah looked at her without saying anything.

Trust me, she mouthed at him.

He nodded, once.

"Nothing to say, Mr. Feldman? No last words?" Chris taunted.

Micah attempted a shrug—difficult, with his arms still zip-tied behind his back. "I recognize when I've lost, Mr. Johnathan."

That, more than anything else, seemed to settle Chris. With his free hand, he ran a hand through Kara's hair, the sheath of the knife butting against her neck, and she held her breath, forcing herself not to recoil, as badly as she wanted to.

"You really think you can make me come?" she said over her shoulder.

She could do this.

She'd done it with Victor.

She'd done it on the train.

Come on, Kara. You're okay. Right now, you're okay. All you have to do is breathe.

And even though she wasn't okay, she forced herself to inhale and exhale slowly. In that exact moment, she was okay. And besides, no one could stave off the panic for her. She had to do that part by herself.

The rest they would do together.

"Oh, Ms. Blum, I know it," Chris said.

Kara never thought she'd be grateful for delusional men, but she was now.

She felt his hand move behind her, heard the snick of his pants zipper. Followed by her men's growls.

"Wait, I almost forgot," Chris said. "The stabbing."

No.

It was now or never. Now or nothing.

"Chris, how about we make a deal," she said, letting the desperation she felt come through. "Please."

He paused in his caresses. "What sort of deal?"

"You can force me. But you and I and everyone here will know how unwilling I was. Don't you think your men will talk? About how I didn't want you?"

Micah's eyes were trained on hers, his face grim, but approving.

"And what?" She could hear Chris's frustration, how he was trying to hide his bruised and scratched ego. She knew him. He loved being wanted—by his students, by New York's literati. By her. Rejection never sat right with creative types.

"And I'll fuck you—willingly. If you just give us all one more day. That's all I'm asking for, please. One more day for us to say our goodbyes."

More growls, more denials from Luke and Conor. She ignored them; she had to. She didn't want to do this. This was worse than Victor, worse than anything she could have imagined. The idea of willingly touching her former lover again, letting him touch her, made her want to puke all over the hard ground, cut off her own hands. She'd promised herself this would never happen again. And yet here she was. She could see the waves of her panic rising in the distance.

What would you do, for love?

For life?

She hadn't heard that voice in a while. Her voice. Curious, gentle, encouraging.

Anything. She'd do anything.

She could do this. She *had* to do this.

She waited as Chris considered, weighing his options. Finally he said, "Alright, but you'll have to prove yourself. Get on your knees."

"Kara." Conor's voice was strained with pain and fear.

"Don't, sweetheart," Luke said, his own voice breaking.

She looked at all three of them, letting tears well in her eyes.

"I love you," she said. And then, "But yes, I can. Remember? I can deepthroat *anything*."

With those telling words, she turned away from them, lowering to her knees and steadying her breathing before reaching for Chris's pants and finishing where he'd left off with unzipping them. The sound of the zipper's teeth opening was one she'd never forget: an echoing *snick snick snick* in the otherwise quiet room.

"Anything? Hmm," Chris said, brushing her cheek with the knife again. "Seems you have new skills. Let's test them, shall we?"

Closing her eyes, Kara pushed down his pants and briefs to his knees. It had been years since she'd seen his penis, and she'd happily have gone an eternity without seeing it again.

Instead, she gripped it in her hand, tight, stroked a few times, listening to his horrible sighs. He was the only one making sounds in the cell; everyone and everything else had gone silent, like the very building held its breath, waiting for what came next.

Kara leaned forward. And as the waves of panic threatened to rise, she banished them again.

In this moment, I am okay. I am going to be fine. All I have to do is breathe.

With that, she took a deep breath, opened her mouth, wrapped it around his disgusting penis.

"Oh, you bitch, your mouth still feels so—"

And then he screamed as she bit down, and down, and down. Not releasing him as he screamed and tried to hit her, accidentally releasing the handle of his cane and the sheathed knife as he collapsed on the floor. Down, down, down, in slow motion, and still she didn't release him, even as blood spilled out of his penis and into her mouth. She held on, teeth clenched around him, and shook her head back and forth like a rabid dog, until with an unholy tearing sound, his penis detached from the rest of his body and he collapsed to the ground with an even unholier scream.

The room exploded into chaos, the two guards in the room seemingly unsure if they should help their boss somehow or start shooting. And Kara stirred the chaos more, rising to her feet and spitting Chris's detached, bleeding, lifeless dick right into the closest guard's face.

The guard yelled in surprise, dropping his gun to the floor as he batted the appendage away. The gun hit the ground and went off.

"Kara!" Her men yelled, almost in synchrony.

"Duck!" she yelled back, spitting more blood out of her mouth.

Fuck, that was disgusting. Satisfying, but disgusting.

The guard recovered and reached for the gun. She reached faster. Grabbing it, she shot him in the chest. With a scream, he dropped to the ground, directly on top of the still alive and shrieking professor.

Before the other guard—the one who had taunted her with "tick tock"—could raise his rifle against her, Kara trained her gun on him.

"You have two choices," she told him. "Drop your rifle, put up your hands, and I'll let you go, or try to shoot me and die. In case you can't tell, I'm a good shot." She tilted her head toward Luke. "He taught me."

"Okay, okay," the single standing guard said. He dropped the rifle and kicked it across the floor toward her, raising his hands. "I—"

He never got a chance to finish his sentence before she pulled the trigger and shot him right in the forehead.

He fell backwards, dead.

"Tick tock, asshole," she muttered.

"Kara? Sweetheart?" Luke asked from her right side, pulling her out of her bloody satisfaction.

"Oh, shit, yeah."

Ignoring the now whimpering Chris, she located the knife by his side. Removing it from its sheath, she ran behind Luke and quickly put the gun and rifle on the floor where Chris couldn't reach them, before sawing at the zip tie around Luke's wrists, avoiding his skin.

"Sweetheart," he said again.

"Got it." With one final cut, the zip tie split and his arms were free. His left one, broken, hung limply at his side. The other was cut up around the wrist from the multiple times he'd tried to break them, but otherwise, miraculously, he looked no worse for wear.

Bending down, he grabbed the handgun with his good hand.

Kara ran over to Micah, making quicker work of his zip tie.

"I'm so proud of you, baby," he told her.

His approval filled her with pride, but it had nothing on the satisfaction she felt when she glanced out of the corner of her eye and spotted Chris's dick on the floor.

"Thank you for trusting me," she told him as she cut her lover free.

There was a gun shot. Kara jumped, only to see Luke clicking the safety back on the gun and Conor lifting his arm away from the wall. The reinforced steel shackle was still around his wrist, but the chains were no longer attached to the wall. He stood, stretching his back, before grabbing up the rifle.

"Am I your bad girl, or your good girl right now?" Kara asked him, so relieved to see them all free, she almost felt giddy.

"Both," he said easily.

"And do you want to punish me or kiss me?" she asked Luke.

"Both," he repeated.

"I for one, am just proud of you, baby," Micah said, love and approval in his voice. More seriously, he said, "Are you okay? That was terrible to watch, I can't imagine how terrible it was to experience."

Kara paused, observing her body. Her heart was racing, but her hands were solid.

"I want to puke," she said. "And I'll probably be a mess later. But for now I'm fine."

She didn't have a chance to say more, as boots pounded down the hallway. The next few moments were a blur of gunshots and yelling, until they were surrounded by a pile of dead bodies.

Kara didn't relax though. Not while Micah and Conor disappeared to make sure the rest of the building was clear.

As they waited, Kara rinsed her mouth out with the single water bottle they had left.

"I'm going to whip your ass with my belt for this," Luke warned her. "Sweetheart, I'm so sorry you had to go through that."

Kara shook her head, feeling vulnerable and a little shaky as the adrenaline began to wear off. "It was awful. Absolutely horrifying. But I'd do anything to keep you all safe."

"Come here," he said gruffly. She leaned against his good side. "I'm proud of you, and grateful," he said as he leaned down to kiss her.

She pulled away. "You can't—"

"Sweetheart, I thought I was going to lose you. Forever. You think a little blood from our enemies is going to stop me from kissing you? Nothing could stop me." And then his lips were on hers, his taste replacing the metallic taste. His mouth, his heat, helped prevent the shakes.

Conor and Micah reappeared in the cell, covered in blood.

"Clear," Micah said. "And I found a SAT phone and made a call to Marcus. Billy's fine—he had to parachute out of the plane, which is what took them so long. They're coming to get us."

Oh, god.

They were okay.

Everything was going to be okay.

Kara inhaled and exhaled, and then suddenly there were three large, warm men surrounding her, holding her tight and wrapping her in love and safety.

Finally, stepping back, they released her.

"What do we do about him?" Luke asked, nodding toward Chris.

"It's Kara's decision," Conor said, and his words galvanized her to move.

She stepped across the small room to where Chris still lay in the center, crushed under the dead guard lying on him. Her feet were soaked in the blood pooling across the floor, and she didn't care. She was covered in blood, she could taste it, and even though she hadn't been lying—she did want to vomit—she'd also never, ever, felt more alive.

"Help me move the body," she said to the others. Micah reached down, easily rolling the dead guard off to the side, revealing Chris. The professor's eyes were glassy with pain and shock, his breathing labored, one hand covering the bleeding stump sticking out from his crotch. Kara surveyed him with satisfaction. She'd done that. She was the reason for his pain. He'd hurt her—but she'd hurt him more.

Good.

"Kara," Chris whimpered. "Please. I'll give you anything," he gasped. "Anything. Money, power, whatever you want, I'll—"

She shook her head, unsure how she'd ever seen anything in him. She wasn't that lost little girl anymore. "No thank you. I have everything I'll ever want, or ever need. And I have you to thank for that, Chris, because I'd never have found them if it weren't for you." She sighed. "Unfortunately, it's not enough to save you."

His already glassy eyes went wide as she held out her hand.

"I have to say, I'm really loving this Dark Phoenix thing," Luke remarked as he handed her the knife. "Beats Kryptonite Pussy any day."

Laughing, both solid in her body and exhilarated in her mind, she accepted it.

"I told you, didn't I?" she asked Chris.

"Told me what?" he wheezed.

"That you're no mountain. You're only a man—a pathetic one, at that. And soon you won't be anything at all. But I should warn you," she added, smiling. "I think this is going to hurt."

And Chris Johnathan, esteemed professor of creative writing and three-time runner-up for the Booker Prize, died to the sound of his own desperate screams and her low, husky laughter.

"I think you did it, sweetheart," Luke said, staring at Kara in admiration and not a little bit of fear. "He's dead."

Kara rose to her feet. There was blood everywhere, splattered in her hair, across her cheek, down her bare body. Her golden-brown eyes were bright with satisfaction and not a little bit of blood lust. The knife was still in her hand, and Chris Johnathan lay at her feet.

She'd never looked more beautiful.

Never looked more alive.

Never looked more *theirs*.

"Come here," he ordered.

She walked toward him, dropping the knife so it clattered to the cement floor. There wasn't a lot of room in the cell, but he'd make do. He needed to touch her, to be inside her, to celebrate that they'd made it. So, he lifted her up with his good arm and, without preamble or preparation, lowered her down onto his cock.

She was already so wet she slid easily onto him, and fuck, *fuck,* she felt good.

She felt like coming home.

He held her like that for a while, just indulging in her tight pussy around his cock, squeezing him, welcoming him where he had always and would always belong.

And then Conor was coming up behind her, moving easily, and he was parting her ass cheeks and pushing in one finger, then two.

"Kara, my sweet girl," he said, "Do you remember when I told you I was going to use the professor's—Christopher's —blood as lube?"

Luke watched as her big eyes went wide.

And then her eyes went wider and she made a desperate sound of pleasure as Conor did as he'd said, working his fingers and then his cock inside her ass. Luke could feel Conor's cock through the thin membrane of her pussy.

They were connected. In love. Whole.

And alive.

And then he was distracted, because Micah was spitting on his hand and then working his own huge, thick cock into Luke's ass. Luke grew impossibly harder, not just at the sensation of fucking and being fucked, but by the way all their bodies pressed close together, the way their hearts beat together, the way Kara cried out as he and Conor took turns pumping in and out of her, and as Micah thrust into him at his own rhythm, one only known to the Machiavellian deviant he loved, and Conor grunted, and Micah groaned and crooned filth and love at all of them, and Luke stared deep into Kara's eyes and knew that he was home, that he belonged here forever, with them.

That they would have forever together.

So, he fucked into her harder, and harder, not ready to come yet, but ready to send her there.

Ready to do anything for their girl.

If you'd asked Kara—back when she lived in Chicago in her sad little life with her sad little belief that being alone meant being free—if she'd ever find herself covered in the blood of a man she'd ruthlessly murdered, she'd have said no. If you'd then asked her if she'd find herself covered in blood while being fucked from both ends by the loves of her life, while the third thrust into the second's ass, she would have told you hell no. But secretly, she would have fantasized about it, and when she did, these three men would've starred in her fantasies.

Life wasn't a fantasy. Life was messy, and bloody, and raw, and so, she had learned, was love. It wasn't going to be easy, and it wasn't ever going to feel like a fairy tale. But then Kara Blum had never been a girl who cared much about fairy tales. Deep down, she'd always empathized with the villains.

Instead, she luxuriated in the present moment. Here, now, with the men she loved, being fucked into orgasm after orgasm, her eyes on Luke's, Conor's kisses on her neck, gripping Micah's hands around Luke's waist. Together, fucking or not, murdering or not, arguing or not, this, this was all she had ever wanted and not known she needed.

This, here, was home. This was where she belonged.

"Home," she gasped out loud, as Luke hit a spot inside her that made her spiral tighter and tighter.

"What's that, sweet girl?" Conor asked as he pushed into her from behind and held himself there.

"All of you—the three of you—wherever we are. Home." They weren't the perfect words, but the fact that her brain was working at all was impressive.

Conor sighed, sliding out, then in again. "Yeah, home."

"Home," echoed Luke on another deep thrust that she felt in her throat. "Keep squeezing me with this fucking pussy, sweetheart."

"Home," Micah said, and he must have punctuated his words with his own thrust, because Luke groaned and began to come inside of her, making her come again, too.

Micah followed them with a roar, and then all that was left was Conor, holding her up from behind, as he began to pound into her, her thighs spread wide and helpless. Micah and Luke took immediate advantage, dropping to their knees and taking turns to lick her pussy, kiss each other, and then lick her pussy some more.

She was so close, aided by Conor pounding into her. But it was his words that sent her over the edge:

"Love us, Kara, like the good girl we know you are."

And, like the good girl she was for them, and the bad girl she was for everyone else...

...she did.

27

———————

Three months later

The mission—Kara's second, if you counted the Chris stuff, and Kara certainly did—had gone off without a hitch. It was a simple hit, but a profound one: a Swedish billionaire had paid them to torture and kill his daughter's abusive husband and record the whole thing for him to watch in perpetuity. Kara had taken lead, playing her honeypot role to perfection, flirting with and leading the target to her hotel room, where her men had been waiting. They'd trussed him up like a turkey, but Kara had done the carving, in part because she'd developed a taste for it, but mostly because she thought seeing a woman doing the work might bring some catharsis to her client and his daughter.

She'd been right. The client hadn't contacted them on the flight home from Europe to Idaho, and she'd worried some, even when Micah had shown her the rest of the hefty payment in their bank account. But as Luke pressed the button on the remote clipped to their Jeep's sun visor, and opened the driveway gate to their home, an anonymous text came in on the burner:

Thank you.

From me, and my father.

Kara's eyesight blurred a bit, making the aspens on both sides of the drive go watery. She leaned her head against Conor's shoulder, sniffling, as she showed him the phone.

"You did good," Conor said, kissing her hair. "I'm proud of you."

Conor, for his part, had let go of his qualms regarding her joining the "family business." If he'd had any more doubts, any more guilt about changing her, they'd died alongside Chris's last breaths. He had insisted that she needed more training, so the months between Chris's death and this hit had consisted of fighting, hacking, shooting, and general hit-person lessons, most of which took place at the cabin. Along, of course, with so much sex Kara thought her pussy maybe deserved a dick vacation.

They lived there now, full-time in Idaho at the cabin. Lola had come to visit, once. At first, Kara's best friend had been reluctant to accept Luke, Conor, and Micah as permanent fixtures in Kara's, and thus, Lola's own life; but after spending a few days with them, and seeing how happy Kara was, Lola had softly said, "I get it now."

She'd been out of contact ever since, but then Lola had always ghosted Kara periodically, so Kara didn't think much of it. Micah kept an eye on her, and would tell her if something was wrong.

Kara didn't tell Lola about the hitwoman lessons. It seemed better that way.

"We're home, baby," Micah said from the front seat as Luke pulled to a stop in front of the cabin.

"I'm fucking starving," Luke said.

"I'm fucking exhausted," Conor added. It was around eight in the morning, but none of them had slept in thirty-six hours. And yet, even without sleep, Kara was still revved. Bloodlust would do that to a person, and she wasn't even ashamed of it.

Luke, Conor, and Micah hopped out of the car. As Kara unbuckled her seatbelt, the door opened, Conor scooping her out of the car and carrying her in through the front door like a bride.

"Conor," she laughed. "I can walk."

"Yeah, but you know I love carrying you," he said.

The house looked more lived in. Bobby the Basset Hound's dog toys were scattered throughout the living room, waiting for him to play with when they picked him up from the boarder's later. They didn't let a sitter stay at their house, because even though they all lived under aliases now, they still had to be careful. Unfortunately, they hadn't extracted a second confession from Chris before she killed him, so there was no way to prove Conor wasn't at fault for Frankfurt, or get their records expunged. And the other two Johnathans had disappeared. But the four of them had agreed it didn't matter, anyway. They preferred their life in the shadows. They always would.

A guitar case rested against the couch because Kara had convinced Conor to start playing again. And on the armchair near the window lay one of Kara's notebooks—because her men, in turn, had convinced her to start writing again.

Home. The feeling spread through her as Conor carried her down the hall and into the kitchen.

Micah's kitchen was mostly pristine—except for Kara's favorite coffee mug still in the sink. It had been a gift from Luke, and said, *Being your regular orgasm supplier should be gift enough...but here's a mug.* Kara loved it, even if she had forgotten to put it in the dishwasher. Which was okay: Micah had relaxed (slightly), and so the kitchen, though still clean, looked a little more lived in, too.

Finally, Conor deposited her on the floor.

"I'm going to go take a nap," he told her, with a brief, hard kiss. "I expect breakfast when I come back."

"I'll tell Micah," she said, and he laughed and slapped her ass before disappearing from the room.

Micah entered, stopping and smiling at her. He did that a lot lately, stopped and smiled—and it no longer felt like there was some hidden agenda beneath it. Just him, happy that they were together. He came up behind her, wrapping his arms around her waist and kissing her neck.

"I love having you in my kitchen," he said between kisses, "even though you forgot to wash your mug before we left. But you know what? For that, I'm putting you to work."

She leaned back against him, enjoying the affection.

"To work? What happened to not letting any of us 'kitchen nightmares' cook?"

He laughed against her neck. "I still don't trust Luke or Conor, and I'm not certain you wouldn't burn down the whole house accidentally while trying to toast bread—"

"—I know how to toast bread."

"—but I still want to teach you to cook."

With that, he left her to turn to the fridge, where he pulled out a carton of eggs, as well as butter.

"Micah, you sexy, manipulative jerk, I know how to make eggs," Kara said, somewhat offended.

He raised an eyebrow. "I'm not talking about a half-burnt scramble or even some sunny side up business. I'm going to teach you how to make a French omelet. It's how restaurants audition chefs, because if you can't make an egg properly, you certainly shouldn't be allowed to do anything else."

Kara joined him at the stove, watching as he heated the pan on high.

"I thought you weren't supposed to cook eggs above medium heat?" she asked.

He stepped behind her. "That's for amateurs. Now, slice off a slab of butter and drop it in the pan, and tilt it around until the butter covers the bottom completely."

She followed his directions, enjoying his warmth at her back and his left hand on her hip as he handed her an egg with his right.

"The moment the butter bubbles, it's time to crack your eggs in the pan. Do not let them set, immediately begin beating them with a fork so they mix properly—but gently."

"Sounds like something Luke would do," Kara said, taking the egg from him and cracking it on the pan, then the next, then the next. Micah handed her a fork, brushing his fingers with hers when he did and lighting sparks within her, but she needed to ignore them, because the eggs were about to set.

"Alright, you're going to want to start tilting the pan again as they cook, so they don't stick. There you go, that's it. You're doing so good, baby," he murmured behind her.

Kara beat the eggs, marveling at how they turned a soft, consistent yellow in the pan.

"Now, you're going to want to flip them. Beginners mostly use rubber spatulas for this, but I want you to pop the pan in your hand like you're attempting to flip a pancake, but keep it tilted at a forty-five degree angle so it folds—exactly. Exactly like that."

Every single word sounded like sex. Felt like being held

after, adored and loved. She'd never see cooking eggs the same way again.

"Okay, baby, take the fork and fold up the bottom, like you're sealing an envelope. Now! You're done!" Out of nowhere, a plate appeared next to her. "Gently slide the omelet out of the pan and voila, you've done it."

She'd done it. A silly thing, cooking some eggs, but it filled her with pride.

He placed the plate next to her, reaching around her to turn off the stove. She turned into his arms and he pulled her away to make sure she didn't get burned by the still hot range.

"I'm proud of you, baby," he said. "Do you know what you just did?"

"Make an omelet?' she tried to tease, but her heart was racing.

"No. Tried something new, something you could have easily failed at, without having a panic attack."

Oh.

Oh.

Elation filled her.

Look how far you've come, his eyes said, the blue as placid as the ocean first thing in the morning, lit by the sparking sun. *Look how far we've taken you, you've taken us. Let's take you further.*

And they had. Back when they'd kidnapped her, he hadn't even trusted her to make a sandwich without poisoning him. And yet here they were, making eggs together, like a normal, well, polycule.

"This," she said, pressing her lips to his ear. "This is what I want our lives to look like. I don't care if the rest of it is bloody, and violent, and dangerous as hell—as long as I get moments like this with you."

He turned his head to kiss her. "Agreed."

Luke was already hard when he and Conor entered the kitchen. The TV was on, turned to a college hockey game.

"Your little brother's good," Luke remarked, pausing to watch as Jack Feldman knocked the puck straight into the net, inches from the goalie's mask.

"Too good," Micah said, sighing. "We need to go deal with that, soon."

"When you're ready," Kara told him, cheeks flushed. To Conor, she said, "We should go see your mom and sister, too."

Conor grunted, but a smile played on his lips. Luke turned back to Kara and Micah.

The two of them were at the island, Kara on Micah's lap, letting him feed her omelet with his fork. When Luke glanced under the counter, he saw that she was clenching her thighs together in time with Micah's fork touching her lips.

Perfect. That was exactly what he wanted. He pushed his soon-to-be in laws out of his mind and looked to Conor, who nodded.

"This is your show, Boy Scout."

His show. Part of Luke had expected his issues with Conor to continue, but Christopher's torture had helped them work through their issues, ironically bringing them closer together, even though the long-dead professor had been trying to pull them apart. Sure, sometimes he and Conor bumped heads, but then Micah and Kara, with both ease and exasperation, helped them talk through their shit.

In the same way that when Kara went quiet, lost in traumatic memories, the three of them held her quietly and let her talk. Just more evidence of why they needed each other. And why the symbolism of this next step was so important to him.

The three tiny gold hoops in his hand, each with the letters *CML* engraved on them, kept him centered, focused, calm. This was a mission, like any other, and he just hoped Kara was good with it.

"Sweethearts," he called from the doorway. "It's time."

A smile, sexy and satisfied, grew on Micah's face.

"Time for what?" Kara asked.

"Time for you to truly give yourself to us," Conor contributed.

Confusion filled her beautiful face. "I've given myself to you in every way possible, haven't I? Is there a hole you haven't penetrated that I'm not aware of?" The joke was almost breathless.

"Baby," Micah said, lifting her face. "We want to pierce you."

She stilled. "Pierce me?"

"Yes," Luke said, striding forward, doing his best to ignore the pain in his knee. He lifted her off Micah's lap and put her on her feet in front of him. "Pierce you. Here," he brushed his fingers against one nipple, which hardened under his touch, "here," he brushed his fingers against the other nipple, which followed its twin's behavior, "and..." he ran his hand down her abdomen to her pussy, stroking toward her clit and tapping on it. "Here."

Kara jerked, her whole body flushing. "Hang on."

Conor moved forward, so she was blocked in on all sides. "Are you ours?"

She nodded. "Yes."

"Are we yours?" he asked.

She nodded again. "Yes."

"Kara, sweetheart," Luke asked, knowing the answer already. "Do you trust us?"

There wasn't even a pause when she nodded. "Of course."

Conor lifted her chin. "Are you using your veto?"

She shook her head, her eyes bright. To Luke, she asked, "It's going to hurt, isn't it?"

And Luke experienced the unfamiliar sensation of his cock going rock hard at the same time his heart went gooey-soft.

"Hell yeah," he said. "It's going to hurt a fuck ton. And it's going to be so, so good."

They decided to do it in the dining room. Conor suggested the kitchen, but Micah was adamant that, no matter how much he cleaned it, he didn't trust it. Plus, the island was too high to get the angle quite right, and apparently the angle really mattered. Kara thought that sounded right; after all, they were talking about putting needles through her nipples and the hood of her clit, so things like getting angles right seemed pretty important.

She was a curious mix of turned on, so excited to be doing this with them it felt like a high, and incredibly sober. Not just because of the pain, although that was a huge part of it, but because this, more than anything else, felt like an irrevocable commitment. It was silly; they'd already made an irrevocably commitment to each other all the times they'd saved each other. But this felt...permanent.

This felt like marriage.

It was fortunate she didn't need a moment to catch her breath, because it was a moment she wasn't going to get. They didn't take things slowly, or pause to process. It didn't matter that they'd only been together for about six months. They decided, they acted. That was it.

And you're it, for them, that voice in her head reminded her, and it was that that guided Kara forward, not fighting Conor when he lifted her in his arms and deposited her face up on the smooth wood table.

Out of the corner of her eye, she saw Micah disappear, then reappear with rope.

"Why are you tying me down?" she asked.

Luke winked at her. "You're going to want to move around, and we'll need you to stay still so the needles go where they're supposed to."

That made her heart thud hard as all three men tied her arms and legs down to convenient little metal loops underneath the four corners of the table. Conor had added them about two months ago. Micah took the final length of rope and wound it around her waist, once, twice, three times, before tying it off. She'd been tied down by these men before, many times, but she'd never felt as caught as she did now—or as safe.

Or as loved.

Or as turned on.

"Oh, bad girl, that made you wet, didn't it?" Conor tsked.

"And her nipples hard," Micah added, moving down the table to pinch one, then the other, making her cry out.

She felt oversensitive already, and they'd barely touched her. What was it going to feel like when the rings were actually in? She was going to be on the verge of orgasm all the time, led around by her pussy and willing to do anything for them, just how her men liked it.

How she liked it, too.

Luke showed her the rings. Two were bigger, one was tiny. All of them had a bump she couldn't discern.

"Are those...letters?"

Luke nodded. "C,M,L. Conor wanted it to say "Property of Conor O'Connell, Micah Feldman, and Luke James, but the jeweler told us it wouldn't fit.""

"Besides," Conor grunted, "No one's going to be seeing you naked, so our initials were enough of a reminder."

Micah leaned down to bite one nipple, then the other, alternating until Kara's hips jerked, only to be stopped by all the rope holding her down. "I thought it was a little kinder than us carving our names into your breasts, although that was thrown out as an option."

"Mmm, knife play," Luke sighed. "One day."

"Veto," Kara said automatically, making her men laugh.

"I think her nipples are hard enough, and her clit is getting there, but it could use some help, don't you think, Conor?" Luke said conversationally.

Conor grunted, and then his mouth was there. He didn't bother with any other part of her pussy, completely focused on licking, sucking, and biting on Kara's clit, until she didn't need to see it herself to know it was—

"Look how red, look how pretty," Conor said, pulling back and showing Luke and Micah, who crowded around him.

"Poor baby," Micah crooned. "Our pussy needs to come, doesn't she?"

This time, when Luke laughed, it sounded sinister. "Unfortunately, she can't come yet. We need her clit to stay hard."

And then all three of them were touching her, stroking and pinching her clit, working it back and forth.

"There we go, out from underneath the hood, just like we needed," Luke said.

"What am I, a car?" Kara moaned.

"Are you really sassing us right now? We're about to stick needles in your most sensitive spots, and you're sassing?"

Then Luke was handing out antiseptic wipes to the others, and all three of them were wiping her clean, making her moan some more. He handed Micah and Conor each a needle, and a nipple ring, keeping the clit ring for himself.

"Sweetheart, we love you," he said. "Very much."

"And we're so happy with our life together. We want to keep living it with you, baby," Micah added.

Conor caught her eyes with his, and she got lost in them, the dark light in them swallowing her down like quicksand, although she didn't want to struggle this time.

"Forever, perfect girl," he said.

Yes.

"Forever," she repeated, she started, then shrieked as, one after the other, they pushed the needles through her nipples. She was on fire, she hurt everywhere, and she was going to—

Luke placed a gentle kiss on her the hood of her clit, and touched the last needle to it, and then, and then, the burn erupted into a supernova, centered around her clit, as she fucking *came*. The orgasm felt like it lasted forever, a never-ending shockwave, pleasure and pain flipped and Kara unable to tell which was which anymore.

Moments, or maybe months later, her heartbeat began to slow, and the pain and pleasure lowered to a background hum.

"Fuck, that was hot," Micah said. "Too bad we can't fuck her for the next month."

His words shook Kara out of her reverie. "I'm sorry, did you, did you say a month?" she gasped.

Luke's grin was evil as he stared at her from the other side of the table, placing soothing gel on her clit. "Sweetheart, you'll need time to heal, and come could infect the piercing. Since I don't trust any of you—or myself, for that matter—we're making your pussy off limits for the time being. But don't worry, you can choke on our cocks or watch us fuck each other as much as you want. Just no touching. Think of it as one very long...edging session."

Oh, *god*. She hadn't signed up for *this*. It made her hot, and apparently, there was nothing she was going to be able to do about that for a long, long time.

"You love this," she accused.

He nodded. "I haven't satisfied my inner sadist in a while. Watching you for the next month, desperate to come, but unable to? It'll do the job, for sure."

His words softened Kara. After the island, Luke had refrained from physically hurting any of them during sex, as if his psyche had needed to heal. This, more than anything, proved he had.

"I love you," she murmured.

"Yeah," he said. "You do."

"I feel like I'm being edged right now," Conor complained. "Either you flip our toy over, so I can come in her ass, or I'm choking her on my cock."

Luke shook his head. "No anal. It's not safe. Not until our...gift arrives, anyway."

Conor sighed, pretending to be put out. "Fine." She heard his shorts hit the floor, and then he was climbing on top of her.

"Open," he told her, and she did automatically.

"Good girl," he sighed. "This will be quick. Don't swallow yet." He pushed his cock into her mouth, and as she sucked, she heard two more pairs of pants fall. He thrust deep into her mouth and throat, his balls resting on her chin, and with a groan, he came.

"Show me," he told her, and she opened her mouth, aware of the way his eyes darkened seeing his come still on her tongue, spilling out of her mouth.

Micah was next. But instead of climbing on her, he leaned over and kissed her, open mouthed, swallowing Conor's come for her. Kara felt a sting, sharp and almost beautiful, from where the ring was stimulating her already overstimulated clit. Then he was taking her hand in his and they were jerking him off together, his cock so thick and heavy it was almost hard to wrap her hand around it. And then he came with a shout all over her stomach.

Finally, Luke was there, tall enough that all he had to do was turn her head toward him and thrust his cock into her mouth. He pumped a few times, then pulled out, coming all over her lips, face, and neck, but careful to miss her chest. And if you'd asked Kara before she'd known them if come on your face could feel like love, she'd ask you what porn you'd been watching. But now, she knew, that love could feel like anything. That it didn't matter how filthy or embarrassing or deviant or depraved it was, there was nothing they could do together that was shameful—not when there was love between them.

Although she really wanted to come, as painful as it would be.

Luke wiped her face with a wet washcloth, tending to her as he murmured how much he loved her.

Then Conor said, "Don't forget the last ring."

Kara sat straight up. "What the hell else are you piercing?"

In answer, someone lifted her left hand, and tight, metal bands slid onto her ring finger: One, two, three.

She peered down at her hand. On her ring finger were three stackable rose gold bands, each with a different stone: a small but brilliant diamond, a glittering pink tourmaline, and an alexandrite that changed colors in the light.

Luke's, Conor's, and Micah's birthstones.

For a moment, Kara forgot how to breathe.

"It's not technically legal," Luke started, his voice thick, "for you to marry three men. And clit and nipple piercings aren't really the same thing as a wedding ceremony. We'll give you one, if you want. But this, to us..."

Micah cut in. "It felt realer than anything else we could do. You've pierced our hearts, it's only fair that we, well..."

"Yeah," Conor finished. "I, just...yeah. We love you, sweet baby girl."

And there it was. Even though he didn't have the words, the wet shine in his eyes, brilliant as the rings on her finger, told the whole story.

Struggling not to cry, she asked, "And you weren't going to ask me, first?"

All three men laughed.

"Baby," Micah asked. "Since when have we ever asked?"

"I want you to have rings, too," she said, taken over by the urgency of it. "I want..."

"Hush, baby," Micah said. "We just need you to pick them out for us."

Conor's phone buzzed with a text, and he leaned over to pick it up.

Then, he laughed.

"What?" Micah asked, as he untied Kara from the table

and Luke checked her circulation. She felt weak as a kitten, and like a kitten, all she wanted was to curl up somewhere soft and let her owners pet her.

"'I'm calling in my favor. I have a kidnapping of my own to coordinate, and I need your expertise,'" Conor quoted. "It's from Marcus."

"Kidnapping?"

Micah shook his head. "Apparently both my brothers are busy."

Kara sighed, focusing on her rings, admiring the way they sparkled in the light, and vowed, in that moment, to never, ever take them off.

The next four weeks were *hell.*

It didn't matter how sweet the assholes were, or how gentle they were with her, they were all sadists—not just Luke. All of them. Something Kara told them, constantly.

It wasn't that there weren't good parts. Kara would catch Luke and Conor wrestling out on the grass, without any of the fraught tension that usually was between them. Conor began to sing, sometimes even in the shower. She hadn't heard that low, smooth baritone of his since they'd first met. And Micah's smiles had become completely guileless—like that same sun was just bursting out of him, and he had to share it with her.

But that barely distracted Kara from the constant throbbing between her legs. The morning after they pierced and bandaged her, Luke disappeared, saying he needed to go to Jackson Hole, and reappeared a few hours later with a box. The guys were too excited about it, sending wariness through Kara. They opened it, revealing some leather, mesh, and metal contraption with two straps, one that would wrap around her waist and the other that would go between her legs, covering both her front and back holes, as well as her clit. When she saw it had a reinforced steel padlock on it, she took off running, thanking Luke silently for his coaching over the past couple of weeks. That said, she didn't get particularly far before they caught her, pushed her onto her hands and knees, and locked the evil device around her.

"This is for your own good, baby," Micah lectured. "We know you too well to think you'll keep your hands off your pussy, and we don't want you to get an infection or anything nasty."

"Whose idea was this?"

She was surprised when Conor pointed at Micah.

"You tattletelling fuck," Micah said with a laugh.

"I know you love us, sweetheart, so it's okay if you hate us for a little while. You're going to end up addicted to it," Luke said, practically rubbing his hands together with glee.

She snorted. "You're way too excited about this."

"Yup," he said, his cheerful tone unable to hide the unholy look in his eyes she hadn't seen since the cabin days. "Like I said, this is gonna be fun."

It wasn't.

The chastity belt felt like a motherfucking thong that had been sent from hell. It didn't chafe, which Kara thanked the sex toy gods for, and it was breathable—important to keep the piercing from getting infected—but it was so ever-present, she could never forget it was there. Especially when her men fucked in front of her, or discussed what it would feel like to fuck her again. Which they talked about, all the goddamned time.

Every day, they removed it, gently checked her piercing, cleaned it, and put on healing gel, but moments before she was about to come from their light touch, their hands disappeared and the belt was locked back on around her body, until she thought she'd go mad from the torture.

One night, they were lying in bed, Kara's head pillowed on Micah's chest as he played with her hair and she tried and failed not to think about sex, when Conor stomped in, naked, his cock so hard it had to hurt.

That was a satisfying thought.

"I can't go three more weeks like this," Conor announced. "I keep dreaming about fucking our bad little girl in her pussy or her ass, and it's fucking killing me. Her mouth is not enough anymore."

Micah sighed, stroking the underside of Kara's breast and making her wiggle in his arms. He liked to gently tease her that way; Kara both loathed and loved it. She could come from just a little bit of nipple play, they were so sensitive, but the men were avoiding them.

As Luke had teased: "If there was a chas-titty belt, we'd use that, too."

It was silly, there was nothing saying she couldn't have nipple stimulation, so she was sure it was just meant to add to her torture.

Luke entered the room. "No anal. For one thing, she'll get off; for another, there's too much of an infection risk."

Conor growled, and then, as if Kara weren't even in the room, they got into an argument about whether Conor was capable of lasting by fucking Luke and Micah in the ass instead.

Micah refereed the argument, and it was also nice to see that some things didn't change, even if the tenor of the argument had.

"Don't I get a say?" Kara asked, raising her hand.

"Nope," all three men said, then carried on with the discussion.

Beyond frustrated, Kara began to yell, desperate to be heard, as they argued in circles. Finally, Luke disappeared for a moment, returning with a ball gag, forcing it into her mouth as Micah held her down.

"Thank god, I thought it would never stop," Luke said, kissing Kara's cheek to reassure her it wasn't meant cruelly.

Kara didn't care. She kept telling them off, even with the ball gag in her mouth.

"I can still hear her, and I know a better way to shut her up," Conor suggested.

"She's probably going to bite your cock off if you do that," Micah said, amused.

Luke flinched, remembering. He turned to her. "You know, I'd never been more proud of you—or more frightened of you."

For a moment, Kara beamed, forgetting her predicament. It was a nice compliment.

Conor laughed. "We still have the spider gag somewhere. You know, just in case we've pissed her off too much."

Anal debate temporarily forgotten, Luke and Conor wandered around the master bedroom, searching through the walk-in closet and various armoires until they came up with it.

"No," Kara tried to say through the current gag in her mouth.

"Yes," Conor told her, understanding, implacable as he approached her.

She put up a good fight, she did, but moments later she was kneeling on the floor, spider gag holding her mouth open, as Conor thrust in and out of her throat, slow and easy. His cock was too big for her to make much noise, and the noises she did make caused vibrations, making him sigh and stroke her hair.

"Good girl," he crooned. "This is so much better."

"Does this mean you're willing to drop the anal thing?" Luke asked.

Conor just groaned. "It's hard to argue with you, when I've got this tight little cockwarmer distracting me."

"You know, the anticipation is good for all of us, not just her," Micah said. "The day we can finally get our cocks back into her two little tight bottom holes, it's going to be so good it's going to blow all of our minds. Just think about it like a prolonged wedding night when the bride doesn't see her husband, but in reverse. And in three weeks, we get to have our honeymoon."

Luke came up behind Kara and kneeled, leaning down to spread kisses along her bare back.

"We should put her in a white dress, shouldn't we?" His voice was husky. "I've never seen her in white."

And even though Conor had withdrawn his cock to let her breathe, Kara couldn't catch any air.

She did want that. She wanted it badly.

"My turn," Luke said, rising to his feet and switching places with Conor. "Sweetheart, you're going to love on my cock for a while."

And as Kara watched Conor flip Micah over on the bed and go at his ass, their fingers tangled together, as Luke pushed his cock into her throat and held her there, something settled in Kara's chest, something warm and easy. Belonging, finally. And even with Luke's cock lodged deep inside her, she found it almost easy to breathe again.

About a week before their sex honeymoon, they made Kara kneel on the bed, arms tied behind her back, and took turns fucking each other while the third whispered in her ear.

Conor was bent over next to her on the bed, hand gripping her thigh, while Luke hit him with a flogger Kara hadn't seen before. It was the promised punishment for Conor's attempt at self-sacrifice, and Kara knew her time was coming. At first, Kara had been almost shocked at how roughly Luke was flogging Conor, until she saw how hard he was. No wonder why her arms were tied behind her back; every time Luke lashed Conor, he squeezed her thigh, hard, and she wanted to touch him so badly she keened in her throat.

Micah sat on her other side, stroking her hair, her collarbone, her ear, making her shake with his touch, while he narrated.

"See how focused Luke gets? He's like that with you, too, you've just never seen it because you're facing the other way. For him, nothing exists but the two of you and the way his hand or belt ties the two of you together. See how hard Conor is right now? It's not only from Luke, or the pain, it's from having you so close."

"Micah," she begged, not even sure what she was begging for.

"Poor baby, you need to orgasm, don't you? It must be

torture, aching down there, clenching against air. Only seven more days before you have us back in your cunt."

"Be a good girl," Conor groaned next to her, "and tell us you love us."

"I love you," she cried, the words now so familiar, saying them felt like breathing—and just as essential.

"Oh, sweetheart, it's going to be so good," Luke added, flogging Conor one last time, and Kara watched, so hungry, as Conor came on the bedding.

And finally, finally, the day arrived.

"It's tiiiiiiime," Luke sang, startling Kara, who was working out her excess frustration on the punching bag in the exercise room.

"It's good that Conor's the singer, and not you," she told him, wiping sweat off her face.

"Just for that, I'm going to beat your ass before we let you come," he told her. "Go upstairs to the bedroom and strip."

She didn't bother to argue or to put up a fight, just ran down the hallway and up the stairs, where she pulled off her sports bra, leggings, and underwear and dropped them on the bedroom floor. She stood straight, completely naked except for the godforsaken chastity belt.

Micah and Conor entered the room, stopping when they saw her.

"You know," Micah remarked. "It doesn't matter how many times I've seen you naked, or how many more times I'm going to see you naked. It never gets old."

Conor didn't say anything, just swallowed when he saw her, and held up the key.

"Wait," Luke said. "She was bratty, so I need to punish her, first."

"Haven't I been punished enough?" Kara complained, even though anticipation lit in her belly at the thought of his hand on her ass.

Or being passed around by the three of them.

She'd take anything at this point.

"You want that sweetheart, don't you?" Luke asked her. "You want whatever we do to you, however we do it, for as long as we do it. You need it all, and only we can give it to you."

"I want anything and everything you ever give me," she told him, solemn.

His eyes warmed with her words. "Good. Say yes, sweetheart," he ordered.

"Yes, sweetheart," she teased.

"You can call me sweetheart whenever you want," he told her, his voice gravel.

And then she was in his arms and he was sitting down and she was over his lap, and he was spanking her: short, quick, gentle slaps, warming her up, followed by harder, longer smacks that burned every time they landed. She sank into the sound of his hand on her flesh, the heat of his body under hers and Conor's and Micah's as they surrounded her on both sides, telling her what a good girl she was, for taking her punishment so well; what a good girl she'd been this past month, submitting to them and the orgasm denial, and how they were going to reward her *until you can't fucking see straight, you'll have come so much, baby.*

She let herself get sucked into their undertow and be swept away.

Finally, when her ass was on fire and she couldn't take anymore, they stopped, soothing her. And then there was a click as the key slid into the tiny padlock and turned, and they undid the chastity belt, leaving her free.

Air washed over her, and her clit and pussy, already throbbing and wet from Luke's spanking, felt so sensitive from the weeks of teasing and from the clit ring, she was going to scream. It wouldn't take much, and she needed it. Now.

"Piercings look good," Luke announced, all business, like she wasn't about to scream at them and demand they touch her. "She's ready."

"Yeah, she is," Micah said, his hand stroking her inner thighs with a barely-there touch, sending shivers up and down Kara's legs. "I bet if we blow on her, she'll come like a geyser."

"Let's see," Conor said, and then his head was between her legs.

He blew a stream of cool air directly on her clit right over the ring, and Kara trembled, wracked with shivers, as she came. It felt like fire, it felt like ice, she loved it, and she hated it, and all she wanted was more.

"Touch me," she begged. "Love me."

"Of course, baby," Micah murmured, and then she was being lifted and lowered onto his cock, and they were rocking together, skin to skin, eye to eye, arms wrapped around each other. They were so close, so in sync, she could almost feel what he felt: the tight, wet heat of her pussy, the pull of the tiny clit ring, the softness of her skin, the piercings in her pebbled nipples pressing against his chest hair. And more than that, she could feel his utter peace at being inside of her, because this was exactly where he belonged.

Home.

For so long, Kara had looked for somewhere to belong,

only to think she'd never find it. And so the reminder that she was home to them, and vice versa? Well, it never got old.

"We'll keep you safe forever, baby," he murmured in his ear. "But you, this? This is our safe place."

The words pierced her the way that those needles had pierced her four weeks ago, and she came with them echoing in her ears.

And then she was being lifted off a still hard Micah and placed on her hands and knees, and Luke was behind her, and then inside her, so long, so deep, she felt him in her fucking throat, felt him everywhere. And she knew, she *knew*, that even after he came, even after he stopped thrusting in and out of her pussy, slow and devastatingly perfect, she'd still feel him there.

"Sweetheart, sweetheart, sweetheart," he groaned, in time with his thrusts, and he seemed to be saying, *mine, mine, mine.*

"Yours," she agreed on a gasp, and although she wasn't sure how he could've heard her, he growled in affirmation.

He placed his lips at her ear, and bit down, hard, just as he hit the perfect spot inside her, so she came. And as she came, she thought she heard him say, "There's no one else for us but you."

And then he was pulling out of her, also still hard, and she was being flipped onto her back, and Conor was coming down on top of her, his arms trapping her between them, as he slid into her, then held still. He didn't say anything, just kept his eyes on her, and she watched him back, her heart full. She reached a hand up, curving it around his cheek, and he leaned into it like a cat desperate for affection. He slid out, then in, out, then in, building something in her that was going to take her down like a tidal wave, and god, with that look in his eyes? She was ready to drown.

He whispered his lips over hers, then pressed down, giving her his whole heart with his kiss, and the sheer, painful sweetness of it crashed over her, taking her with it. He murmured, "I don't care who I am, as long as I'm yours, perfect girl," and she came again, his words like perfect circles on her clit, stretching her tight and then releasing her, stretching and releasing, so she came, and came, and came.

She was still mid-orgasm when Conor slid out of her, also still hard, and they rearranged her. Micah kneeled on the bed, holding her tight in his lap as he buried his nose in her hair and smelled her, one hand pulling on her nipple rings, the other playing with her clit piercing, prolonging the orgasm until it was sharp and almost painful and wetness gushed from her, drowning her thighs in her pleasure.

"Micah," she moaned, overwhelmed.

"More, baby," he told her. "Always more."

Conor and Luke were lying, side by side, Luke's hand gripped around both their cocks, holding them together. Micah lifted her by her hips and began to lower her down, but even in her sex-drunk state, she knew enough to say, "Uh uh, no way. They're not going to fit."

"Oh, we'll fit, sweetheart," Luke said darkly. "We're going to stuff you full with every last fucking inch."

"And you're going to take it like our good girl, aren't you?" Conor asked.

It wasn't really a question, and she clearly wasn't meant to answer, because suddenly the tips of both their cocks were inside of her, Luke's first, because he was longer, and then Conor, thicker, and even though it hurt, it hurt, it *hurt*, it felt more right than anything ever had, especially as Micah forced her hips down, forced her to take them, slowly but relentlessly, as determined to fill her pussy together as they had been to get inside her heart.

And just like she'd made space for them in the latter, she let them fill the former, as well.

She felt every inch of them, pushing against her pussy walls on all sides, until there was nowhere left for them to go, but there still was more, and more, and more. Until finally, *finally*, they were all the way inside, so deep, so thick, she couldn't move, just succumb to the sensation of them inside her.

"How does it feel, sweetheart?" Luke asked, his voice pure gravel.

"Full," she said, or moaned, or gasped, or cried. She wasn't sure; she'd never made a sound like that before. "So full."

"You're about to get fuller," Micah promised, and she heard the click of a plastic bottle being opened, and then she was being pushed down over Luke and Conor, so her head was in the groove between their bodies, and she was being trapped by them so she couldn't fight, so she was safely held for what came next.

"Better than blood," Luke gasped out his joke.

And Kara would have laughed, if she could have. If she wasn't so full—and aching to be fuller.

Then there was cool gel being pushed inside her ass, and Micah was crooning, "You want to let me in, baby, don't you? You know it's going to be so good, the four of us like this," and Conor was praising her, calling her "our good girl," and Luke was brushing back her hair, murmuring "sweetheart, sweetheart, sweetheart," and then...

And then.

Micah was pushing his cock inside her ass, and if she'd thought she'd been full before, she hadn't known what the word meant. Micah's thick girth redefined the word, as he pushed deep into her ass, and all she could do was make that same unfamiliar sound, a sound that meant pain and pleasure and submission and love, complete and encompassing, love that stuffed her full until she was about to burst with it.

"You okay, baby?" he murmured in her ear, and she realized he was all the way inside.

"Fuck," Luke groaned, "I can feel you. I can feel all of you, *fuck*, I need to move," and the filthy honesty of his words made Kara cry out again as she came around their cocks, pulsing.

And then they began to move, in and out, slow but deep. There was no orchestrated rhythm, no flow, no orchestra conductor or choreography. Just a relentless push and pull, and a sweet, perfect ache that took over everything, until she became nothing more than the bones and flesh holding them together, their safe space where they could all belong, and she could belong to them, too. Words bubbled in her chest, perfect, beautiful words, but she wasn't sure what they were, only that her three men responded with their own words of love and adoration, and groans and growls as their speed picked up inside her and they held her tighter and all she could do was take it, submit to them as they powered into her, and she came, so many times she didn't know who she was outside of an orgasm. This was it, everything she wanted.

Theirs, she was theirs.

"Mine," Luke growled, and came, filling her with his release.

"My good girl," Conor groaned, coming inside her.

"Ours," Micah sighed, as he finished in her ass.

Slowly, they withdrew, shushing her through the aftershocks. Gently, they carried her to the shower, bathing her body and washing her hair and soothing her, praising her, as she cried from the intensity of it. They dried her with a towel, and then they were back on the bed, and then they were fucking her again.

"We're not done?" she managed to ask.

"We'll never be done," Conor told her.

And there, on their massive bed, in the cabin they'd built for her out of desperation and hope, she and her men proved that very thing.

That no matter what they did, or who they hurt, they belonged to each other.

That they loved each other.

And for that, Kara Blum was glad.

EPILOGUE

Five years later

As soon as Micah opened the door, he heard the screams.

But he just stood there and watched as a naked woman wearing ridiculous fuzzy socks skidded around the corner, saw him, screamed again, and went running in the other direction.

Luke just swaggered after her, not even breaking a sweat.

"You know, you should just give up now," he called.

"You'll never catch me, motherfucker!" she yelled back from some other part of the house.

Smiling, Micah glanced in the window. His tattoo, now complete, shone in the reflection. The army rifle shooting out the green stem now had a strawflower poking out at the end, red and gold like the colors of Kara's hair and eyes. They'd all gotten tattoos together: Conor had covered up his old Semper Fi tattoo with an eagle holding a bunch of bee balm in its claw; Luke, an ocean wave crashing over a mountain; and Kara now had a knotted rope made up of their names wrapped around her inner right thigh. When she'd gotten the tattoo done, all three men had hovered over her, glaring at the tattoo artist as if warning her to keep her hands from wandering. Kara had laughed for a few minutes, until the pain zoned her out entirely. She'd been putty in their hands afterward.

"I give it two minutes," Luke called to Kara, winking at Micah.

Micah watched as Luke put a finger to his lips and stepped into the shadows underneath the staircase. At first, Luke's abandonment fears hadn't gone away, rearing their ugly heads when Kara left to go see Lola, or Conor visited his mother and sister, or when Micah went to talk some sense into his little brother. He'd been extra harsh with his punishments after. But each time they came back, each time they made it clear he was essential to their foursome, he became more and more relaxed.

Kara, for her part, threatened to send all of them to therapy, but when they pointed out that they couldn't talk about their "day jobs," she'd given up, calling them macho men with affectionate exasperation.

"I guess you'll have to rely on the healing powers of my pussy," she'd said, and they'd all agreed.

Kara appeared around the corner, holding water balloons, which she threw at both Luke and Micah. "Two minutes, huh?" she called, then disappeared again.

"She's going to ruin the floors," Conor commented from beside him.

Micah glanced over. His lover had a soft smile on his face. There was an ease to him these days, a self-acceptance that had been missing before.

"They're her floors," Micah pointed out, trying not to grimace at the water potentially warping the hardwoods.

They'd put the deed in her name, reasoning that, if anything ever happened to them, she'd be safe and cared for. Besides, the house had always been meant for her.

He heard the woman in question shriek from the kitchen.

"You can't use your height against me!"

"You're using your tits," came Luke's reply.

"You know," Conor said, watching Micah, "I'm onto you."

Micah smirked. "Are you?" he asked.

"You pulled our strings like marionette puppets to get us here."

"You could argue that," Micah admitted. "But it was more setting things up so you could all find your own way."

Conor shook his head. "You fucking manipulative mastermind." Then: "Thank you."

Micah backed Conor up against the wall, and kissed him, one of the rare times between them when he took blatant control. Conor let him, before kissing him back and taking over, conquering Micah with licks and bites until they were both panting and hard.

Kara re-appeared in the hall, hands on her hips. "He stole my water balloons, and you assholes are what, making out? Help me."

Conor laughed. "No, bad girl. You take what's coming to you."

She glared. "Goddamn traitors."

Footsteps, loud and ominous, sounding behind her.

"Shit, shit, shit," she gasped, looking around for a place to hide.

"Okay, that's it," Luke warned, and as she laughed hysterically, he pounced, grabbing her by the ankle and then catching her, rolling so she landed on him and not the floor.

Micah leaned over to Conor, whispering, "What did I tell you, huh? More fun to chase her when she loves us."

"Fine, you were right," Conor said.

He was always right.

"That's what I like to hear."

The laughter had turned into pants and then moans as Luke grabbed Kara's ass and thrust inside her.

"I guess that's our cue," Conor said, and, Micah, completely fucking content with the world as it was, followed Conor and joined his family on the floor.

THE END

(*For real this time.*)

DELETED SPICY SCENES...

Want to read some deleted spicy scenes? (I swear, these four would not stop fucking.) Subscribe to my newsletter and see what they got up to while they were misbehaving!

Curious what else I've been up to? I have a story called The Stepbrother *that I'm releasing on Kindle Vella and my Patreon! And if you join my Patreon, you'll receive other goodies as well, like early releases.*

And finally, an author's career is built on reviews. If you enjoyed Meet Me In The Dark *(and the* Bad Heroes *trilogy), please leave a review on Amazon or wherever you like to review! I'd truly appreciate it.*

SNEAK PEEK OF THE STEPBROTHER

Want to get a glimpse into my Vixen and Vice *world? Here's a sneak peek of* The Stepbrother *(now on Kindle Vella):*

Episode One

James

She was the most beautiful girl I'd ever seen in my life.

And I wanted her more than I wanted anything.

I watched as she spun around and around in another man's arms, laughing on the dance floor at my father's wedding. She was tiny and delicate, a pale, black-haired butterfly in a blue dress with hair like satin and skin like silk, and as my eyes followed her, it felt like I was also spinning, like the earth had tilted off its axis and even gravity had been thrown into chaos.

At eighteen, I'd been with dozens of girls around my age, and a handful of older women, too. All gorgeous, all sexy, all eager to please. But this little slip of a thing caught my attention and held it like no one ever had. And even though I was only eighteen, I already knew no one ever would captivate me the way she did.

I wanted her.

I would have her.

I didn't know the guy she was with—some young, thin jackass who clearly didn't realize what a loser he was—but it wouldn't take much to scare him off. I was on my way to do so, and to get my hands on her tight, sweet, supple body, when a hand fell onto my shoulder and gripped hard.

"James," my father said.

"Paul." I'd stopped calling him Dad a long time ago. He'd stopped *being* a dad, after Mom had died and he'd abandoned me in his grief.

He coughed. I knew he hated when I called him by his first name.

"I'd like you to spend some time getting to know your new stepmother and stepsister. Anna's still mingling with guests, but I'd like us to spend the rest of the weekend together. And I see that you've spotted your stepsister, Leslie."

My whole body went cold. I ripped my eyes off the butterfly in blue to turn and look at him. "What do you mean?"

He nodded toward the dance floor, face grim. "That's your new stepsister."

Stepsister.

The earth, no longer spinning madly, stopped so immediately I almost stumbled.

My fantasy of introducing myself to her, seducing her, and seeing what her body looked like underneath that blue dress disappeared quickly as reality intruded. She was my stepsister. Not only could I not have her—*never* have her— she was the daughter of the woman I hated, the woman who was trying to replace my dead mother. I wanted nothing to do with this new family my father was assembling in an attempt to forget the love of his life who had given him everything.

I continued to watch her, my stepsister, the lust and awe burning into ash.

"Listen, James. I know I'm not your favorite person, and you're angry at me for remarrying, but I'm telling you—treat our new family right, or I'll make sure you regret it." He squeezed my shoulder again. "You hear me?"

"I hear you," I said through gritted teeth.

"Good." He lifted a hand to his mouth. "Leslie, come join us."

The butterfly paused, saying something to her partner. He kissed her—a light peck, but just the image of his lips against hers made me want to break something.

I couldn't help but stare at her bare legs as she made her way toward us. Even walking, she looked like she was dancing.

When she reached us, she stared up at me, her dark eyes curious.

"Leslie," my father greeted her warmly, wrapping an arm around her and kissing her on the cheek. And even though I knew his affection toward her was nothing more than fatherly, I wanted to rip him away from her.

"Hi, Paul," she said fondly. Her voice was high and clear, wrapping around me with a sweetness that made my chest ache.

"Leslie, I'd like you to meet someone. This is James, my son."

She tilted her head back to look up at me. Her dark brown eyes were warm and friendly. "I guess that makes you my stepbrother, doesn't it."

I laughed bitterly. "I see you get your intelligence from your mother."

She reared back, offended. "Excuse me, what did you just say to me?"

"James," my father warned.

I shrugged, showing her my teeth. "Sorry."

Glaring, she shrugged, mirroring me. "Apology not accepted."

I laughed despite myself. An aggressive butterfly, then.

Before she could snap at me further, Anna, her mother, appeared next to us. My father put his arm around the buxom blonde as well.

Leslie must take after her father, whatever had happened to him.

"Oh, I see you two have met!" Anna trilled happily. "I'm so glad. James, Leslie just graduated from Brooklyn Arts School. Leslie, James about to start his freshman year at Harvard. But you'll both be home this summer, so James, I hope you can show her around town and give her the lay of the land."

"Oh, I can give her the lay of the land, all right," I said smoothly.

Leslie's cheeks turned pink.

"Mom, I thought we talked about this. I don't want to spend the summer in Westchester. Bea said I could stay with her and her parents in Harlem. I'll be closer to ABT that way..."

"Leslie! You spend all year with Bea, completely focused on dance. Don't you want to spend some time with your family? Don't you miss me?" her mom wheedled.

So she was a dancer. That explained the toned legs, perfect posture, and ethereal way she moved.

It didn't explain my desperate need to rip that dress off of her and get my mouth between those toned thighs.

It wasn't going to happen.

I wanted the butterfly nowhere near me. I wanted to make her fly far, far away, before I did something that we'd both regret.

"Excuse me," I said. "But I need to be somewhere right now."

"But we haven't even gotten to the toasts yet!" Anna protested.

My father stared at me.

I nodded my head toward Tiffanie, my on-again, off-again girlfriend I'd forgotten on the side of the dance floor the moment I'd seen Leslie dancing. "I've been a bad boyfriend and left my date alone. She deserves some of my time, no?"

Anna relaxed, smiling. "Oh, that's nice. Young love," she trilled. "Maybe you can double-date with Leslie and her boyfriend, Spencer."

There was no way in hell I'd be doing that.

From the expression on Leslie's face, she felt the same way.

"Nice to meet you, Lily," I said.

She raised an eyebrow. "Nice to meet you too, Josh," she retorted, and as I walked away, I couldn't help but smile at her attempt at a power play.

But my smile dropped off my face as I remembered that was the only time we'd ever be playing.

I grabbed Tiffanie by her arm and dragged her off with me without saying anything.

"Where have you been?" she asked in what I'd always thought was a sexy voice until now.

I had a growing fear I'd never think a single voice was sexy if it wasn't high and clear and sounded like bells over water.

I didn't bother to answer her. "I need you to suck my cock."

"Of course, baby," she said.

I dragged her into the pool house, ignoring the other guests, the sound of metal on glass as the toasts began. I ignored everything as Tiffanie got on her knees, unzipped my slacks, and pulled my hard cock out.

"You were that excited, thinking about me, weren't you, baby?" she crooned, and I didn't bother to correct her.

I wasn't hard for her.

I was hard for a butterfly who would remain just outside of my grasp, unless I set fire to her wings.

As Tiffanie's mouth worked my cock, I imagined Leslie in front of me instead, her dark hair falling around her shoulders as her pert mouth gave me pleasure. I imagined coming down her tight little throat, on her tiny, perky tits, or on her perfect, beautiful face.

Pleasure rushed through me at the thought, followed by anger.

Some people pinned butterflies to keep them close.

I was going to make this one fly far, far away.

After all, she was the most beautiful girl I'd ever seen in my entire life.

And I hated her more than I hated anything.

Want to read more? Check it out on Kindle Vella or subscribe to my Patreon!

SNEAK PEEK OF PUCK IT

Want to see what Jack, Micah's little brother is involved in? Here's a sneak peek:

I guess I should start by saying that, despite all the terrible things humans do, all the terrible things I've done, and all the terrible things people have done to me, there's only one thing in this world I actually hate:

Liars.

Which is why Jack Feldman and I don't have a future—and never should've tried in the first place.

Not that Jack cares about that. He wants me close so he can inflict his special brand of torture on me forever and call it love.

He's a liar.

And because I hate liars, I'm telling the truth now.

Yes, I did it.

I burned down Halister Hall.

But even though I technically started the fire, Jack—Jack, with his manipulation and domination and inability to accept a world where he didn't get exactly what he wanted, Jack, who stole my heart and then broke it—lit the match.

This is my story.

Spoiler alert: It doesn't have a happy ending.

Preorder Puck It *now.*

ACKNOWLEDGMENTS

I honestly don't even know where to begin. So many of you have played such a huge role in making this trilogy a reality, and I don't want risk these acknowledgments turning into a whole fourth book, so here goes:

Jen, my beloved editor, friend, and fan of commenting: "JO. NO." in the Word documents I send you: This series wouldn't be what it is without your help. Thank you for taking on a trilogy (!) with cliffhangers (!) and all sorts of other stuff besides. Thank you also for pointing out when I was too scared to let my characters do bad things or experience bad things—you helped me put gas back in the engine.

Jasmine, my publishing life was disorganized chaos before you showed up. Thank you for all that you do. Please never leave me.

Brittney, thank goodness Karen Marie Moning brought you into my life—and thank god you stayed. I don't know what I'd do without you. Love you, bestie.

Sabrina, there are not words to express how grateful I am to have you as a friend. Hopefully we can both take a break from it being "our turn" in the text thread for a while.

Poppy, thank you for your friendship, your wisdom, and your feedback on all the things—including but not limited to on this book. I hope I did you proud.

Liz, thank you so much for alpha reading this mess—and not throwing it, and me, into the trash. I'm so grateful for your friendship and so glad Kara brought us together.

Shosh, I love you. Don't send geese when you get to the end.

To my beloved ARC team: I put it in the ARC note itself, but the fact that you all spent so. much. damn. time. reading and reviewing this series! It means the absolute world to me. Thank you, thank you, thank you.

To my intrepid street team: Thanks for your tireless promotion of my work, and thank you also for not murdering me about the SpongeBob thing.

And, finally, to my readers: None of this would exist without you. My stories would just sit on my computer and languish forever—you give them life.

Thank you, as always, for reading.

ABOUT THE AUTHOR

A lover of dogs, mountain adventures, and HGTV, Jo Brenner writes romances that are little bit twisted, a lotta bit sexy—and always have an HEA.

Stay in touch and get the latest publishing updates, book teasers, book recommendations, and more by joining her Facebook readers' group, Jo Brenner's Bar, and by subscribing to her newsletter!

facebook.com/AuthorJoBrenner

x.com/jo_brenner

instagram.com/jobrennerbooks

tiktok.com/@jobrennerbooks

goodreads.com/Jo_Brenner

amazon.com/author/Jo_Brenner

bookbub.com/profile/jo-brenner

ALSO BY JO BRENNER

BAD HEROES

You Can Follow Me

Lose Me In The Shadows

9 780996 019644